Lessons in Fusion

Yellow Dog
(an imprint of Great Plains Publications)
320 Rosedale Avenue
Winnipeg, MB R3L 1L8
www.greatplains.mb.ca

Design & Typography by Relish New Brand Experience
Printed in Canada by Friesens

Library and Archives Canada Cataloguing in Publication

Title: Lessons in fusion / Primrose Madayag Knazan.
Names: Madayag Knazan, Primrose, author.
Identifiers: Canadiana (print) 20210259957 | Canadiana (ebook) 20210259965 |
    ISBN 9781773370682 (softcover) | ISBN 9781773370699 (ebook)
Subjects: LCGFT: Novels.
Classification: LCC PS8626.A312 L47 2021 | DDC jC813/.6—dc23

Canadä

FSC
www.fsc.org
MIX
Paper from responsible sources
FSC® C016245

LESSONS IN FUSION

Primrose Madayag Knazan

yellow dog

For Baba Syl
I miss our family dinners

Chapter One

If you like salty buttery popcorn, make it extra extra by adding the briny flavours of furikake and the nuttiness of sesame oil and browned butter. I eat this by the fistful; it is soooo good. Ugh, I'm craving it right now.

Furikake Popcorn with Sesame Browned Butter

2 tsp furikake seasoning (or make your own with crushed nori, toasted sesame seeds, and kosher salt)

1 tsp salt

3 tbsp butter

1 ½ tbsp sesame oil

½ cup popcorn kernels

Mix furikake and salt in a small bowl. Set aside.

In a small pot, heat butter on medium heat until it turns brown and smells nutty. Remove from heat and set aside.

Add sesame oil and 2 popcorn kernels to a heavy-bottomed pot. Set to medium heat. Cover.

When you hear both kernels pop, one after the other, remove pot from heat, remove cover and add the rest of the popcorn kernels.

Cover and place pot back on the hot element. Jiggle the pot back and forth to coat the kernels.

Once the popping starts, listen for it to slow down. Jiggle pot intermittently for kernels to fall to the bottom of pot.

Once the popping slows down and you can hear the popping of individual kernels, lower the heat slightly.

Lift the lid just a bit and place slightly askew to let out steam or you'll end up with soggy popcorn.

When 3 seconds pass and there's no more popping, turn off heat.

Remove lid, wait 10 seconds.

Dump popcorn into a wide bowl. Use a spoon to drizzle butter over popcorn.

Toss the popcorn with a large spoon to coat. Drizzle more butter. Toss again. Repeat until all butter has been added.

Sprinkle the salt and furikake evenly over the popcorn. Toss with the spoon.

Serve while still warm. And be ready to make more because it's THAT good.

Winnipeg

"My girl is going to win. You'll see. I will bet money, like, real money."

I had just stuffed a handful of popcorn into my mouth. I chewed quickly and gulped the salty puffed kernels, chewing too fast to savour the nutty flavour. I carefully wiped the seasoning off my fingers with a napkin before picking up my phone to reply to Lena. Out of habit, I swept my tongue across the front perimeter of my mouth to ensure no bits of sesame seeds or nori were stuck to the front of my teeth before holding the camera lens at eye level and starting to speak.

"Where are you going to get 'real' money, Lena?" I asked, somewhat smugly to the video image of my BFF. "I haven't touched cash in almost a year."

Lena rolled her eyes so hard they could have rotated the orientation of the screen.

"You're always such a smartass, Sar," she said with a smirk. "You know what I mean. Twenty bucks on Nessa. Those whipped ricotta crostini were epic."

"Fine," I agreed. "You can transfer it to me right after the show when Lai takes the title. Her bun bo hue blew my mind."

My phone vibrated and started to play the midi theme from an 8-bit video game I love. I got a notification that someone was trying to join our video chat. Typical. Jay was always late. I tapped a button and let him into the chat. His image popped up on the screen next to Lena's, her box shrinking to accommodate his. I placed my phone down on a stack of books on the table, laying it sideways to give their images more space.

"Sorry, sorry, sorry," Jay said in his usual quick, clipped notes. "Just got home. What'd I miss?"

"E-ve-ry-thing!" Lena stretched out each syllable. Jay did miss everything. It was the season finale of *Cyber Chef* after all.

My friends and I were OBSESSED with *Cyber Chef* since it aired a couple of months into the pandemic. Unable to produce the standard cooking competition television show with on-site cooks creating dishes for a panel of judges, the Food and Drink Channel came up with the idea to hold a virtual competition between food bloggers who never had to leave their homes. FaD Channel had an instant hit on their hands with a version of the show now airing in several countries. With only seven episodes each season and six weeks in between, FaD was churning them out quickly. It was February, and we were already at the end of season three.

"I'll recap," I said, turning down the volume on the commercial. "For the appetizer round, Nessa made whipped ricotta cheese with blood oranges on toasted baguette. They looked better than

Lai's salad rolls, but Lai definitely took the entrée round with her spicy beef soup. Nessa's chicken 'n waffles looked too basic for—"

"WHAT?! They were, like, sooooo good! Anyway, I don't care if they're basic," Lena said, arms crossed. "I'm still making spicy chicken 'n waffles for dinner tomorrow. That chili marmalade looked ah-may-zing."

Lena was Team Nessa from the beginning. I was Team Lai since episode three when she made turkey larb. I made the Thai meat salad recipe the next day, and I was hooked. Ground turkey with mint, fish sauce, lime juice, and chillies in lettuce wraps. Salty, fresh, and funky. Who knew? The best part of the show was that the links to the recipes and videos were posted on the *Cyber Chef* website that night. You could even order the ingredients right off their site with just the click of a button. Not that my mom would let me use her credit card. I always texted her a list of the ingredients so she could add it to the family shopping list.

"They just started the dessert round," I finished explaining.

"Sure, sure, sure," Jay said. "Thanks."

"It's star-ting!" Lena yelled.

We stopped talking as the show returned from the break. I heard a doorbell ring. Not mine. Jay probably ordered pizza again. He always ordered junk food on days he was working at his family's Argentinean cafe. After laying off most of their staff last year, his parents depended on him and his siblings more than ever to carry the slack.

Overhead shots of Lai dredging under-ripe banana slices in a light batter filled the screen.

When our high-definition televisions were taken over by shows featuring streaming videoconference boxes, many of us of the younger generation adapted quickly as we were already using video to talk to friends and family long before the pandemic. I spent the last few months of grade ten learning through group chats and video meetings. I had to teach my parents how to use video meetings for work. Talk shows, news, even reality shows had jumped on the streaming format. Why not cooking?

As I watched Nessa infuse oat milk with Earl Grey to add to frosting, I thought of how I would attempt infusing the bergamot tea flavour. I would grind up half of the tea leaves into powder and mix them into the icing sugar. The frosting would have a stronger Earl Grey flavour and would have pretty specks throughout. There might even be a little bitterness from the straight-up tea leaves, but we like a little bitter with our sweet, right?

This was probably why I was so into *Cyber Chef*. It piqued my imagination. It also gave me ideas for my own food blog. I started creating my own recipes when I was fourteen. I filed the Earl Grey frosting recipe in the back of my mind to test out later. *Hmm, we have butter and vanilla. I'll need Earl Grey tea, icing sugar—*

"Who's winning?" my mom asked as she plopped down next to me on the couch. She grabbed a handful of popcorn. My Furikake Popcorn with Sesame Browned Butter was one of her favourites. She loved how the briny saltiness combined with the nuttiness of the sesame browned butter. My mom was my taste tester whenever I would experiment and she wasn't shy about giving me feedback on the many, many, many times I had ended up with a fail.

"Lai is deep-frying bananas," I recapped. "And Nessa is making London fog macarons."

We watched in silence as my mind whirled. *You need colour, Lai!* I wanted to shout as she pulled out homemade mango ice cream from the freezer. Yellow on yellow. So boring. As if she heard me, Lai tore up basil leaves and threw them into a pot of boiling sugar. *Basil syrup on fried banana and mango, what?!*

"The fried bananas remind me of something my mom used to make," my mother said wistfully. I wasn't familiar with my lola's cooking. She lived in British Columbia with my uncle Christoffer.

"It was called turon. It was fried saba banana wrapped in spring roll wrappers."

"Do you know the recipe?" I asked before remembering there was no point in asking.

"I have no idea." She turned to me and smiled. "It's a pretty common dish. Turon should be easy enough to Google. Auntie Cher probably knows how."

My mom turned back to the TV, grabbing another handful of popcorn.

"I like Lai," she commented between bites. "But she's a little too avant-garde sometimes."

"It doesn't matter what show we're watching," I said, taking the bowl back before she finished it. "You always cheer for the Asian woman, just because you're Filipino."

"And you don't?"

I smirked. My Filipino half didn't grant anyone my automatic allegiance.

"I'm cheering for the one with the best recipes, and that's clearly Lai. Besides, the Philippines and Laos are thousands of kilometres apart. I think. I have no idea where Laos is. It's near Thailand, right?"

My mother cocked her head at me.

"Do you know where Thailand is?"

"Asia." I smiled back.

"Shh, you two!" Lena called out. I forgot they could hear us.

The show cut to Nessa's video as she assembled the macarons, lavender in colour and flavour. She artfully placed a matchstick salad created from julienned green and red apple next to each macaron. She mixed a bright orange passion fruit sauce that would likely be dotted on the white plate or added as an artful swipe. The dish was the beginnings of something you could get in a restaurant.

Cyber Chef contestants were stacked with YouTubers, food

bloggers, Instagrammers, even Twitch or Tik Tok accounts. One time there was a podcaster. Every week, each contestant submitted short videos of themselves preparing what was supposed to come across as an easy-to-follow recipe. Sometimes they were eye-opening and mouth-watering. Some were total disasters.

In a separate box in the corner of the screen were the three judges: a celebrity chef, a FaD Channel social media exec, and a professional Food Content Creator—yes, you can actually do that for a living. The judges would have the ingredients in front of them and we would watch as they furiously tried to replicate the recipe in their own homes. After all, the mark of a good recipe is that it turns out the way it's described.

The recipe videos were typically three to ten minutes long in real life. Making the recipe always took longer, but all footage, including the videos, the cooking, the interviews, and the judging, were edited to fit the one-hour format, including commercials. The season finale required recipes for a three-course themed dinner.

Suddenly Lai's screen was in the forefront, and Nessa's was pushed to the background. Lai dipped a spoon into the green grassy syrup, pulling up a string of superheated green sugar. She drizzled the syrup in thin zigzags across the bottom of an oiled inverted metal bowl that had just come out of the freezer. I had seen this technique on other cooking shows. My mom was right, Lai is super fancy.

"Oh no!" I shouted.

One of the judges gave a tiny scream. She had burned her wrist as she flicked the melted sugar instead of using a slow, methodical drizzle. We all said the words out loud: FOLLOW THE INSTRUCTIONS as they scrolled across the bottom of the screen. Every few weeks, the judges missed one of the instructions of the recipe. When the contestant forgot to add something to a recipe, we would say ADD IT TO THE RECIPE. The judge quickly rinsed the burn under cold water and returned to the counter. I took a breath in, then out. It wasn't a deal breaker. Cooks burn themselves all the time, right? I had enough burns across my own hands and arms to compare myself to professional cooks and chefs.

The soft sugar threads formed a lacy coating on the outside of the upside-down bowl. As the sweet structure cooled and hardened, she placed the crispy banana next to a rounded scoop of mango ice cream. She dotted raspberry sauce in the negative space of the white plate then picked up the metal bowl, carefully sliding out a glittering sugar strand dome, placing the semi-transparent sparkling cloche carefully over the dessert, concealing the sweet surprise within.

"Nessa! Nessa! Nessa!" Lena chanted. I tapped a button and muted her voice. As the person who hosted today's video call, I had the power to mute whomever I wanted. I could see her bouncing on the couch, her blond ponytail swinging back and forth. Her lips silently mouthing *Nessa! Nessa! Nessa!* Jay ate a slice of pizza. All I could hear was his chewing. I muted him, too. All season he was indifferent, except for when Ethan was eliminated in episode four. I could tell Jay was disappointed because he couldn't even finish the tacos he had ordered for delivery.

Each camera on the screen panned over the completed dishes. My mom and I audibly oohed and aahed over the elegant presentations, the judges' dishes almost carbon copies of the originals. I thought Nessa's macs were fancy; Lai's upscale dessert was breathtaking.

Images of the two bloggers appeared in the top corners of the screen as the judges discussed the dishes. Images from the contestant's videos were placed side-by-side with the judges' versions. If the recipes were written correctly, they should be similar. That wasn't always the case.

Nessa told a story about how her mother's favourite hot drink was a London Fog. She learned to make it as a teenager and would bring her mother the sweet, foamy hot beverage whenever she had a hard day. Her mother was an ER nurse and hadn't been in the same room as Nessa and her children in almost a year. Last week she was diagnosed with COVID-19.

"That's going to be tough to beat," my mother commented.

"It's about the recipe," I insisted. "Not the story."

She patted my hand. I reached into the now-empty bowl of popcorn. I licked the crumbled seaweed and toasted sesame seeds off each fingertip.

Lai gently reminded the audience and judges that she had attended culinary school but stopped cooking professionally when she became a single mother of twins. From previous episodes, we already knew her mother had helped raise her sons as Lai transitioned from cooking in a restaurant to teaching in a Red Seal culinary program. Her mother died of breast cancer when the boys were seven. A twist on a Lao-Thai dessert, fried banana and mango, was her mother's favourite treat. Lai wanted to elevate it.

Both of them had touching stories of their mothers, the theme for today's finale.

Lai instructed the judges to tap on the fragile sugar bowl with the flats of their spoons. As each judge tapped, the sugar bowls gave way, cracking into grassy looking shards throughout the platter. My mother and I whoa-ed at the same time.

As the image of each contestant faded to black, the judges discussed amongst themselves the pros and cons of each dish. Just as Lena and I had surmised, Nessa clearly won the appetizer round, and Lai ran away with her entrée. The judges were split on desserts. The image of the show's host appeared, a gorgeous Canadian-Moroccan model with a snarky wit that gave her a huge social media following. She let the audience know that the judges would announce the winner live after the break.

I brought back the volume of my friends as my mother stood up for a quick bathroom break.

"...Nessa! Nessa! Nessa!" Lena was still going.

"Have you been cheering for Nessa this whole time?" I asked.

"Of course!" she said proudly. "Did you not see those macs? Want, want, want!"

"But Lai's dessert was a masterpiece!"

"Way too complicated for me." She dismissed the thought with a wave of her hand. "You shouldn't need an instruction manual to eat a glorified banana split. Seriously."

"Jay, what do you think?" I asked. "Who's going to win?"

He turned towards his tablet and gulped down the bite of pizza he was chewing.

"The one the third judge likes."

I sighed, then muted them both and picked up the big bowl to bring to the kitchen. I poured a quick glass of water and headed back. My phone was blinking. I picked it up and saw three texts from Lena.

Lena

WHERE R U?

WATCH THE LAST COMMERCIAL!!!

NOWWWWWWW!!!

All caps were pretty common for Lena, but punctuation in the right place wasn't normally her style, so it must have been important. I picked up the remote and was able to rewind on my television through the magic of digital cable.

"Do you want to be the next Cyber Chef?" a deep voice said dramatically over clips from the previous season. "For our upcoming season, the Food and Drink Channel is searching for the next recipe superstar and this time, we're looking for the next generation of Cyber Chefs! Do you create recipes? Do you have a food blog? Do you have a food channel? If you are between the ages of thirteen and seventeen, the next Cyber Chef can be YOU!"

My phone buzzed again.

Lena

do it

do it

DO IT!!!

Buzz. Another text.

Jay

u shoud enter

I sat down and quickly looked up the *Cyber Chef* website. I scrolled through the requirements. Fill out a form. Send a short video of a recipe. Send the link to your platform—your webpage, social media, podcast, or YouTube channel. Have your parents sign a waiver.

Could I do this? Me? The next Cyber Chef? No, that's the wrong attitude. I CAN do this! Me! Sarah Dayan-Abad, the next Cyber Chef!

My phone buzzed again.

Lena

in ur face Sar! Nessa rules!

u o me 20!

I grabbed the remote and fast forwarded to until I reached live TV. I forgot I was behind.

Lai's image, with eyes the same shape as mine and my mother's, faded to the background and was replaced by Nessa's blond hair and blue eyes taking up the centre screen. She hugged her husband and kids. Another box popped up, the caption *Nessa's Mother* underneath. She wore a hospital gown, a sterile white wall behind her. She looked frail. I decided I didn't want to rewind and witness Lai's defeat.

I turned back to the *Cyber Chef* website and tapped on the button to open the application form.

Ten months ago
Toronto

An executive paced back and forth in her high-rise condo. Two years ago, Poppy had been promoted to Vice-President of Talent Acquisition and Development, a position she had been working towards for the past eleven years. However, all her corporate momentum had come to a grinding halt. Filming on all shows was put on pause at the FaD studios over a month ago and already, the unions and accountants were breathing down their necks. The pandemic wasn't going away anytime soon. People were dying, literally dying, and the bills were piling up.

She sat down and opened her laptop. Her email contained the link to the video conference interface they had all started using last week. She had straightened out the painting on the wall behind her and had angled her desk in order to get the best lighting on her face.

Poppy wore a cornflower blue blouse with a fashionable wide bow at the neckline, loose sleeves, and wide cuffs with mother-of-pearl buttons. On her bottom half she wore comfortable pink-striped pajama pants and her feet were bare. She crossed her legs yoga style and tucked her legs under her desk. She checked her lipstick one more time before logging on to the meeting.

The faces of the other network executives appeared on screen, each in separate boxes. All of them were older White men. Most wore shirts and ties. One wore a turtleneck. She wondered how many of them were also wearing pajama bottoms, sweats, or shorts.

Victor, the president of the network, logged on and they all sat up in rapt attention. He gave a spiel about how the company wanted to support everyone in these trying times. After rattling off phone numbers for mental health aid and promising a better work-life balance, he finally got down to business.

"We will be short thirty percent of our usual content in two months," he said bluntly. She watched as the team clenched their jaws. "After four months, we will be down by fifty-five percent. We need ideas, fast."

A couple of the men were speaking over each other. Poppy sat back as everyone was quickly silenced with the click of a button. Each person who wanted to speak had to tap an icon of a white palm to appear in the corner of their video image, raising their digital hand as if they were all back in grade school.

Poppy was fine with this arrangement. Her ideas were stolen too many times by men rephrasing her words. She knew from experience that her voice was better heard if she let the blowhards get their thoughts out first. Victor wasn't one to jump on the first few proposals. She did her best brainstorming after she heard other people spout ideas that she could tell wouldn't work.

"Recorded interviews…"

"Re-edit old footage…"

"Blooper reels…"

Poppy's twenty-year-old daughter popped her head in the doorway, just out of view. She'd come back home from university when in-person classes were cancelled.

"Mom," she said in what was clearly going to become a sing-song whine. "Can we buy a new stand mixer?"

Poppy knew that the term 'we' meant 'you'. She leaned forward and quickly tapped the button to turn off her camera. During their near-daily meetings, every so often one of her fellow execs would bow out of the video conference to tend their spouses or children or to simply go to the bathroom. There was that one time that one of the execs brought his laptop into the bathroom without turning off the camera. Awkward was an understatement.

The voices continued to drone on. Someone was badly explaining their idea to have a live cooking show where viewers called in with questions. Ugh. Poppy spun around in her chair to face her daughter.

"Why do we need a new mixer?"

"This recipe says that it's best to use a dough hook and our mixer doesn't have one."

When she should have been studying and completing online courses, her daughter spent most of her time trying to bake. She seemed to be out of the cupcake and cookie phase and was moving into the wide world of breads.

"Just order a dough hook," Poppy explained. "You don't need another five-hundred-dollar mixer."

"Oh, you can do that? Huh," she answered, flicking her fingers upward on her phone screen. "What about cake yeast? This blogger says it's the best kind to use. This site has a sale."

"Fine," Poppy waved her away. "Whatever you buy, nothing over thirty dollars. My credit card is in my purse."

"Thanks, Mom." Her daughter blew her a kiss. "This is going to be the best brioche ever."

She quietly shut the door. Poppy didn't mind the interruption. The past few weeks had brought them closer together, mostly because of her daughter's baking obsession. They finally had something in common. Poppy had met pastry chefs at the top of their field, but she already knew that her daughter's brioche would be the best she'd ever had.

Poppy had read somewhere that since the pandemic started, people were baking and cooking more than ever. With restaurants and bars closed, people had to learn how to become their own chefs, bakers, bartenders, and baristas.

Her daughter was always showing her new recipes she found on the internet, usually from food bloggers or YouTube. In fact, she and her daughter had spent hundreds of dollars on baking equipment and specialty ingredients in the past two weeks, from silicone cupcake liners to intricate cookie presses. Then there was the money spent on pour-over coffee supplies—

Poppy turned back towards her laptop. She clicked her camera back on and put up her digital hand. She grabbed a pen and nearby notebook and started to jot down notes. She grabbed her phone and quickly looked up a few sites while the current executive who had the floor yammered on and on about science-based cooking lessons. Nerd.

It was finally her turn.

"Food content creators," she said with authority. She knew she had to explain further. "Bloggers, YouTubers, podcasters, Instagram, Facebook, Snapchat, Twitter, anyone who uses digital media to create recipes. We give them a show, no, a competition. And we do it like this."

She pointed to the invisible box that framed her face, the box that only her colleagues would see on the screen.

"A completely digital competition filmed remotely on their own devices." She held up her phone for dramatic effect. "They film it. We edit it. All the talk shows are doing it. I watched a sketch comedy show pull it off last weekend. It can work and it can be made cheaply. We can also milk the advertising and sponsorships. I see a positive return."

She knew she said the magic words.

"Flesh it out," her boss said. He might as well as have given her a trophy as the boys sulked. "Send me a full proposal by tomorrow morning."

"Thank you, sir."

Poppy sat back, satisfied. Maybe she would buy a new stand mixer after all.

Chapter Two

I made latkes, or potato pancakes, with my baba every Chanukah, sometimes for Shabbat dinner, and sometimes for a Sunday brunch. When I suggested we start making them with sweet potatoes instead of russets, we started experimenting with Indian spices. Instead of traditional sour cream or applesauce, we would serve them with raita made with yogurt, green apple, and mint. It was Baba's idea to add the green apple. She was a pretty cool grandmother, open to new flavours and accepting of everything. She saw fusion as bringing together the best of two worlds.

Sweet Potato Latkes
4 cups shredded sweet potato
1 shallot, chopped thin
2 cloves of garlic, minced
1 tbsp ginger, minced
⅓ cup flour
1 ½ tsp kosher salt, divided
1 tsp cumin
1 tsp cinnamon
½ tsp turmeric
Oil for frying (peanut, avocado)
½ tsp chilli powder (optional)
2 eggs, lightly beaten
½ tsp garam masala

Place the sweet potato into a triple layer of cheesecloth (or a clean tea towel that you wouldn't mind being stained orange). Twist the top and squeeze out all the liquid from the sweet potatoes.

Add the sweet potato into a large mixing bowl. Fluff up with a fork to separate the shreds.

Mix together sweet potato, shallot, garlic, and ginger.

In another bowl, mix the flour and spices, except the garam masala and half a teaspoon of salt which should be mixed together in a separate bowl and put aside.

Sprinkle the spiced flour on top of the sweet potato mixture. Mix until evenly combined.

Add enough beaten egg to hold the mixture together. It should be gloppy like cookie dough, not wet like pasta.

Add oil to a heavy frying pan, or better yet, cast iron, about 1 cm depth.

Heat pan on medium until the oil shimmers.

Add a tiny bit of potato mixture. If it starts to fry, you're ready to cook.

Add a spoonful of potato mixture to the oil. Flatten slightly with the edge of a spoon. (You want it to have nooks and crannies.) It should be about the same size as the bottom of a drinking glass.

When the edges lighten in colour and start to get crispy, approximately sixty to ninety seconds, flip over carefully and fry the other side. The latke should be golden brown.

Drain on a rack and keep in a warm oven (300F) while frying the rest.

Sprinkle a pinch of the garam masala salt over the latkes just after setting on the rack.

If the latkes fall apart while cooking, add a bit more egg to the mixture.

Only fry 3 or 4 latkes at a time. Do not overcrowd the pan. If the oil starts to smoke, lower the heat for a couple batches then return heat to medium.

Serve with applesauce, or a raita with plain yogurt, chopped Granny Smith apple and mint. No measurement needed. Make it as loose or as chunky as you'd like.

Winnipeg

Scroll, scroll, scroll, scroll, scroll, scroll, click 'I agree'.

After over an hour of filling out online forms, I was finally nearing the end of the application process. They asked for the standard info. *Name, address, phone number, mobile,* etc. Type, type, type. *Workplace name, number, occupation, job title, name of company.* Type, type, type. *Emergency contact name, address, phone number, mobile,* etc. Type, type, type.

On and on it went, *birthdate, pronouns, parents, medical info.* I wish there was a mobile-friendly form. I normally used my laptop for school, a hand-me-down from my mom. I used my phone for everything else, but I don't think I had a choice this time. The font and boxes were tiny, and the page didn't expand well. My phone would've auto-filled some of the basic info that I had to keep entering over and over again. *Name, address, phone number, date.*

What platform do you use? There were several choices. *Website, blog, videos, podcast, other.* I checked the box for *food blog* and added the website address: www.fusiononaplate.com. There were also various social media platforms. I checked off Instagram. Of course I had other social media accounts, but I didn't associate them with my blog. I liked to keep it simple. And they didn't need to see sixty-second videos of me dancing in my room.

I added a brief description of my blog, one hundred words or less: *Fusion comfort food, a mash-up of East and West and everything in between. Easy recipes of your classic cravings with a twist.*

What is the focus of your cuisine? This question was harder. I liked all types of food, whatever I'm craving at the time. I was lucky that my parents raised me to have an adventurous palate. The website listed different types of cuisines: *Chinese, Japanese, Indian, Caribbean, French, Modern…* The instructions indicated to check all that applied, which was almost the entire list. I added to the box where I could list 'Other': *Indigenous, Laotian, Scandinavian, Brazilian…* I ran out of space.

The next form was optional for statistical purposes, a series of questions asking about my race. The list read like the types of cuisine: *Chinese, Japanese, Indian, Caribbean…* The instructions indicated to check all that applied.

Filipino, check. I prefer the gender-inclusive term Filipinx, but that wasn't an option.

My mother is first generation Filipino-Canadian. She prefers the term Filipino, but I think that's out of habit. She's coming around. She was born in Winnipeg. My maternal grandparents had come to Canada in the seventies, "in search of a better life" so I've been told.

Scroll, scroll, scroll. I couldn't find Ashkenazi Jew, i.e., a Jewish person of Eastern European descent as opposed to Middle Eastern or Mediterranean.

My father is Jewish, third-generation Canadian. My baba was born in Saskatchewan and moved to Winnipeg to work in an office as a receptionist at my grandfather's company. She eventually became a bookkeeper and then an accountant for another company when my zaida had to shut the business down. Her grandparents were farmers, originally from Russia. My zaida died when I was four. My great-grandparents on his side were Holocaust survivors, born in the Poland ghettos. After the war, they had also come to Canada in search of a better life.

I checked off Polish and Russian and added *Ashkenazi Jew* to the 'Other' box.

Then came the essay questions, each of them 1000 words or less. *Why do you want to be the next Cyber Chef? What would you want to teach kids your age about food? What do you want to be when you grow up? Who taught you how to cook?* Type, type, type. It was like being in school.

My phone would have also auto-corrected a lot of my spelling mistakes. I'd have to get my mom to look everything over when I was through.

"Mom!" I shouted. "I need you to sign something!"

She popped her head in.

"How do I sign something online?" she asked. "Do I print it out?"

I scrolled down more. "You have to type your name, phone number, and the date for each of the different pages. They'll send a code by text or email to verify."

"Ooh, very tech-savvy."

I rolled my eyes. She knew it annoyed me when she was impressed by things that seemed basic to me. She's not as tech-obtuse as she pretends.

I stood up to let her take the chair. She sat down and pushed the laptop further away to a comfortable distance. My mother had been working from our home office since the very beginning of the pandemic, when almost all government offices had shut down. Luckily, she was already working one or two days a week from home as a project manager with the Feds and already had the right tools in place. I still don't quite understand what she does for a living. My dad works at the National Virology Lab in procurement. He worked from home a couple of days per week but was usually at the office. I don't quite understand what he does either, but I'm going to assume it has something to do with fighting the pandemic.

My mother scrolled to read through all the terms and conditions. Ugh. Who does that? This would take forever. I picked up my phone and looked at my video submission one more time.

I decided on a recipe that Baba and I had created together.

Baba made the best latkes. We would stand at the counter and grate potatoes into bowls by hand. We'd wring them out in old but clean tea towels, specifically put aside for pulling moisture out of shredded potatoes. Then we'd add flour, garlic powder, and salt, before adding the egg. Baba would tell stories as we prepped; about planting potatoes, caring for chickens. She grew up with food being made from seed to plate.

We had modernized the recipe using sweet potatoes and Indian seasonings of ginger, cumin, turmeric, and garam masala, further adding to the vibrant colour. Instead of sour cream or applesauce, I would make a raita with yogurt, green apple, and cucumber, a striking contrast against the bright orange of the sweet potato latke. It was one of our favourite dishes.

Lately when I made the recipe, I used a spiralizer, a gadget I got last Chanukah. I could load a vegetable into the contraption, turn a handle, and end up with a whole bowlful of noodle-shaped veggies within minutes. With Baba gone, there was no need to prolong the prep time. And besides, spiralized potatoes were far starchier and made for super crispy latkes. No need to wring out liquid with a towel. It always made my mom mad when I stained the towels orange.

I had to adjust the recipe for the competition. Not everyone owns a spiralizer. Not everyone has homemade garam masala sitting in their pantry. Not everyone is born with the innate knowledge of how big a latke is supposed to be.

I re-watched the video and pictured Baba's hands next to mine, grating the potato, adding the flour and the spices. The kitchen would smell rich with exotic scents. She would smile when she heard the sizzle of the latkes hitting the hot oil. When her fingers became too stiff to pinch the salt and garam masala to sprinkle onto the latkes as we pulled them out of the cast iron, she insisted we fill an old saltshaker because we made the dish so often.

I wiped away the tear gathering in the corner of my eye. It'd been two years since Baba passed away. I started my blog to pay homage to her recipes. I still dream of her matzah ball soup. I can almost smell the broth simmering on the stovetop—

"Okay, done," my mother announced. "And I took a look through the rest of your application and made a few corrections. Looks good, Sar."

She stood up, and I sat down. I uploaded the video then took a breath and hit the Submit button.

Now we wait.

Winnipeg

> From: M. Dunkirk (mdunkirk@fadchannelcanada.ca)
> Sent: Feb 24, 2021 12:48 PM
> Marked: High importance
> To: Sarah Dayan-Abad (sarah.da@email.ca)
> Subject: Application – Cyber Chef: Next Gen
>
> Ms. Dayan-Abad,
> Thank you for submitting your application for Cyber Chef: Next Gen.
>
> You have been screened in for the next stage of the application process. We would like to speak to you via videoconference.

Please read the attached PDF with the video conference details and required documentation. Please confirm your availability.

Thank you.
Marlee Dunkirk (she/her)
Team Leader   Talent Acquisition
Food and Drink Channel – Canada

"Mooooooommmmm!" I shouted, holding my phone up. "They want to interview me!"

"Oh, congrats!" my mom looked up from her desk. "That was fast. When is it?"

"Tomorrow!" I shrieked. I could hear the over-excitement in my voice. I tried to calm down. "I have a lot to do."

I shot off a quick text to my dad, then my Auntie Cher—pronounced 'chair', then Lena, then Jay. They each replied in turn.

Chair

i got an interview w cc !!!!!!!!!!!

Thats awesome sar!

Knew you could do it!

Lena

i got an interview w cc !!!!!!!!!!!

ahhhhhhhhhhh

!!!!!

Jay

i got an interview w cc !!!!!!!!!!!

nicee

Daddy

i got an interview w cc !!!!!!!!!!!

That's excellent, honey.

I'm so proud of you!

FaD had taken two days to reply to my application. I had been trying to put it out of my mind, keeping busy, trying new recipes, playing with new ingredients. I picked up artisan cheese, fresh bread, and pickled asparagus at a nearby grocery store that specializes in local products. I started creating cheese boards. My family was getting sick of stinky cheese.

For the past year, my parents have given me a portion of our grocery budget. As long as I fed the family, I was free to pick out whatever I wanted, but even they had their limits.

On the day of my video interview, my mom helped me set up my laptop in the den. Behind me, the kitchen island held a bowl full of mandarin oranges. White plates in neat stacks and narrow glasses in rows sat on our open kitchen shelves. It was like a kitchen straight out of a cooking show, exactly what I was going for.

However, I wouldn't be cooking during the interview. The notes said that they wanted to know more about me, my methods, my life, my influences. My mother was welcome to sit in during the interview since I was only sixteen, but she knew that would make me more nervous. She said she would be in her office down the hall with the door open.

A short melody played on my phone at two pm sharp as the video call request came in. Though it had been hours since I had lunch, I swept the front of my teeth with my tongue. I answered the call and put on my best smile. I wore a simple light blue scoop neck top, and I'd used my flat iron to give my long dark brown hair just a bit of a wave. A swipe of universally flattering coral-coloured lipstick coated my lips. I had been wearing a mask for so long, I almost forgot the feeling of lipstick on my lips.

"Hi, Sarah," the woman said, pronouncing my name *SEHR-rah,* her voice bubbly. "My name is Marlee. I'm the Team Leader of Talent Acquisition at Food and Drink Channel. Thank you for making yourself available."

She was blond with a messy bun piled on top of her head. She wore a bright pink crew neck sweatshirt that said *FaDulous* in script across the front. A huge, grey dog sat beside her on a large, overstuffed brown couch. Her hand wandered over to pat its back.

"Hello," I said, a little nervous. My heart twittered. "By the way, it's pronounced SAH-rah, with a short A."

"Pardon?"

"Sarah, it's the Hebrew pronunciation." I said gently. "I wrote in my application that I'm half Ashkenazi Jew."

Marlee's brow furrowed slightly. She wrote something down.

"Sorry about that," she apologized. As requested in the email, she asked me to show a copy of my ID. I pulled out my medical card and student ID, holding it up to the camera. She asked if I consented to have the video recorded for future review.

"Now, Sah-RAH," she said, overemphasizing the wrong syllable. I didn't want to correct her a second time. "Why do you create recipes?"

I took a deep breath.

"My grandmother was the first one to teach me how to cook," I started. After watching three seasons of *Cyber Chef,* I had an idea I would be asked this question. "When I was really little, like three years old, I started asking how I could help her prep for weekly family dinners. I would measure ingredients and sort veggies. By the time I was five, she taught me how to use a knife.

"I didn't really watch kids' programs or cartoons. I liked to watch cooking shows and videos. I learned about techniques and the science behind food. My aunt was classically trained and is the chef and part-owner of a local restaurant. She taught me more about technique.

"As I got older, I learned about different kinds of foods and cuisines. When I was helping my grandmother in the kitchen for family dinners, she would listen to my suggestions. I started playing around with her recipes and introduced her and the whole family to ingredients like miso or burrata or kimchi. Eventually I started writing down my ideas. After my grandmother passed away, my aunt suggested I start the blog."

"Fascinating," Marlee said, not looking up. She continued to write in her notebook. She turned back a page and looked up at me. "Did your grandmother pass down any family recipes? Her special pancit or lumpia?"

I bit my lip. Pancit and lumpia were traditional dishes from the Philippines. I hated having to correct her, but I didn't want her misinformed. I should have been clearer.

Even though it was a video conference, I became self-conscious again of food in my teeth. I regretted having a salad for lunch. The lettuce, the hemp hearts, the pickled asparagus—what if she could see? I knew she wouldn't be able to smell the stinky cheese on my breath, but maybe I should have brushed. I swiped my tongue across my teeth as I thought of how to frame my response.

"My baba is from my father's side," I said, trying to keep my tone gentle. "My Jewish half. We would hold Shabbat dinner every Friday night with the whole family. She passed away two years ago."

"Hmmm," Marlee turned back to other pages in her notebook. I was surprised to see so much handwriting. I was used to typing everything out on my phone or tablet when I had to take down information. Writing in a notebook was so analog. "We looked through your blog. There aren't very many Filipino recipes."

"I didn't grow up eating a lot of Filipino food," I admitted, using her term. I didn't want to get into semantics. "My mom doesn't cook. My dad is a good cook, but he usually makes comfort food, like chicken and steak and pasta and stir-fries and stuff. He's good at tacos. We also eat out a lot. Well, a lot of takeout and delivery."

"Do you eat at any of your relatives' houses?" she asked. "Extended family? Lolo? Lola? Debuts? First birthdays?"

"I have cousins, but they live in Penticton, BC," I said, wracking my brain. She had mentioned all the typical Filipinx family members, the grandfather and grandmother, the typical Filipinx events—the debutante party for eighteen-year-old girls, the over-the-top first birthday celebration, all things that I had heard of but were not part of my upbringing. "My grandmother lives in BC, helping my uncle and auntie raise my cousins. We've visited my family in Penticton a few times, but I wouldn't say we're close."

"Filipino friends? Family friends?"

I could feel my excitement ramping. She was asking so many questions. She wants to know me better. That's a good sign, right?

"No, I go to private school with a Hebrew immersion program. I was the only Filipinx—I mean, Filipino kid in my grade, maybe in the whole school. I did most of my activities through school or the Jewish community centre or through the synagogue. I went to Jewish camp and was away a lot of the summer. Not last summer, obviously.

"I hear about Filipinos having this big extended family consisting of family members related by blood and friends of the parents and grandparents, but that's kind of a stereotype. My parents don't have any Filipino friends. If my grandmother did, I never met any of them. For family, I just have my Auntie Cher. She lives here, in Winnipeg."

"Chair?"

"Yes, Cher. It's short for Cherish."

"You said she was a chef? A Filipino restaurant?"

"Uh, no," I answered. I smiled wider. "A fusion tapas restaurant. She's the one who taught me about taking flavour from one type of cuisine and mashing it with others to create something new and amazing. That's where the blog came from, because the idea was like me. I'm half-Filipino and half-Ashkenazi Jew. I am the definition of fusion."

She wrote something on another page in larger letters, but I couldn't see what she wrote. She smiled.

"I think I have everything I need." She closed her notebook. "Your story is fascinating. Thank you so much for your time, Sah-RAH. You'll hear from us very soon."

She logged off immediately. I still had the smile plastered to my face.

Winnipeg

> From: FAD Channel Canada (info@fadchannelcanada.ca)
> Sent: Feb 26, 2021 9:32 AM
> To: Sarah Dayan-Abad (sarah.da@email.ca)
> Subject: Cyber Chef: Next Gen

> Hello,
> Thank you for submitting your application for *Cyber Chef: Next Gen*. While you have not been selected as one of the contestants for this season, we were impressed with your submission and your recipes. We have received over four hundred applications across the country and were amazed at the quality of content and diverse voices from young people such as yourself.

> Please join us to watch the new season of *Cyber Chef: The Next Gen* premiering in April 2021.

> Sincerely,
> Poppy St. Martin-Dubois
> Vice President   Talent Acquisition and Development
> Food and Drink Channel – Canada

I shut off my phone as hot tears burned in my eyes.

This sucks.

Toronto

"Ms. St. Martin-Dubois," the FaD junior researcher spoke with trepidation. "I hate to bring this up, but I couldn't get a hold of Marlee."

Poppy could tell she made the researcher nervous. The girl appeared young, probably only a few years out of university, but she couldn't be one hundred percent sure based on the image of the girl on her screen. How she envied Black women for their age-less skin. She was positive she had met the girl before, but couldn't remember her name. A quick glance at her email confirmed the girl's name. *How do you pronounce that? Tonisha? Tanisha?*

Since the switch to having office staff work from their homes, Poppy felt disconnected from the team. Not that she made it a regular habit to wander the low-walled third-floor cubicle maze of researchers, copy editors, and other staff that supported the creative teams of Home & Life Canada, the parent company that owned FaD and a handful of other specialty cable networks. Food, travel, home, self-care; there was a channel for everything nowadays, all of them competing for the same viewers who could watch three minutes of condensed content on YouTube for what they perceived as 'free'.

Once in a while, Poppy would stroll past the narrow hallway alongside the cubicle village and feel the eyes of the underlings who either cowered under her gaze or worshipped the ground she walked on. She never bothered going to the fourth floor that held the high-walled cubicles where the number crunchers and paper pushers kept the bills paid. None of them would have recognized her if she walked by. This Toni girl clearly knew who she was, but was she afraid or in awe?

Working from home had its advantages, but Poppy missed the incredible meals the development team brought up from the studios to the creative floors and support staff. They never brought food up to the executive offices or the accounting and tech sections. It was an inverted hierarchy where the higher your salary, the less cool the perks. The employee lounges on the lower floors were known for their Zen décor and meditation corners. She coveted the space so much that just before the first lockdown she had requested a meditation corner be added to her office. She mused whether she should have one added to her bedroom or the unused dining room that no longer saw dinner parties or drinks with friends.

"What's wrong? Your email was cryptic," Poppy said curtly. She was known for being no-nonsense and professional at all times. Today she wore her dark hair back in a low bun and a grey jacket over a pink silk shell. For bottoms, she wore leopard print leggings and bare feet. Conversely, the junior researcher had her hair pulled into a high but neat ponytail, tight curls crowned on top. She wore a red hoodie and white tank top. She clearly took her work wardrobe cues from her supervisor, Marlee, who always wore crewnecks and sweats, her camera always pulled back far enough to show her stretched out on her couch next to her giant dog. The girl should have considered changing before sending the email with "URGENT: Contestant Problem" written across the top.

"There's a problem with one of the contestants."

"That was the subject line of your email," Poppy struggled to hold on to her patience. "And the body just said, 'Call me' which is why I'm calling."

The email was addressed to Marlee, with Poppy added as a CC, most likely for situational awareness. The girl was likely expecting Marlee to call her on mobile, not the VP of Talent Acquisition and Development on video less than a minute after the email was sent. Poppy was used to correspondence through texts and emails; however when someone asked for a call, it meant there was a problem, and she didn't want Marlee to sanitize the issue before sending it her way.

"I was doing a final check on the candidates before we sent out the promotional packages." The researcher appeared to grow in confidence as the shock of seeing her boss's boss began to wear off. "I discovered an issue with Johanna Castillo, the Prairie Region contestant, while I was doing a spot check on a recipe from her blog. I'll share my desktop."

With a click of the mouse, a website popped up on the screen. Both women were looking at Johanna Castillo's food blog, *Regina, Rice, and Everything Nice.* The girl clicked on a recipe.

"I did a random content sweep and plugged her recipe for Pork Belly Adobo over Chinese Broccoli, and it showed up on another site."

"That's not unusual," Poppy said. "Ingredients don't fall under copyright law, or else only two or three people in the world would own every cake recipe."

"I know. Recipe developers only own the recipe part, the method for making a dish." The researcher pulled up another website with a *.ph* end in the address bar. "And they own the pictures. I also did an image search, and this site came up on both searches."

Poppy frowned as the researcher scrolled through the Filipino website.

"I pasted the instructions into a translator and they're also a match." The researcher scrolled down to other recipes. "I recognized some of the other pictures. I translated those as well and they're the same as others I've seen on Ms. Castillo's site. We would have caught it earlier but no one on staff is Filipino."

"Any chance she's the same author?" Poppy asked hopefully. "Could she have created the blog in the Philippines before she immigrated here?"

"The website hasn't been updated since 2009. She would have been four years old. It looks like she was just translating the recipes into English and claiming them as her own."

"Ms. Castillo is a plagiarizer."

"It appears so."

"Thank you for bringing this to my attention. I'll give Marlee a call." Poppy exhaled in resignation. She glanced at her email quickly. She had to make a decision about how it was pronounced. She'd just go for it. "Good job, Tonisha."

"Uh, no, thank *you*," the girl said, smiling a little too widely. "Ms. St. Martin-Dubois."

Poppy knew then that she'd pronounced the name wrong. She also knew the girl was in category two, not afraid of her, but an admirer. Or at least she used to be.

T-A-N-I-Z-I-A. How do you pronounce that? She would have to ask Marlee when they spoke next.

Poppy forgot the girl's name by the time she sent a text to Marlee, asking her to give her a call, ASAP.

Chapter Three

Golden Latte, aka turmeric & black pepper in hot milk, is super healthy with anti-inflammatory properties and antioxidants. All I know is that it's super trendy and kinda spicy but really good, with a creamy and warm burn. Instead of a hot latte, why not make it a summer drink and add some immune-boosting ginger.

Iced Ginger Golden Latte
¾ cup coconut milk
1 cup almond milk
1½ tsp ground turmeric
2 tsp grated fresh ginger
1 tsp freshly ground cinnamon
1 tbsp raw honey
3 turns freshly ground black pepper
2 glasses full of ice

Heat coconut and almond milk in a pot on medium until it starts to steam. Don't let it boil!

Drop heat to low and whisk in spices, ginger, and honey. Simmer for 5 minutes.

Remove from heat. Cool for 30 minutes.

Use an immersion blender or pour into a blender and blend on high until foamy.

Strain into a large measuring cup. Pour into 2 glasses filled with ice.

Winnipeg

"I *hate* these things," Lena said as she plopped down on a chair on our covered deck. She threw her reusable mask down on the table.

"You're the one who wanted one made of velvet." I rolled my eyes. "Just stick with the cotton ones your mom made you."

"Yeah, yeah, yeah," she said, stuffing the hot pink and turquoise sequined mask into her pocket. "Health over fashion, whatever."

"Want a skull one?" Jay offered. He pulled out one from his backpack as he sat down. "I got extra."

"No," she sulked and brought out a white cotton one with pink polka dots. It still matched her parka.

As a side gig, Lena's mom made and sold customized masks out of clean recycled clothes. She asked Jay and I to purge our closets last summer before our back-to-school shopping and made us five complimentary masks each. My mom bought a dozen more for herself and my dad.

I went inside to finish our drinks, pouring the slightly warm turmeric-infused milks over ice cubes in tall glasses. Spring had come early to Winnipeg, and the snow had started to melt away, revealing dead grass and dog poop under dirty snowbanks. For mid-March plus five Celsius was practically shorts weather after our minus twenty-five winter mornings.

In celebration of the thaw, I wanted a cold yet spicy drink to warm our insides. I had placed the glasses artfully on a grey wooden tray that also had ginger root and cinnamon sticks off to the side. I added steel straws to each glass and topped off each drink with one more turn of black pepper to add visual texture as well as increase the efficacy of the turmeric's health benefits. Before passing out the drinks, I took a few quick photos for Insta. I made sure not to touch the props so they would remain unscathed before being returned to the pantry. My friends were used to waiting for me to take pictures of our food. It was a small price to pay for free drinks and snacks.

Lena grabbed her drink off the tray before I set it down. Jay picked up one glass and placed it in front of me politely before taking his. We each sat around the patio table, somewhat distanced. Although our infection numbers were low in Manitoba compared to other parts of Canada, and far below the rest of the world, my mother insisted that we maintain our social distancing, even outdoors.

Lena pulled out her phone, holding her drink in the other hand. We brought our glasses to the centre and pulled out again as she took a quick Boomerang video that would repeat the short clip over and over again.

"Cheers!" we said in unison.

Lena, Jay, and I had met in Hebrew school and had been in the same class from kindergarten to grade six. We were each outsiders that only felt a sense of belonging amongst each other. Lena's family had come from Russia when she was young and knew little English when entering school. When I had met Jay, his family had come from Argentina and had been in Canada for over a year. I was the only biracial child in the class.

We ended up going to different middle schools as we lived in different areas of the city. I was the only one of us who stayed at our private Jewish school. The three of us ended up attending back-to-back bar and bat mitzvah classes and even volunteered for the same food bank as part of our mitzvah, i.e., mandatory charity work. I had other friends from school, but Lena and Jay were my crew.

We went to different high schools too, and by that time, we had already started drifting apart. Then Covid came to town. Strangely, being forced to contact our friends through virtual means actually brought us closer together. We were already used to communicating through text and video, but our isolation made us reach out to each other more often. Once our parents gave us the okay to hang out in-person, we couldn't get enough of each other. Even though we were only allowed to get together outdoors, we were like long-lost family.

"Are you putting this up on the blog?" Lena asked, loudly sipping air from the bottom of the glass. "And is there more?"

I took her glass and slid open the doors to the kitchen. I got a couple more cubes of ice from the freezer. I had made a double batch and there was one serving of the turmeric latte left.

"I posted the recipe last month," I said. "You'd know that if you actually read it."

"I skim through the pictures," she said, taking the glass.

"Read it," Jay said. "It's a good recipe. Easy."

"Did you make this before or after the break?" Lena asked.

I had taken a couple of weeks off from posting recipes. After being rejected by the FaD Channel, I wanted to avoid anything that had to do with photographing or writing about food. I sulked in my room eating dry cereal, spoons of peanut butter, and cold ham and cheese sandwiches. I wasn't in the mood for going to the tented farmer's market in the south end of the city or checking out the vegan taco pop up from one of my favourite caterers.

Then a few days I got a DM from one of my followers on Instagram.

Knotacatlady92:

> I'm a huge fan of your blog. I have a question. For Christmas my neighbor gave me a small jar of spices. She said it was chai masala. But what is that? It smelled amazing. I thought it was chai tea powder. I mixed a spoon of it with hot milk but it was so spicy! I'm too embarrassed to ask her about it. If it's not tea, then what is it and what do I do with it???

She had attached a picture of the jar in question. I opened it up and expanded the image with my fingertips. I imagined the ground up cinnamon, cloves, cardamom, pepper, and likely a mixture of other exotic spices from a recipe handed down from mother to daughter.

Sounds like a great gift! It's probably a mixture of the chai spices in their pure form. Brew a cup of regular black tea and add a quarter teaspoon of the masala to the cup. Mix well before adding the milk and a bit of honey, then adjust for taste. You'll end up with your own customized chai latte!

Head to my blog and search for my recipe on chai rice pudding. Use your masala instead of my spices. It's a great dessert for this time of year. I'm considering working on a cookie recipe. And if you post a pic, remember to tag me!

Knotacatlady92:

Thank you so much! I knew you could help. I made the latte and it was soooo good! I even made your rice pudding and I gave a tub to my neighbor. She now follows your blog. You are so awesome! You're one of my favourite bloggers! Can't wait for the cookie recipe!

She had sent several pictures of her latte and chai rice pudding. I could practically smell the warm spices.

I had checked out the woman's profile. She lived in Montana. She had two cats and seemed to have a nice, comfortable life. And I helped her. I had followers from all over the world: Japan, England, Romania, Korea. I hit four thousand followers on Instagram last month and had just under a thousand email subscribers. I didn't create my blog for some TV show. I created it to share my love of food with people like Knotacatlady92.

Toronto

"There's only two to choose from?"

Poppy was scrolling through the different applications that appeared on her tablet. Marlee's face was on her screen as well as two other researchers: the girl with the weird name along with another researcher named Tom, which was so much easier to remember.

"You said you needed a Filipino girl to replace the last one," Marlee answered. "If we were trying to find one in Toronto or Vancouver, we would have had more selection, but in the Prairies this was harder to come by."

"I thought Winnipeg was supposed to have more Filipinos per capita than any other city outside the Philippines," Poppy said smartly. She had done her research.

"We had three more applicants," Marlee said, exasperated. "But two of them had thick accents and the last one was just too shy. I could barely hear his voice during the interview. He doesn't do video on his website, just pictures. Cute kid though."

"He's fifteen, Marlee," Tom said lightly. "So inappropriate."

"You're gross, Tom," she retorted.

Poppy flipped through the rejected candidates.

"How strong are their accents?"

"Subtitle-strong."

"That won't work." Poppy closed their applications.

They had a Singaporean immigrant with a thick accent on the show in the first season. Viewers never connected: seventy percent fewer click-throughs on the links to her blog posts, sixty percent less purchases for products. The judges did not have the luxury of subtitles and could barely understand her when she spoke. She was gone by episode two.

Poppy looked at the last two applications.

"Why'd we reject this one?" Poppy opened a video of a young woman making an ube mousse. "She seems polished."

"Her brand is too strong," Marlee answered. "She rakes in a couple thousand in ads each month. We can't use her."

"She's only seventeen?"

"My daughter watches a seven-year-old unwrap toys on YouTube. The kid makes a million a month on ad revenue," Tom piped in. *A young go-getter with kids.* Poppy thought. *This guy will do well in our company.*

"Why did we reject this one?" Poppy asked.

She pressed play on a video with a young woman making sweet potato latkes. The vibrant orange leapt off the screen. A sprig of rosemary sat next to the bowl for no other reason than to add green to the shot. The girl knew how to make colour pop.

"Out of eighty-seven recipes on her blog, only two feature Filipino dishes," the Black girl answered. *What was her name again? Tunisia? Isn't that a country?* Poppy thought. "But she has a lot of variety, some Korean, Japanese, Indian—"

"But she does a weird thing with her mouth," Marlee said. Poppy could hear her flipping through her notebook. "I knew you wouldn't like that. I'll pull up her interview. You can see it at 1:27 and again at 2:58."

"My grandmother was the first one to teach me to cook..." The girl's voice prattled on, then she did that thing, running her tongue across her teeth. Poppy clicked forward. *"...When I was helping my grandmother in the kitchen for family dinners, she would listen to my suggestions..."* Then she did it again.

Poppy sat back and tapped a key with her fingertip to pause the video.

"She's really focused on her Judaism," Tom pointed out.

"That's not a bad thing," Tunisia piped up. *No, that's not right. Not Tunisia.*

"But it's not what we're looking for," Tom countered.

Poppy continued to think.

"I like her," Poppy said after thirty seconds of silence. "She's bubbly and has the potential of a good story, but she needs work. She has to show her face more in videos. We can't have her limited to overhead shots. Tell her she does a weird thing with her mouth and she'll stop."

"What about her recipes?" *Was her name Tammy? Toni?* No, she would have remembered a Black girl named Toni, like the singer Toni Braxton. She loved that song, "Unbreak My Heart." A beautiful low soulful voice. "They don't check the box."

"She's Filipino," Poppy decreed. "She has to have something from her mom or her grandmother. She probably just doesn't want to share the recipes on her blog for public consumption. Just give her some encouragement."

"You think she'll share them with us?" Tom with the blunt questions, the important questions. She would have to consider him for the senior research position that would be available next month.

"Of course," Poppy said with confidence. "We're FaD."

Winnipeg

My phone rang, interrupting Lena's story about the gel manicure kit she bought online. She was flashing her sparkly nails in the sunlight as I glanced at the screen. UNKNOWN NUMBER. I put it down to let it go to voicemail. I don't pick up numbers I don't recognize. Most of the time it's a robocall letting me know about a credit card I didn't own. If it was someone I actually knew, they would've texted me. The home phone rang a minute later.

"SAR!" my mother called from inside the house. "Phone! It's important!"

I stood up, shaking out the pricklies from my foot that had fallen asleep while I was sitting cross-legged on the wicker deck chair. My mom slid open the door. She looked excited. I took the phone from her and sat down on the stool at the kitchen island.

"Hey."

"Sarah Dayan-Abad?" The caller had pronounced my name SEHR-ruh Diy-ANNE AH-bed. Nothing was said correctly.

"SAH-rah DAH-yuhn uh-BAHD," I corrected her. "That's me."

"Right, right," the woman said dismissively. She wasn't going to remember how to say my name. "We talked just over a month ago. This is Marlee from FaD."

I sat up straighter. Lena and Jay stood in the doorway to the deck. I had forgotten to slide the door closed. I mouthed the word FaD.

"Oh, hi, Marlee," I said, trying to sound casual. "What's up?"

"I hope you're doing well."

"Yeah, I'm okay," I said, trying for nonchalant. "School has kept me busy."

"Good, good, good." I heard turning pages. "We had an issue with a contestant and we would like you to take her place."

I tapped a button to quickly mute the phone and squealed. I stood up and motioned for Lena and Jay to come inside. They stepped into the kitchen cautiously. Screw the regulations. I motioned for them to hush and tapped the speaker button.

"Ahh, yes. I'd love to be on *Cyber Chef*." I raised my palm up to keep them from squealing as well. "What do you need me to do?"

"I'll send you an email with the details." Marlee turned another page. "Your mother will have to sign another waiver. You should expect some packages to arrive in a few days. Your media manager will be in touch shortly. You can ask them questions when they arrive. However, we do want you to do one thing, ASAP."

"Sure, anything."

"We want at least three Filipino recipes on your blog before the show premieres and two more before episode two. Can you do that?"

My mind was spinning. Jay nudged me.

"Yes, of course."

"I know that's a lot of content to dump at once," she said, attempting to be understanding. "But I'm sure you have some family recipes you can upload quickly."

"Yes, yes, of course I do." I turned to my friends with wide eyes.

"Excellent." I heard a notebook shut. "Welcome to *Cyber Chef.*"

She hung up. I put my phone down and SCREAMED. Lena and I wrapped our arms around each other and hugged tightly, jumping up and down. Jay gave me a fist bump. He wasn't a hugger.

"Hey!" my mom shouted, leaning in the doorway. "Social distancing! And you're supposed to be outside!"

I ran up to hug her and tell her the good news.

Chapter Four

What to do with day-old rice? Spice it up with Korean and Filipino flavours! Not your typical fried rice. Salty and sour and loaded with garlic. And there's Spam. YES, SPAM!!!

Kimchi Java Fried Rice with Spam & Egg
Half a can of Spam, diced
1 tbsp oil
3 cloves garlic, minced
½ cup shelled edamame beans, frozen is easiest
1 cup snow peas, ends trimmed and strings removed
2 cups day-old rice
2 tsp turmeric
1 tsp ground annatto
1 tsp oil
1 egg, lightly beaten
½ cup kimchi, roughly chopped
1 tsp gochujang (optional)

Dice up some Spam, dice it big, dice it small, up to you.

Fry it up in a large non-stick pan or wok on medium high until reddish brown on all sides.

Drop heat to medium. Add oil. Add garlic, edamame, and snow peas. Cook for 30 seconds.

Add rice. Break up clumps with the back of a spoon.

Mix garlic, veggies, and Spam through the rice.

Sprinkle turmeric and annatto over the rice. Mix through until rice is evenly orange.

Mix together kimchi and gochujang. Mix evenly into rice.

Push the rice to the outer edges of the pan, leaving space in the middle.

Add oil to the middle, heat for 10 seconds.

Pour beaten egg into the middle of the pan. Wait 30 seconds.

Scramble the egg up in the middle of the pan until soft-cooked. It's okay if some rice gets mixed in.

Once at the soft-cook stage, mix egg throughout the rice.

Serve in bowls or as a side dish.

Winnipeg

"Salt, aroma, acid," Auntie Cher chanted like a spell. "Soy, garlic, vinegar. Say it to me."

"Salt, aroma, acid," I repeated. "Soy, garlic, vinegar."

We were in Auntie Cher's kitchen with the huge gas stove and butcher block countertop that spanned the wall and peninsula. She didn't have as much natural lighting as my kitchen, but her kitchen was designed for function rather than form.

She had a rare day off from the restaurant where she was the executive chef and part-owner. Her Asian fusion tapas restaurant and bar had survived the pandemic storm by diversifying their business, offering takeout, delivery, meal planning, and even groceries. The restaurant was open with strict capacity limits that had only recently been increased to fifty percent. For the past couple of months, the regulations also only allowed members within the same household to sit together, a rule that had decimated the hospitality sector. Guests from different households could share a table on outdoor patios, but Auntie Cher couldn't justify spending thousands of dollars on heat lamps to keep guests comfortable during Winnipeg's fluctuating temperatures. The extra services kept Auntie Cher's business afloat. Unfortunately, due to vaccine shortages and a third wave on the horizon, she was still stressed out about the future.

"These are the staples to authentic Filipino cuisine," she lectured as I took notes. "Chicken adobo is chicken pieces marinated in soy sauce, chopped garlic, and rice vinegar. Pancit is noodles and vegetables sautéed in soy sauce and garlic, served with a wedge of calamansi for the acid. Tapsilog is served with garlic fried rice, usually with a side of atchara. Lumpia is often served with garlic sawsawan—"

"You're going too fast. I don't know what any of these things are." I checked my notes. "What's calamansi? What's tapsilog? What's atchara? What's sa-sa-sa?"

"Wow, Grace really raised you Whitewashed," my aunt said, referring to my mother, her older sister. I frowned. "Sorry, I meant Jewish." I crossed my arms. "Kidding, kidding. You know I love you, you little bagel."

I punched her in the arm and she laughed. I didn't mind my aunt's teasing. My mom would get pissed when her sister teased her, but my dad howled in laughter when he was the target. We understood she roasted us from a place of love.

"Why would I know anything about Filipino food?" I asked. "I don't have Filipino friends or any other Filipino family except for you, and you never bring any food over."

I knew the basics, chicken adobo: Filipino braised chicken. Pancit: Filipino chow mein. Lumpia: Filipino eggrolls. But those other terms were foreign to me.

"Then this is going to be a crash course on Filipino cuisine," she said. "I hope you like pork."

I grew up Jewish, but we didn't keep kosher in our household, only during Passover. *(Why is this night different from all other nights? Because it's the only night we keep kosher! And for the other seven days too!)* I learned to love a variety of food and was never confined to one cuisine except for Jewish holidays when our table was graced with traditional dishes.

"What dish should we start with?" I asked.

"You could have googled any Filipino recipe." My aunt took my phone out of my hands. "But you came to me, and that means no phones in my kitchen."

"But it's my phone!"

"When I catch my kitchen staff using their phone during service, they're on de-grease duty for a month. I'll bring you to the restaurant if I have to. You feel me?"

"Yes, Chef!"

"Kanin." She brought me to the pantry in the corner of her kitchen where she kept a large woven bag of rice sitting on the lowest shelf.

"That's huge."

"This is a five-kilogram bag. Most Filipinos buy bags ten kilograms or bigger. Those would be kept on the floor." Auntie Cher passed me an off-white opaque plastic cup. "Get three cups of rice and put it in here." She held the inner pot from a rice cooker in her other hand.

"What size cup is this?"

"It doesn't matter."

"What do you mean, it doesn't matter?"

"It came with the rice cooker. Measure the rice."

I levelled off three exact cups of rice as my aunt leaned in the doorway of the pantry. Maybe the plastic container was half a cup? I wanted to dump the rice into a proper measuring cup to get the exact volume, but she refused to bring one out. She explained how to rinse the rice and drain. Then rinse and drain again. She insisted on three rinses. She then said we had to add the water for cooking. When I asked her how much to add, she stuck her hand into the pot until the tip of her index finger touched the top of the wet rice grains.

"Until here." She pointed to the line marking the first knuckle.

"Until the line on your finger?" I asked incredulously. "I'm supposed to know how long your finger is?"

"Not my finger specifically. You're cooking the rice, so we'll use the line on your finger."

"That's not precise," I said. "My hand is bigger than yours. What if my dad was making this? His hands are huge."

"This is the recipe for white rice."

"What?!" I shouted. "That's not a recipe! It's not even real instructions! It's a guess! Enough rice till here? How are you a chef?"

"I'm not a chef right now. I'm a Filipino daughter whose mother taught her to cook rice."

Auntie Cher took the pot away from me and filled it with water, exactly up to the first line on the inside of her index finger. She stirred it gently with her hand until the grains settled evenly. She placed the pot into the rice cooker, put on the glass lid and pressed a single button that gave a deep audible click.

"Why doesn't my mom cook rice like this?" I said after a couple moments of silence. "She cooks rice on the stovetop or the microwave, sometimes the pressure cooker. That's how she taught me. We don't even own a rice cooker."

"Your mom knows how to cook rice this way. That's how our mom taught both of us. She just doesn't want to do it this way anymore."

"Why?"

She patted me on the hand. "We have to get some cold rice."

"But we have this fresh rice cooking."

"It's the magic of television."

"I don't mind waiting for the rice to cook."

"My recipe needs day-old rice."

"Then why did we bother to make new rice?"

The rice didn't take long but we had wasted ten minutes. I needed to learn real recipes.

"So I could teach you the way your grandmother taught me." She passed me a covered plastic container. "And to replace the rice in the fridge. I always have cold rice on hand to make Java Fried Rice or Lugaw."

My aunt had me set up the mise en place, placing the prepared ingredients in little dishes, ready to add to the dish when needed. Chopped garlic, turmeric, ground annatto, shelled edamame, trimmed snow peas. We fried the garlic in oil until the bloomy aroma filled our nostrils. We then added the now room-temperature rice, spices, and green legumes. The end result was a bright orange fried rice with a savoury scent.

Aroma...

"We should serve the Java Rice with something salty and fried." She brought out a rectangular metal can.

Salt...

As my aunt chopped up the luncheon meat into matchstick pieces, she explained how my grandmother would slice it into thin cards and fry them until they were crisp. She and my mom would get three slices each while my uncle got four, '*because he's a growing boy!*' she mocked in a Filipino accent, imitating my grandmother. She pronounced 'because' as Be-COWS. I remember giggling when I was little, vaguely remembering my grandmother's accent.

Nowadays, my aunt prefers her Spam in smaller pieces to get them crispy like bacon bits, adding some oyster sauce for a bit of salty, sticky sweetness and chilli oil to add some heat.

She filled teacups tightly with the cooked Java rice and inverted the cups on two plates to create orange mounds. She added the crispy Spam sticks on top of each rice hill, cascading down the sides like crimson waterfalls. She garnished with a couple of cilantro leaves, then dripped a soy sauce and rice wine vinegar mix on one side of the plate.

"Salt, aroma, acid," she announced.

"Spam, Java rice, vinegar and soy."

"Sawsawan," she picked up the small bowl of pungent brown liquid. "Vinegar and soy."

I looked at the artful dish. So simple, but also complex. I reached over to my phone to take a quick picture. I glanced up at my aunt. She nodded in approval.

"I don't think this is how a typical Filipino dish would be served." I stood up on a chair to take a photo from overhead.

"I had to add some soigné," she said proudly, referring to fancy plating. "Now eat it and try to get a bit of everything in each bite."

She handed me a spoon and nodded. Filipinos ate rice with a spoon. That was something we did do in our household, passed on by my mother, which must have been passed on by my grandmother, my lola. I broke into the rounded rice dome, mixing it with the sauce on the plate. I heaped rice and Spam into my mouth. Aromatic rice. Salty Spam. A hint of sour. Balanced.

I kept eating, realizing I was hungry. I asked for more sawsawan. The hamster wheel in my brain turned. I could combine this with my kimchi fried rice recipe. I could add an egg to give it some richness. But the Spam I would keep. This salty crispiness couldn't be substituted.

Before I left that afternoon, my aunt gave me a big hug and a small two-cup rice cooker she didn't use anymore. I would be back again to learn more after school tomorrow.

Toronto

Victor

It was a good gamble. Pangea Trading finally agreed to a 4% increase for the sponsorship deal.

Good job Poppy.

Poppy smiled at the text from the network president. By the second episode of *Cyber Chef: Next Gen*, FaD planned to put out the call for auditions for the next adult iteration. They would use the youth version as filler between seasons of the real show, with the premiere only a week later. By airing the shows nearly back-to-back, they could get continuous sponsorship from the high-end international grocery chain they had been working with since the first season, but she suggested the network push for an increase to the terms of the deal. More money, more power.

Victor

What about the Australia deal?

You were right about that too.

They'll start filming by September.

South Korea is also biting.

You definitely have a knack for this.

Poppy gave herself an inner high five. When she was an assistant at Home & Life Canada, she watched silently as show after show geared towards women centred on men as the hosts. Straight men, gay men, old fatherly types, strapping sex symbols. It didn't matter.

I'm a man. Let me show you how you should decorate your bedroom.
I'm a man. Let me show you how you can unclog your sink.
I'm a man. Let me show you how you can plant a vegetable garden.
She was sick of men being the authority on things that women actually do. Why did it always have to be a man?

She also noticed that it was usually a White man. A tall guy with dark hair and a fitted button-down shirt. A burly redhead with muscles. A lanky blond with a deep tan. No Black men, no Asians, no Indigenous men.

When an opening popped up at FaD sixteen years ago, Poppy made the move to Talent Acquisition and Development. She clawed her way to the top chair with a purpose of increasing diversity. FaD did have female leads in some of their top-rated shows; however, the content was often geared to working moms, single women, and health freaks.

Dinner in 20 with Laura Eastman
Table for One with Sally French
Skinny Sweets with Greta Schmidt
Correction, the shows were geared towards White working moms, White single women, and White health freaks.

Poppy wanted to develop female chefs in power positions. She wanted to feature women in commercial kitchens in commanding roles. She wanted to bring in chefs from all ethnicities, cooking diverse cuisines from all over the world. Globalism was the future and FaD needed to grab the attention of an audience that had largely been ignored.

She brought in Clara Shenzu, owner of Michelin-starred Xiao Bao in Montreal. She brought in Dionne Binds, a Caribbean-Canadian caterer to the most elite events in Vancouver. She brought in Sona Parvati, an Indian cookbook writer in Ottawa.

She brought in potential superstars who would appear in competitions, one-off features, and as guest stars. Unfortunately, she could count on one hand how many of the cooks she had personally recruited ended up with their own shows. The rest were wasted.

Poppy knew the real power was in programming, which dictated not who, but what would air. She had bided her time. She had come up with pitch after pitch of show ideas, only to have her male superiors take credit. She was patient, and she learned. She had come up with a couple of successes, but *Cyber Chef* was her baby. She had influence over the directors and shaped the show in the most diverse and profitable ways possible.

Roger, the VP of Programming, always sat back, letting everyone else come up with the ideas for him. He was a salt-and-pepper-haired dinosaur. He no longer knew how to innovate, but he was good at delegating others to innovate on his behalf. Poppy was determined to make her ideas known. Surely the network president realized how valuable she and her ideas were to the company. She could lead FaD to the future.

"Mom," her daughter popped her head into her office. "The mixer is finished kneading the dough. It's time to pull the noodles."

Poppy smiled at her daughter. She wanted to build a network with shows for her daughter and her future. She had adopted Leng from China after she found out she was unable to have children of her own. Poppy wanted her daughter to see women that looked like her on television, in positions of power and not relegated to teaching working moms how to throw together a week's worth of meals with four ingredients or less.

"Coming." Poppy shut off her laptop. The new stand mixer and dough hook were a great investment after all.

Chapter Five

These are too easy to make. And they're gooood. And addicting. Sure, you can use dark chocolate chips, but creamy white chocolate mixed with spicy chai masala reminds me of one of my favourite lattes and is too yummy to resist. Plus, your kitchen will smell AMAZING!

White Chocolate Chai Almond Butter Cookies
½ cup brown sugar, firmly packed
1 tsp ground cinnamon
½ tsp ground cardamom
½ tsp ground cloves
¼ tsp freshly grated nutmeg
3 turns of freshly ground black pepper
  (You can replace the above with ½–1 tsp of chai masala spice if you already have a recipe. Amount will depend on the strength and ratio of the spices.)
1 cup almond butter
1 egg
½ cup white chocolate chips

Preheat oven to 350°F.

In a bowl, mix spices with the brown sugar. Set aside.

Before measuring, stir the almond butter in its own jar to incorporate the oil.

In a bowl, mix almond butter and egg until smooth. Gently mix in spiced sugar.

Fold in chocolate chips until evenly mixed. The dough will be loose and chunky.

Drop by the rounded tablespoon onto a cookie sheet lined with parchment paper or a non-stick mat. Leave space in between cookies, approximately twelve to fifteen cookies per sheet.

Bake for thirteen minutes.

After removing cookie sheet from oven, do not move cookies to a rack to cool. Leave on the cookie sheet to cool completely, wait thirty minutes before devouring.

Winnipeg

"Hi, I'm Del. I'm your media manager."

A gorgeous tall woman with mocha skin and the commanding stare and stature of a goddess stood in my doorway. With her lanky build and impressive height, I thought she was a model. She had intense hazel eyes with long eyelashes, precise eyebrows, and dark brown cornrows braided tight to her scalp. A bulbous messenger bag was slung over one shoulder and she held the handle of a boxy nylon case in her other hand. She wore slim grey-washed jeans and a black leather belt with brushed metal grommets and an ornately carved silver buckle. A black mask with *FaD* screenprinted in italics in the left corner covered what I imagined to be a sharp jawline.

"Hi," I said, a nervous butterfly in my chest. "I'm Sarah."

I did a bow with my head, a standard greeting I had grown accustomed to. Del nodded in response. I'm glad she didn't extend her hand for a handshake or a fist bump as most adults tended to do. That would've been awkward.

"Good to meet you, Sarah." She was careful to pronounce my name correctly.

"Come in," my mother said, opening the door wider. "You've already met Sarah. I'm Grace Abad. This is my husband, Aaron Dayan."

"Welcome to Winnipeg!" my dad said in a boisterous voice. Del was the same height as him, but she had more hair. "Do you need help with your bags?"

"No, I'm good," she said, holding up the case with ease. "Just point me towards the kitchen and I'll set up."

My mom showed her our kitchen. Del placed her bags on the floor and walked the perimeter of the room, looking at the space from all angles. Del had emailed me a few days ago to explain her role.

Every *Cyber Chef* contestant was assigned a media manager to liaison with FaD as well as manage filming, editing, interviews, promotions, and more. The media manager held the contestants to the tight timelines and would upload footage to be included in the show. They would assist with some editing, for time only, not esthetics or anything that could affect the recipe. I had wondered how the contestants managed to get their videos so polished.

"You can remove the mask," my dad said. "You said in your email that you tested negative, and we were all tested as the network requested, also negative."

I shuddered at remembering the burning sensation at the back of my throat as a nurse stuck a long cotton swab up my nose for the COVID-19 test. It was the second time I had to take the test. Last year I had a cold a couple of weeks after school ended and after my mother had returned from a business trip. Our doctor recommended I take the test, which was uncomfortable but negative. We still had to quarantine for two weeks.

I looked over at my mom, who was giving my dad the side-eye. She wanted masks on at all times. We had talked about it last night. During set up and discussions, she wanted me to wear a mask. I would not be wearing a mask during filming. I couldn't even put on a mask between takes as I would have to keep reapplying makeup. On a regular set, someone else would be touching up my makeup, but we didn't have that luxury when the set was my kitchen. Del looked between my mom and dad.

"That's alright," she said. "I have no problem keeping it on."

"It's okay," my dad reassured her. "We talked about it."

Since getting the news about *Cyber Chef*, my dad has been a little star-struck with the idea of me being on national television. My mom was more practical, fearful of a team of camera operators and crew traipsing all over the house. She was relieved when we were told only one person would be on-site.

"No, I'm good," Del said firmly. "Safety is the highest priority, and we want to ensure your family is kept safe."

She exchanged a quick nod with my mother, who subtly exhaled. My dad's lip pouted slightly.

Del dropped her bags on the ground. We all watched as she took out a measuring tape, a high-end digital camera, and her phone. She placed each on our cordite kitchen island.

"I live in Winnipeg," Del said as she measured our kitchen island. "You don't have to worry about me travelling in from Toronto. FaD sourced all the media managers locally. I've done some freelance editing and camera work for Home & Life Canada, but only a few jobs with FaD. I live in Corydon Village."

"Not too far from Wolseley," my dad said, referring to our neighbourhood. Both areas were trendy parts of the city, Corydon known for its many restaurants and patios, including my aunt's. Wolseley was considered the hippie neighbourhood known for organic shops and activist residents. Both communities had older character houses and tree-lined streets, part of the canopy of green that covered the heart of the city.

"I'll be spending a lot of time here, so I am grateful for the short commute." Del took out her phone to snap photos from different angles. "Sarah, you do most of your work here?" She referred to the kitchen island. I was impressed that she said my name correctly.

"I do my prep here, but I usually stand on the other side for better lighting, and I do my cooking on the stove."

Del nodded and stood where I would usually stand. The large picture window above the sink gave great natural lighting during daylight hours.

"How do you get your overhead shots?" Del squatted and took pictures from the ground looking upwards.

"I use a tripod and a ring light." I opened up the walk-in pantry where I stored my equipment. "I usually only do angled shots on the tripod above the stove."

Del looked at what I had and made some notes on her phone.

"You got the packages from FaD?"

"Yeah, just give me a sec to get it. Dad, I'll need your help."

FaD had sent several boxes of stuff required for the show. I received some promotional items—a black canvas apron, three masks like Del's, a leather notebook and pen, all stamped with FaD. I also received a set of cookware, utensils, measuring cups, 18/10 stainless steel flatware, a thick butcher block cutting board, and a few plates and bowls of different sizes and shapes. All were branded names that were featured prominently on the show. The most remarkable item was a brand-new phone with the highest-rated camera on the market.

"Yes, it's all yours to keep," Del said after I asked about the promo packages. My father and I hauled everything onto the kitchen island. "I'll also get you a new tripod with some more weight and height that will give us better angles. We'll normally use my lighting kit. I'll bring it tomorrow."

The oven beeped. I went over and opened the oven door. The scent of cinnamon and spice that had already been hovering in the air doubled in strength. I pulled out a rack of cookies.

"Wait," Del said. "Do that again. I want to film it." She pulled a huge camera out of the nylon case on the floor.

"But I'm not wearing make-up or anything. Should I change—"

"No, you look great the way you are."

I ran my tongue across my teeth out of sheer nervousness.

"And you have to stop doing that with your mouth," Del cautioned. I immediately pursed my lips together and tried to keep my mouth neutral. "You got Marlee's note, right?"

I nodded. I knew it was a terrible habit, but I never realized I did it subconsciously. I had to break it before the show started.

Del had me place the cookie sheet back into the oven and reset the timer for one minute. Once beeping started, I re-enacted my movements. I walked across the kitchen, opened the oven door, and pulled out the cookie sheet. I picked up a still-warm cookie from the tray I had taken out of the oven before Del arrived. I closed my eyes and smelled the aroma of warm spices—cinnamon, cardamom, nutmeg, and cloves. I took a bite and smiled. Perfect.

"Cut," Del said, snapping me out of my sweet reverie. "That was great. You're a natural."

Halfway through racking the cookies, I had forgotten about the camera, just like when I was filming a cooking video. Easy peasy, as my baba used to say.

Toronto

Chuck

Looks good. Send to editing.

You got it boss

Text was so much easier than email. Poppy was drinking her second glass of chardonnay that evening and she didn't want to open her email and find a hundred items in her inbox demanding her attention.

She had just finished looking over the final list of videos that were ready to go to the editing department. The first show would premiere in three days and there was still too much to do. She didn't have to be this involved, but this was her choice.

Each season of *Cyber Chef* grew exponentially in terms of popularity, social media, and franchising. If half the international affiliates chose to produce a *Next Gen* show in addition to the original version, her annual bonus should cover the rest of her mortgage on the cottage.

Home & Life Canada had their fair share of reality show competitions—cooking, gardening, home repair, relationships—almost any subject could be exploited. Most competitions were filmed weeks, even months in advance of airing; however, when they created *Cyber Chef*, Poppy insisted on an interactive component. She saw the potential of social media and wanted to increase traffic to their website. She had underestimated the response.

At first, the audience response was slow, but as more people streamed the show from the FaD website, more people recreated the contestant recipes. More importantly, the audience began to take advantage of the convenience of purchasing the ingredients directly from the website.

Something simple like their grilled cheese challenge resulted in thousands of orders for organic butter, artisan sourdough, and gourmet cheese. With three percent of each purchase going to FaD, the show paid for itself. The network added affiliate links to all of their FaD recipes; however, with a built-in rabid customer base confined to their homes in the early months of the pandemic, the *Cyber Chef* recipes sold the most goods. Now that they'd increased their commission to four percent, their revenue would go up an additional twenty-five percent, all thanks to her.

As America and Europe caught on, Home & Life Canada decided to share the concept with their international partners. Again, they received revenue for each franchise. Eight countries last season, eleven countries for *Next Gen*. Networks around the world were hungry for content. Audiences were craving something other than binge-watching streamed series.

Home & Life had already taken the *Cyber* format and created a show featuring bloggers with make-up tutorials for the *Fit & Fashion* channel, but the concept bombed with test audiences and the idea was eventually scrapped. Good. She enjoyed the exclusivity.

Poppy picked up the last bite of cookie she had been eating. Her daughter was back to making cookies and treats after a week of noodle pulling attempts. She had gotten the recipe from a blog for flourless white chocolate chai cookies. When her daughter had opened up the handmade chai masala given to her from a FaD America celebrity chef, Poppy had hidden her fury. However, the spices had been sitting in her cabinet, vacuum packed and never used. The cookies were delicious, not too sweet, outrageous with spice, and had a wonderful chew.

Her daughter was considering starting a cookie business just in time for Mother's Day. Good timing. The chai cookies would have to be on the menu. And something pink. Rhubarb would be in season. Poppy got up to pour herself a third glass of wine. While at the counter, she opened the canister that held the cookies. Just one more.

Chapter Six

Salty, Sweet, and Sour. Or Super Star Sauce. Whatever you want the three S's to stand for.

Triple-S Sawsawan
¼ cup rice vinegar
2 tbsp soy sauce
1 tsp raw honey
1 tsp shallot, finely chopped
1 clove garlic, minced finely chopped
1 bird eye chilli, seeded, finely chopped (optional if you
    want your fourth S to be Spicy)

Add all ingredients to a mason jar. Seal, shake, and let stand an hour.

Use for dipping, a dripped garnish, or spooned over rice, noodles, meats, anything.

Winnipeg

"This would be so much easier if it was farmer's market season," I complained as I placed another bottle into our shopping cart. "I hate that I can't use local produce."

"If it was May or June, or even worse, July or August, you would be overwhelmed," Del said from behind a camera as she followed a few feet behind. "I've seen too many anxiety attacks when contestants realize how much harder these competitions are in real life."

FaD had sent me a gift card to Pangea Trading, a gigantic chain store that specialized in international foods. I rarely shopped there because the prices were far higher than the smaller Asian stores I usually frequented, and my parents had raised me to support local businesses instead of faceless corporations. Del cautioned me to avoid saying any of this out loud.

I wore my teal thigh-length A-line belted wool coat and dark jeans purposely frayed at the front of my thighs. My dark hair was pulled into a ponytail to keep it out of my face, which was concealed by my black FaD mask. Del wore all black—slim-fitting cargos, black leather jacket, black t-shirt, black mask. She matched the black camera perched on her shoulder.

There were other shoppers in the store, but much fewer than normal. The store's usual capacity limits were reduced further in order for Del to film unimpeded. It was all for B roll, background shots. The shoppers were told that FaD was doing some filming. The few that were allowed into the store had to sign a waiver and agree to ignore the camera. I learned that Pangea was *Cyber Chef*'s main sponsor and *Cyber Chef*'s audience was a huge source of customers for Pangea. Win-win for everyone except the little store down the street! *Shut up, Sarah, and use your gift card*, I kept telling myself.

I'd wanted Auntie Cher to come with me, but Del said it would be better to see me shop alone. FaD wanted to portray me as independent, despite the fact that I looked young.

I'm sixteen, but my whole life people have assumed I'm younger than I am. With pale skin, dark almond eyes, long dark hair, and a cherubic face with round cheeks, regardless of my age, I was often compared to a China doll. I was small for my age in comparison to my peers, but my mother often told me how tall I was for a Filipino girl. That didn't provide me any comfort when I would be picked last for teams in gym class all through elementary. In middle school, I shot up and became taller than Jay at 1.6 meters, but Lena still towers over me at 1.8 meters. No one would ever call Lena any kind of doll other than a Barbie.

"Do you want to pick out some vegetables?" Del asked.

If I were to make Del into a doll, she would be a mocha-skinned Wonder Woman action figure with cornrows. I'd buy that comic and watch the movie in a theatre.

"Sure, I have a few items on my list."

Auntie Cher had given me a detailed list of Filipino items for stocking my pantry. Soy sauce. Banana ketchup. Calamansi juice. Rice vinegar. Coconut vinegar. Rice—a five-kilogram bag. Chicharon—deep fried pork rinds. Garlic—lots of it. I drew the line at Bagoong—shrimp paste. The flavour was too pungent for my tastebuds.

Auntie Cher had taken me with her to order take-out at several Filipino restaurants over the last three weeks. She would point out the dish on the menu and place the order, saying the name of the dish with a Filipino accent.

"Lumpia Sariwa. Bistek. Sago at Gulaman. Salamat po."

Fresh egg roll. Steak and onions. Filipino bubble tea. Thank you, sir.

"Kwek kwek. Embutido. Maja blanca. Salamat po."

Deep fried quail eggs. Pork meatloaf. Coconut pudding bars. Thank you, ma'am.

"Combosilog. Tapa, longanisa, and tocino. Sunny side. Salamat po."

Filipino breakfast with fried beef jerky, sweet chorizo, sweet cured pork, served with garlic fried rice, and sunny side up eggs. Thank you, respected elder.

Almost every dish was served with atchara—Filipino pickled vegetables, and sawsawan—vinegar dipping sauce. These were two easy recipes I could make my own. I still added fusion elements such as swapping out the type of vinegar or adding raw honey.

Last night, my aunt forked a piece of tender grilled pork belly and held it up. "What do you think of the liempo?"

"It's really good. It's perfectly seasoned. Soy. Garlic." I dipped a piece into the little bowl of sawsawan I had made an hour before. "And the vinegar dip really makes the flavours pop. Salty. Sour. Aromatic. What's this red sauce?"

"Banana ketchup."

"Is it made of bananas?"

"Read the bottle when you buy it tomorrow."

As I stood in line at the Pangea Trading checkout, I picked up the bottle of banana ketchup to read the ingredient list. Saba banana, sugar, vinegar, spices, colouring. I smiled.

The lady at the cash register leaned close to me on the other side of the fibreglass partition.

"Are you going to be on *Cyber Chef*?" she asked quietly.

"I don't think I'm allowed to say."

The lines around her eyes above her mask told me she was smiling.

"Good luck," she whispered.

"Thank you." I returned the smile, though it was unseen.

I only bought about sixty dollars' worth of groceries, but I didn't have to buy everything now. Once the show started, on Monday of each week, the contestants would be told the theme, an ingredient, or a type of cuisine. We had to shop and create a recipe and video by Thursday afternoon at the latest. The judges would recreate each of the recipes in their own homes all day Friday and Saturday morning. The contestants had a video chat with the judges on Saturday afternoon; time was dependent on when they finished making the dishes. The show would air Sunday night. The cycle would start again on Monday, with one less contestant.

Luckily some of my classes were online so I would be able to do schoolwork in the evenings if necessary. My mom said I could even miss school if needed. The show was only seven episodes long and my grades were solid.

Del put her camera away and helped me load my dad's car. We had come in separate vehicles.

"You're going to have to get used to that."

"To what?"

"Being recognized."

"It's not going to be that bad, is it?"

"You're not going to have paparazzi following you around." Del shut the hatch. "But you'll get a lot of 'I'm a huge fan! You're my favourite!' especially from kids."

"Because I'm a teenager?"

"Because you're on TV."

I leaned against the car, keys in hand. My dad's car was always spotless, so I didn't worry about getting dust on my back.

"Do you want to go for coffee?" I asked. "I don't have to have the car back for another hour."

Fifteen minutes later we were sitting at a patio table outside of my favourite café on Broadway. Del was sipping a Flat White, and I was holding a London Fog, warming my fingertips. The afternoon had a mild chill, but the sun was shining and almost every table was occupied, spaced two metres apart.

"How did you get into camerawork and editing?" I asked. The tea was sweet and foamy, with a hint of lavender. Our FaD masks sat in front of us on the table. "You go to school for it?"

"Yeah, I started out in a vocational program in high school." Del nodded at the cup in approval after she took a sip. "Then I took some college courses in video and sound engineering. I'm not in Toronto and I didn't want to work for a news station. Freelance was the way to go."

"Is there a lot of work?"

"A lot more now since the beginning of the pandemic. I have a large web portfolio and I understand streaming. Mostly it was being in the right place at the right time. What about you?" she asked. "I read your grandmother got you into cooking."

"My baba."

"Ah, on your dad's side. I kinda figured."

"How'd you know?"

"There are a lot of pictures of relatives from your dad's side, very few from your mom's side."

"Yeah."

"I'm not trying to pry. Just an observation." She put down the cup. "Sorry, I shouldn't have said anything."

"I don't have any of my mom's family here except for Auntie Cher." I put my cup down. "My grandmother has lived in BC my whole life. We don't visit her often. She's helping my uncle and aunt with my three cousins."

"That's kind of expected for the grandma, right? Filipino grandparents help raise the grandkids?"

I shrugged. "I wouldn't know."

"I have a lot of Filipino friends," Del said. "I grew up in the Maples. Most of my friends were Punjabi or Filipino. I grew up on samosas and egg rolls."

"Then you've had more experience with Filipino food than I have."

"Really? But you've been making Filipino food all week."

"It's for the blog. Marlee asked me to add more Filipino recipes. I have one more to make before this Sunday's premiere."

"I'm not surprised." She gave a slight snort. "Expect more of that."

"More of what?"

"I've already said too much."

Del stood up, picking up our empty mugs and taking them to a table next to the door. A woman with a short blond bob sitting alone leaned to the side and turned away as Del passed her by. It was subtle, but definitely noticeable. I frowned. A year after the protests and this shit still happens. I shot the woman a dirty look as Del returned to our table, unfazed or indifferent to what happened. She picked up her mask and leather jacket.

"Shall we?" she said.

"Yes, please."

Thirteen years ago
Winnipeg

"This is bullshit, Grace."

Cher could tell from the look on her face that her sister thought she was being a drama queen. Takes one to know one.

"I told you to not bring anything," Grace said gently, keeping her voice down.

"It's not as if you keep kosher." Cher was still holding the warm pan. "Can I at least put this down somewhere?"

"Fine."

Grace led her sister into the kitchen and pointed to the counter. Cher put the pan down. She lifted a corner of the foil, a luxurious savoury steam releasing into the air. Grace took a step back in disgust. Cher was annoyed at herself for feeling offended.

"You had ribs at my house last week."

"It's Shabbat and Aaron's parents are here." Grace glanced over to the doorway of the dining room. "You should've figured that out when I invited you over on a Friday."

Cher felt a little bad. Aaron's family were good people.

She thought for a moment. "Is Esther here?"

"Of course."

Aaron's mother was one of the nicest people she had ever met. And with Sarah, she was a Jewish version of a Filipino lola, an influence Sarah needed.

"I'm sorry," Cher acquiesced. "I've been working every night for three weeks straight. I have no idea what night it is. Don't you usually have Friday night dinner at her house?"

"She's remodeling her kitchen. You'll be happy to hear she's getting the gas stove you recommended."

Cher sealed up the liempo with foil.

"Fine, what should I do with this?"

"Just stick it in the fridge. Aaron loves your liempo."

Grace left the kitchen to entertain her guests. A toddler skipped into the room, her dark hair in pigtails.

"Auntie Cher!"

"Hello, Princess Sah-rah." Cher always loved to exaggerate Sarah's name, stretched out like the notes in a song. "I have something for you."

"What is it?"

Cher pulled the foil up again, and Sarah hopped onto a kitchen chair to peek into the pan. A heavenly scent of pork, garlic, banana ketchup, and soy wafted out. Cher could practically see her niece's mouth watering. Sarah reached out a tiny hand like she was going to swirl her finger into the rich red sauce.

"Sarah!"

The little girl pulled her hand back and bolted upright guiltily as her mother towered in the doorway.

"Go say hi to Baba and Zaida."

She smiled at Cher and hopped out of the room like a bunny rabbit, her pigtails swinging as she bounced.

"I told you, I don't want Sarah eating that crap." Grace seethed.

"It's organic pork."

"It's fried fat and salt," Grace lectured. "Filipino food is a gateway to junk food."

"It's not like Sarah is a vegetarian."

Cher reached into the pan and pulled out a slice of grilled pork belly, thinner than a pork chop, thicker than a slice of bacon, about the length of her finger. The meat bent from tenderness. The fat was perfectly rendered, the top crispy. Her fingers were covered in the sweet and salty red glaze.

"When Tatay used to make this, it was your favourite." Cher

bit into the meat, soft enough so her teeth cut through easily. She licked the sauce from her lips. "He made some sort of pork belly every weekend but called it thick bacon: saucy red bacon, crispy chunky bacon, hot and sour chopped bacon—"

"Whether he called it liempo or fancy bacon, that's why my daughter never met her grandfather, because of this crap." Grace stepped towards Cher. "I changed my mind. When you go home tonight take that pan of heart attack back with you. Aaron needs to watch his cholesterol anyway."

Grace grabbed a pitcher of water out of the refrigerator and took it to the dining room. Cher took another bite of the liempo piece in her hand, closing the foil over the pan. A little head peeked around the corner.

"Can I come in now?" Sarah asked.

"Of course." Cher waved her in. "Do you want to try this?"

She held out the piece of pork belly to the toddler. Sarah grabbed it right away and smelled it. She smiled and stuffed it into her mouth. She closed her eyes as she chewed.

"Can I have more?"

"Maybe later, Princess." Cher wiped Sarah's hands and mouth with a dishcloth. "We're having dinner soon. It looks like…" She peeked in the oven. "Brisket. Thank God, I think your baba brought it. I was worried your mom cooked."

The little girl didn't have liempo again until another thirteen years had passed.

Chapter Seven

My take on Sago at Gulaman, a refreshing Filipino drink
sweetened with arnibal syrup, with unflavoured gelatin
and small boba-like pearls made of cassava starch instead
of tapioca. While the drink isn't as sweet as one would
think, I wanted to introduce the chewiness of the delicate
transparent sago pearls and the sweetness of arnibal brown
sugar syrup, to the much deeper flavoured milk tea. No
gelatin required.

Milk Tea with Sago
Lots of filtered water for boiling
¼ cup dried sago pearls, large size, white or rainbow coloured
2 cups hot water
2 tbsp loose or 5 bags black tea (I prefer Earl Grey, but
    English Breakfast will do)
¼ cup brown sugar
Ice
1 cup milk (dairy or non-dairy)

Prepare Sago:
Fill a medium-sized pot two-thirds full with filtered water.
Cover and bring to a boil.

Add sago pearls. Mix. Cook uncovered for 10 minutes on
high. Stir occasionally.

Drop heat to medium. Continue to boil and stir.

After 20 minutes, add more water to reach the two-thirds point.

Bring back to a boil on high then drop heat back down to medium.

Cover and cook for 30 more minutes. Stir every 5 minutes.

After 60 minutes total cooking time, turn off heat, stir one more time, cover, and let cool completely, 2 hours or more. Most of the pearls should be translucent.

Prepare tea:
At some point, while the sago is cooking, prepare the tea. The tea is strong because it will be watered down with ice and milk.

Steep tea in hot water for 5 minutes. Strain out loose tea or remove tea bags.

Let cool completely.

Sago in Arnibal Syrup:
Strain sago using a colander for two minutes.

Place the drained sago back into the pot. Add brown sugar.

Heat on medium until sugar is dissolved. Remove from heat. Cool 15 minutes.

Prepare drinks:
Ladle the sago and syrup among 4 glasses. Fill the glasses with ice.

Divide the tea evenly among the glasses.

Carefully pour milk into each glass. Take a picture while it swirls with the brown tea.

Mix before drinking. Use a wide boba straw.

Winnipeg

Lena

i m soooooo nervous for you

!!!!

stop that

ur making me more nervous

I put my phone down on the coffee table next to the concrete coaster where my drink sat. Condensation beaded on the glass. I hadn't drunk much of the milk tea. I knew it was delicious though. It was the latest recipe I had posted on my blog, based on random ingredients my aunt and the internet had assured me went together.

"Where are the other musketeers?" Auntie Cher asked, pointing to my phone. She had taken a rare night off from the restaurant, leaving her sous-chef in charge.

I wanted my friends to come over and watch the premiere with me, but my parents said no, as they always did since the most recent lockdown. I was hoping they'd make an exception this time, but they were straight edge when it came to the pandemic rules. Each household was only allowed two designated household visitors, which meant a bubble of only two other people. My aunt was one of those designates and Del was now our Number Two.

I sat between my mom and my dad on the couch in our den. Auntie Cher sat on the loveseat. I was hoping Del would come over, but she said she had to watch on her own in order to take notes and possibly make a few calls.

"I can't handle Lena's screaming, even if it's over video chat." I picked up my phone to check for the latest text. I turned the screen towards my parents and my aunt.

Lena

4 mins 2 go

how can u stand it

?????????????

i m dyinggggggg

I could handle her if I was still an outsider and we were watching the show as regular fans, but I couldn't take her excitement when I was the subject.

"What about Jay?" my aunt asked.

"Working."

Jay was my calming influence with his stoic three- or four-word comments, but he had to work as a busser at his family's restaurant. He usually didn't work on Sundays, but he'd been called in to take over for someone. Sundays were great nights for tips. He got a percentage of what the servers received. He was saving for his half of a car. The other half would come from his bar mitzvah account.

My parents gave me the same offer, but I was in no rush since my parents had two cars, one of which was almost always available. I wasn't ready for a job anyway. Too busy with school and the blog, and now *Cyber Chef.* I was considering getting a job this summer, but what if I win? OMG, I shouldn't be thinking this way. I could be jinxing myself. Or am I being confident? My mom is always telling me to believe in myself, that I had permission to let myself believe I can accomplish something.

My phone buzzed.

Jay

gluck

Jay always kept it short and simple.

I took another sip of the creamy milk tea, then spooned some tapioca. I loved Hong Kong and Taiwanese boba but never realized Filipinxs had their own version with cassava-sago and gelatin. I had tried sago before at other boba houses, usually with coconut-based drinks. I think I prefer the lighter sago to tapioca bubbles.

My phone buzzed again.

Lena

here we gooooooooooooooooo

Thanks, Lena. I picked up my phone and turned off the vibration. The show was starting.

Four days ago
Toronto

"How's this? Black girl in One. Gay guy in Two. Chinese guy in Three. Green Gables in Four. Métis girl in Five. Filipino girl in Six."

Poppy arranged the pictures of the six contestants in front of her on her desk. She had printed them off and cut them out like a kindergarten project. They were trying to determine the grid in which they would display the six *Next Gen* contestants on screen and in ad copy.

Kendra Black Quebec 17	Geoff White, Gay? Vancouver 15	Li Calgary Chinese 13
Harriet White Nova Scotia 14	Cindy Metis Toronto 17	Sarah Filipino Winnipeg 16

"You can't have both Asians in a column like that." She didn't like the esthetics. This had to look perfect. This grid had to reflect the diversity of Canada. She needed the perfect colour palette. Poppy moved the pictures around again. She consulted the names on the back. "Switch around Sarah for Harriet."

"Which one is Sarah?"

"The Filipino girl."

"Okay, got it."

Poppy consulted her list.

"Jenna sent in her host vid?"

The Digital Director consulted the files in his inbox.

"Just got it."

"Perfect." She sat back. "When it's put together, send me rough copy, okay?"

"You got it, boss."

Poppy logged off. She was pleased with the host they had chosen this season, a nineteen-year-old Inuit singer from Nunavut. Jenna Akeeagok had gone viral in the fall with her covers of Beatles classics with drums and throat singing in the background. She sang like a pop diva. Jenna was also gorgeous with high cheekbones, tall and thin, and had a bubbly personality. People gravitated towards her creativity, and she had just the right look. She had gotten the attention of the right people and was due to release a song in May. Nabbing her as host of *Cyber Chef* was Poppy's idea, bringing her name back into the conversation. Win-win for everyone.

Poppy had her hand in all facets of the production. She had even hand-picked the audition videos and suggested the clips that should air. She didn't usually get so involved in production, but last week she heard a rumour that the network president was considering retiring. Everyone knew Roger Eddington, VP of Programming, would get the job. He'd been with the network for almost twenty-three years. He was a dinosaur, but he was good at surrounding himself with the right people. Poppy was eyeing the soon-to-be vacant programming position, which she had been coveting for years. Surely Roger would know that she was the right person.

Dammit. Poppy looked down at the grid again. She couldn't have the two guys next to each other. She didn't care that one of them was clearly gay. She moved the pictures around again and opened her laptop. The Digital Director answered right away.

"Chuck, we have to make another change."

Winnipeg

"...seventeen-year-old Sarah started her blog *Fusion on a Plate* two years ago, inspired by her grandmother's recipes..."

"It's you, Sar!" Auntie Cher shouted.

A video clip of my hands grating sweet potatoes graced the screen.

"She didn't say your name right," my mom pointed out. "Do you think you can tell them to fix it? Maybe ask Del?"

"Shhhh!" I waved away her concerns, too enthralled by my image on our eighty-inch TV.

My smile filled the screen as I picked up the sweet potato and loaded it into the spiralizer. I was suddenly self-conscious of my thin eyebrows, and I probably should have worn a slightly darker lipstick.

"Grating is great, and traditional, but if you have a spiralizer, the higher starch content will create a super crispy crust, like biting into a funnel cake.

"My grandmother was the first one to teach me to cook." A clip of my interview with Marlee started to play. "When I was really little, like three years old, I started asking how I could help her prep for weekly family dinners. I would measure ingredients and sort veggies. By the time I was five, she taught me how to use a knife."

The shot changed to me spooning the latke mixture into the oil as my voice continued to speak over the video.

"As I got older, I learned about different kinds of foods and cuisines. When I was helping my grandmother in the kitchen for family dinners, she would listen to my suggestions. I started playing around with her recipes and introduced her and the whole family to ingredients like miso or burrata or kimchi. Eventually I started writing down my ideas."

The shot cut back to my face, this time tighter.

"She passed away two years ago."

The shot cut to the picture of the final product, a close-up of the plated latkes.

"Sarah's crispy sweet potato fritters are loaded with Asian flavours representing her culture and family. Inspired by her lola's recipes, her love of fusion cooking knows no bounds."

Lola? What about Baba? I don't even know my lola.

"What was that?" my mom asked, turning down the volume as a commercial about stomach acid remedies started to play. "First they said your name wrong and now they think your blog is based on your 'Lola's Recipes?'"

She put air quotes around 'Lola's Recipes'. She looked almost angry. I looked over at my aunt. *Help me,* I pleaded with my eyes. *You got me into this.*

"Well, technically a lot of the recipes I've been teaching her over the past two weeks came from Mom, and Sar has adapted those recipes for the blog." Cher explained. "Maybe that's what they're getting at."

"It's probably just a misunderstanding," my dad said, trying to calm down my mother, her eyes even wider. "We can call Del after the show."

"Mom, it's not a big deal," I said, feeling a small squeeze on my heart. "I can correct them about how they say my name. And Auntie Cher did teach me Lola's recipes."

My mom crossed her arms and sat back. I picked up my almost empty glass and sipped on the last of the sweet drink. I didn't dare pick up my phone. I didn't want to see messages from Lena or any of my friends. We weren't the only ones who were watching *Cyber Chef.*

After returning from commercials, they showed clips of the judges watching different videos and trying to recreate the recipes, some that turned out great and some that turned out terribly wrong. Not only was the host different from last season, but the judges had been replaced as well. The three new judges were younger, hipper, cooler. A chef in her early twenties that had a show on FaD. A young baker with a hugely successful YouTube channel. A well-known comedian from Toronto who enjoyed cooking. They showed a clip of the baker grating a sweet potato as she watched my video on a tablet propped on her kitchen counter.

Finally, the host announced the six contestants from the clips of twenty videos they had shown throughout the episode. A video of each person waving would take up the space of the whole screen and shrink down to a box in one of six spots. Del had filmed my clip three days ago. The host, Jenna, spoke each contestant's name with passion.

"Kendra from Quebec with her doubles; Harriet from Nova Scotia with her fish tacos; Li from Calgary with his hand pulled noodles; Geoff from Victoria with his grilled lamb; Sarah from Winnipeg with her sweet potato fritters; and Cindy from Edmonton with her bannock pizza. One of these six contestants will be the next *Cyber Chef: Next Gen!*"

My family broke into applause, my father and aunt enthusiastically pulling me up to hug me. My mom, not so much. She picked up the empty glasses to take them to the kitchen.

I picked up my phone, swiping away the dozens of messages from Lena and texts and DM's from other people who were watching the show. I went straight to the *Cyber Chef* site, the address bookmarked from my previous fandom. I clicked on my name and the recipe I had sent in.

Sweet Potato Fritters.

Not Latkes. Fritters.

I went to my blog to make sure I changed the name of the recipe. It would make more sense if they matched.

Chapter Eight

Salty and sour glaze. Use it for wings, chicken, pork, or as a dip.

Adobo glaze
1 tsp oil
2 cloves garlic, minced
¼ cup chicken broth
¼ cup + 1 tbsp white vinegar
¼ cup soy sauce
3 bay leaves
2 tbsp water
2 tsp cornstarch
Black pepper

Heat saucepan on medium. Mix oil and garlic, add to pan. Sauté until fragrant, about 1 minute.

Add broth, ¼ cup vinegar, soy sauce, and bay leaves.

Bring to a light boil. Reduce heat to low.

Mix cornstarch in water to make a slurry. Stir a spoonful at a time into soy sauce mixture until thickened. Turn off heat.

Stir in remaining 1 tbsp vinegar. Remove bay leaves.

Winnipeg

Lena

u don't think i should say anything

srsly

?

its not that bad

and ur on tv

my moms real mad

UR'ON CYBER CHEF

cmon

"Sorry, there was construction. I got stuck in traffic." Del placed her bags on the ground. "Sherbrook was down to one lane."

I put down the remainder of my breakfast smoothie. I was used to hearing complaints about construction. I had gotten used to all the roadwork but was rarely in a rush, so it didn't bother me as much as it did my parents.

"My dad already left for work and my mom's in her office. She's just on the phone. Do you want coffee?"

"No time. We have to set up right away."

"Really? I thought the call wasn't until eight."

"You're meeting with the other contestants at seven forty-five and we'll need time to prep."

We quickly set up the laptop in our breakfast nook, which had the best lighting. It was a sunny morning, but luckily the gauzy sheers on the bay window diffused the bright sunlight. Del set up a camera on a tripod about a meter behind me, above my shoulder. She said it would be out of shot. She also clipped a small camera onto my laptop. My mom popped her head into the room to say hi and tell us that she'd stay out of the way but keep her office door open. She nodded at me before leaving. We had discussed last night that I would talk to Del.

"Del, the host, Jenna, she kept pronouncing my name wrong."

I heard the uptick in my voice that phrased the sentence as a question instead of a statement. It was one of my mom's pet peeves—people that continually spoke in questions, as if they were asking for permission to have their own opinion.

"Yeah, I heard it too." She didn't look up as she fiddled with the cords and looked at the screen of her laptop on the other side of the kitchen island. "We can't really do anything about it at this point."

"Why?"

"We have to maintain consistency."

"But my name is SAH-rah, not SEHR-rah—"

As I heard the words come out of my mouth, I started to wonder if I was making too big a deal about it. People often said my name wrong. I'd correct them and if they still said it incorrectly, I would silently judge them for their short attention span. But this was different. It was out there for thousands of people—no, tens of thousands, maybe more. Someone would be at work or school the next day and say, *"Hey, did you see what SEHR-rah made last night on Cyber Chef?"*

"Sar, we have to go along with it." Del turned to me. "It's part of the continuity. Besides, SEHR-rah is easier to remember. The judges will remember it. The audience will remember it. That's what's important here."

Maybe she was right. Hundreds of applicants wanted to be in my spot. I should be grateful that anyone was saying my name at all, no matter how badly it was butchered.

Del picked up her phone and sent a text. She got a response immediately.

"They're ready for us."

Apparently, we had to log in about fifteen minutes before the actual call with the host and director for the candidates to get to know each other a bit, something Del and the other media managers had arranged. It was apparently a *Cyber Chef* Monday tradition.

I was already prepared for school, although I expected to arrive late for the first period. I was lucky to be in the literal centre of the country. Harriet in Nova Scotia and Cindy in Toronto would have already missed class this morning. Kendra was in university and was almost finished with exams. It was nearly seven am in Calgary where Li was located, and Geoff in Vancouver had just rolled out of bed for six am.

"It's too early for this," Geoff complained. "I didn't even have a chance to make my matcha latte yet."

"I drink matcha in the morning too!" Cindy said.

Kendra had cold brew coffee each morning. Li had green tea. Harriet and I had a smoothie that doubled as breakfast. Kendra, who lived in Quebec, had a lovely French accent. Harriet, from the east coast, had a Maritime lilt to her voice. We all talked for a while about our breakfast drinks. Geoff wandered away to make his latte. We could hear his media manager getting annoyed in the background. He rolled his eyes as he sat down.

"Hey, hey!" A pretty young face popped on screen in a new window, waving both hands, palms out. She had logged in at exactly eight am. "I'm Jenna! Great to finally meet all of you!"

All of us waved at the screen, giant smiles on our faces to match that of our host. We were introducing ourselves as an eighth person logged in.

"Hey, kids. I'm Chuck," said a guy wearing bulky black headphones with a mike attached. He had pandemic hair and a bushy beard. "I'm the digital director for *Cyber Chef.* You won't see my video box in the final edit. I'm here to guide things along."

"Oh, like a real director, like on TV?" Li asked.

"Yes," Chuck said, not hiding his annoyance. "Like a real director on TV."

Li was the youngest of the group at thirteen, but one of the most experienced. He had been cooking in his parents' restaurant in Calgary since he was nine years old. When he was eleven, in pursuit of the YouTube dream, he started taking videos of himself performing his daily job of prepping vegetables.

One video had gone viral last year where he had expertly chopped carrots, onions, garlic, bok choy, and cabbage, his tiny hands wielding a giant cleaver. He added a bit of oil, whole shrimp, garlic, and chilli peppers into a searing hot wok, the items dancing in the pan with heat. After a bit of tossing, he added the veggies into the wok, adding dashes of various sauces that sizzled at the bottom of the pan. He stirred it just a little longer and held the handle of the wok with both hands to pour the contents into a large bowl with an oriental design along the trim. He then held the bowl towards the camera, which panned out to reveal the short and sure eleven-year-old chef.

"Jenna is going to reveal the mystery ingredient for this week," Chuck explained. "Then we want all of you to react. I'll call your name and I'll unmute you. Tell us your first impressions; maybe tell us what you're thinking of making. Any questions?"

Several of us nodded, others gave a thumbs up. I saw the microphone icon in the corner of my screen switch to red, indicating that I was on mute. I saw hands take the latte away from Geoff. He pouted. Several of us suppressed giggles.

"I'm excited to announce this week's mystery ingredient," said Jenna in a bubbly voice. "This is actually one of my favourite foods. I've been eating these since I was a little kid—yes, I know that wasn't very long ago. In fact, I had these for dinner last night. Today's mystery ingredient is... chicken fingers!

"Specifically, Beck's Panko Breaded Chicken Tenders, available in the frozen section at Pangea Trading!"

I turned to look at Del who stood off to the side, the only person in the room. She pointed at the camera on my laptop. That's right, I'm supposed to be focused on the video chat. I placed the smile back on my face.

"Okay," Chuck said, bringing back our attention. Some of the other contestants were writing notes. Another was talking to someone off to the side. "I'll give you a few seconds to come up with ideas then I'll call on you individually to give your thoughts."

Chicken fingers. Not a fan. I realize this is the teen version of *Cyber Chef*, but was the entire season going to be like this? What's next? Mac n cheese? Corn dogs?

"Okay, Kendra, you'll be first." Chuck signalled Jenna.

"Hi, Kendra," Jenna said, right on cue with a beaming smile. "Do you like chicken fingers as much as I do?"

"Not really."

"Kendra," Chuck interrupted. "This is a sponsor. You'll like them. It's deep-fried chicken. We all like deep fried chicken. Jenna, again."

"Hi, Kendra," Jenna started over, the smile even wider. "Chicken fingers are awesome, right?"

"Yeah, they're pretty good."

"What are you thinking of making?"

"As you know from my blog, *Caraibes avec Kendra*—ah, *Caribbean with Kendra*, I like adding some traditional spices to all of my dishes. I'm thinking of using some jerk spice and perhaps some mango or pineapple chow."

"She's polished," Del said, watching her screen. "Smart to mention the blog and the theme."

"Should I do that?" I asked.

"You don't want to copy her directly, but this is the time to create your brand."

I started to take down notes for an idea for a dish. Chicken. Breaded chicken. Versatile.

"Geoff, you're next."

He took a big swig of water before starting.

"I'm barely awake and Joanne took away my matcha latte."

"Then wake up," Chuck instructed.

"Glad you could join us, Geoff," Jenna said, continuing her exuberance. "What about you? Your thoughts for a chicken finger recipe?"

"Like, I'm thinking of some kind of take on Chicken Parmigiana. Homemade marinara, a fuck-ton of cheese—"

"You can't say that," Chuck admonished. "Start again."

Geoff took a breath. "I'm thinking Chicken Parmigiana with marinara, cheese, a LOT of it. It'll be awesome."

"Thanks, Geoff!" Jenna looked down at unseen notes. "Cindy, you're next."

"I'm ready," Cindy said in a confident voice.

"Hi, Cindy!" Jenna said. She never lost her cheeriness. Luckily it seemed sincere or else it would have grated on me. "What are your chicken finger ideas?"

"First thought that comes to mind is Indian Tacos."

"Uh, Cindy," Chuck interrupted. "You can't say that."

"You know I'm Métis, right?" Cindy pointed out. "I can say Indian."

"But we prefer if you use the term Indigenous."

"But Indian Tacos is the name of the dish. I can't call them Indigenous Tacos. That sounds dumb," she insisted. "My parents came from Manitoba. It's a common thing there. Sarah, you've heard of Indian Tacos, right?"

"Uh, actually my name is—"

Del cleared her throat loudly. I looked over at her.

"You're still on mute, Sar. And don't." She gave me a stern look. "Just answer the question."

"Sorry, I was on mute," I said, clicking on the microphone icon. "Yeah, I've seen Bannock Tacos at a lot of places here."

I was also uncomfortable using the term 'Indian Tacos'.

"That's perfect," Chuck said. "Use those words, 'Bannock Tacos'. Thanks, Sarah. Okay, Cindy, start again."

Cindy appeared to give me a dirty look, even though I knew she was only frowning at her screen and not at me directly. She took a deep breath and plastered a smile on her face.

"I'm thinking of making Bannock Tacos," Cindy said flatly. "Basically tacos on fry bread, which is fried bannock. Cause that's what Indigenous people like to eat. Bannock."

"Thanks, Cindy," Chuck said, oblivious to her demeanour. "Sarah, we might as well go to you."

"Hi, Sarah!" Jenna beamed. "What are you thinking of creating with chicken fingers?"

"I'm all about fusion cooking, taking different cuisines and mashing them together."

"Ooh, what are you thinking of combining?"

"I love making sushi, so I was thinking maybe a chicken finger sushi."

"That's it?" Chuck asked. "I can get sushi with chicken fingers pretty much everywhere. Add some creativity. Maybe add a cultural spin?" He looked over to the right, maybe at another screen. "Something in line with your *Fusion on a Plate* cooking blog?"

Del pushed a note over to me. *He wants you to add something Filipino.*

"Of course, I wasn't finished." My mind kicked into hyperdrive. "I was considering making a chicken finger sushi with a chicken adobo glaze. Lots of soy, garlic, vinegar, the staples of Filipino cuisine."

"That sounds delicious!" Jenna clapped her hands. "Thank you so much, Sarah!"

Each time someone said my name, it was like nails on a chalkboard.

"You did good, Sarah," Del said once my microphone was muted.

I was glad to hear my name out loud the way it was supposed to be pronounced. Now I had to figure out if I could pull off the food that they wanted me to make.

Twelve hours earlier
Winnipeg
"Chuck, Jenna said Sarah's name wrong."

Del had called the digital director as soon as the first episode of *Cyber Chef: Next Gen* had ended. Her job was to keep her assigned contestant on task and upload footage for the show. She was basically the director on this side of the screen; however, she wanted to ensure her contestant was treated with respect. It was only fair.

"How did she say it?" he said, exasperated.

"SEHR-rah," Del enounced carefully. "It's supposed to be pronounced SAH-rah, the Hebrew pronunciation."

"Yeah, that's not a big deal."

"It's a pretty big deal to her and her family. Aren't you worried about offending them?" Del cautioned. "What if they consider it anti-Semitic?"

"Del, don't lecture me. I'm Jewish." Chuck sounded annoyed. She knew she had to back down. "Trust me, it's not a big deal. Jews don't care how their name is pronounced."

"But, Sarah—"

"Listen, she's not even supposed to be on the show. She was a last-minute alternate. Did you know that Del?"

"Yeah, I knew that—"

"And they didn't even want her." Chuck was ramping up into a tirade. "They settled for her because they needed a Filipino girl. They always design the season to check certain boxes, and they needed her to check a goddamn box. Something about the sponsors needing to promote a variety of international foods and they needed a Filipino this season.

"Now you're telling me she's Jewish, not Filipino. Well, that's too bad because they needed a Filipino and that's what she's going to be. She doesn't even look Jewish. She looks Filipino."

"I never said—"

"She should be happy she's on TV. She has a chance to win a bunch of money and prizes and get a shit-ton of hits on her blog. That equals money too. She can help out her family and get her fifteen minutes of fame. If she has a problem with how we say her name, you can tell her to get over it. If she gets pissed off and corrects the host or one of the judges on how they pronounce her name, you can bet that she is done.

"My name is Chaim, as in HIGH-Eem. Everyone said it wrong, so I changed it to Chuck so that goys could deal with me. Do you think I would be where I am with a name like Chaim? And this kid's name is Sarah. SEHR-rah! Everyone says it that way! That's the normal way to pronounce it! It's not a bat mitzvah. The world doesn't need to know the Hebrew pronunciation. You can tell her that she needs to grow the eff up!"

Del had pulled her phone away from her face, distancing herself from the volume of Chuck's rant. She had so much to say, but she knew she could be replaced. She clenched her jaw, forcing herself to keep words locked inside.

Last spring it was easy to be vocal, to fight back. *#BLM* Everyone wanted to listen and for a short while she felt heard.

But as time passed, the jobs stopped coming. It had nothing to do with the colour of her skin, and more to do with less work to go around. With the economy coming to a standstill, fewer people needed her services. She was only able to secure work with the Home & Life Canada group because of her experience in digital and streaming technology. She needed the work and she couldn't burn a bridge. And this job was a good get. Media Manager looked far better on a portfolio than Camera Operator or Digital Editor. She had bills to pay, and paydays only come to those that toe the line.

"Yes—" She stopped herself from saying yessir, the same words her ancestors said to their masters. "I will talk to her."

"Good."

Del was seething as Chuck hung up the phone. Her hands vibrated with anger. She put her phone down for fear she would throw it across the room. She grabbed her gym bag. It was late, but she had a membership at a twenty-four-hour gym in the Village. You were supposed to book your time in advance, but there was rarely anyone in so late. She would call on the way. Del was hoping to get on the punching bag. She had her own set of gloves. She decided not to wear the FaD mask and wear one with a raised fist on the cheek.

She made up her mind that she would do everything in her power to keep Sarah on the show as long as possible. Del wanted her to win.

Winnipeg

"Great to meet you, Sarah," said Robyn Douglas, the judge with the baking channel on YouTube. "I really enjoyed your recipe. You showed us your personality and your directions were very clear. I loved your story about making sushi being one of your first grown-up foods. I was impressed."

"You forced me to make sushi for the first time," Gary Jonas, piped in, the comedian from Toronto. "It wasn't as hard as I thought it would be. It looked great, it tasted great. I think my Friday night sushi takeout order may not be necessary anymore."

I was perched in my regular spot at the kitchen island with my laptop open. Each of the judges, Jenna, our host, and Chuck, our director, were on screen. I had sent in my recipe and video two days ago. After the judges informed Chuck they were finished attempting all of the submitted recipes, each contestant was scheduled for a video session. I was most nervous about what the next judge would have to say.

"I've had chicken adobo many times before," said Chef Kelly Kwan of Le Fleur Rouge in Montreal. "You use Filipino flavours in the sauce, but the rest of the dish screamed basic teriyaki sushi roll—"

"One of the things I order every Friday night is a Teriyaki Chicken Roll," added Gary.

"And that's what makes you Basic, Gary," Chef Kwan spat out.

"The adobo glaze was not Basic at all."

"Sarah," she continued. "I do agree with Gary. The sauce was good. I liked the flavour, salty and sour with a strong hit of garlic, just as you describe, but I was hoping for something more cohesive. Your blog is about fusion cooking, but this recipe wasn't fusion. It was piecemeal. If your plan was to incorporate Filipino flavours into a basic Japanese-ish dish, then that has to be present throughout, not just an afterthought thrown on top."

She saw right through me. I was a fraud. I was a failure. And in the first round too. I'm going to be eliminated in the first round because I have no idea what I'm doing.

"Thank you, Sarah," Jenna said in her cheery voice. "We'll see you soon for the results."

I was dismissed from the chat so they could discuss me and my recipe further, then go on to talk to the next contestant.

Last Monday, after we were given the mystery ingredient, I was obsessed the entire day about figuring out the recipe. Instead of taking notes during history class, I was jotting down ingredients and ratios to figure out the measurements.

Soy, garlic, vinegar. Broth could tamper down flavours. How do I make it sticky? Thicken it with a slurry, a common hack used in Asian cooking.

I had met Del at Pangea Trading after school that day. She said the chicken fingers would be shipped to my house later that day. I wanted to start right away to create the perfect recipe.

However, once I started making the dish, I realized the flavours weren't right. I had tried using apple cider vinegar, but it added an unnecessary sweetness. The heat had cooked out the tartness of the vinegar. I had to drop down the cooking time, even though I knew that it would give less of an opportunity for the bay leaf flavour to infuse. I upped the number of leaves and added an extra tablespoon of raw white vinegar.

I tried tossing the chicken fingers in the glaze, then making the roll, but it was messy and unappetizing, with the brown sauce oozing everywhere. Instead, I ended up with a basic Teriyaki Chicken Roll—sushi rice, chicken tender, greens, carrots, all rolled into nori. I drizzled the glaze on top of the roll and sprinkled with furikake seasoning for some texture and more Japanese flavours.

Looking back, I realized it wasn't enough. I should have incorporated other flavours. I could have used java rice in the roll. I could have used camote or sweet potato leaves for the greens.

"Sarah, they're ready for us," Del said.

"That was fast."

"There was only one other person after you."

All the contestants were now on the screen along with the judges, Jenna, and Chuck. We were all on mute. I was curious what the judges had to say about the other contestants' recipes, but I had no way of knowing until the show aired on Sunday.

"Hello, everyone!" Jenna waved. Most of us waved back. "I'm so happy to see all of your faces. You've all met the judges. You've heard their comments. Now let's talk results.

"The judges' favourite this week will not only be guaranteed a spot in the next round, but will also win a special prize. This week's prize is a one-year supply of Beck's Chicken Tenders!" She clapped her hands in delight. "Beck's Chicken Tenders, Wings, and other frozen products are available in-store or online at Pangea Trading. Or order directly on the *Cyber Chef* website for ten percent off and free delivery on orders over thirty dollars!

"Now, the moment we've all been waiting for. This week's winner is…"

I didn't hold my breath. I knew my name wouldn't be called.

"Kendra, with her Jerk Chicken Tender Recipe!"

"Ah, merci! Thank you!" Kendra said happily. Her recipe was so simple. Chicken tenders tossed in jerk seasoning like wings. "Mon petit frère… ah, my little brother will be very excited."

"And you'll be happy too, right Kendra?" Chuck interrupted.

Kendra appeared to nod to an unknown person off to the side, probably her version of Del.

"Mais oui, d'accord… of course," she said. "I… ah, hope to take these chicken tenders and make some good meals for my family. Merci beaucoup!"

"And now," Jenna brought down the tone in her voice. "We need to find out which contestants are in the bottom two. Chef Kwan?"

"This was a hard decision," the distinguished chef said in a serious tone. "But the bottom two are Li and Geoff."

I exhaled. I wasn't in the bottom.

"We'll see all of you soon!" Our feeds were cut off as Jenna's last words were spoken. I guess we wouldn't know who was leaving until the show aired.

"They kick you out so you can't tell people in advance," Del explained, as if reading my mind. "You've all signed NDA's, but this is another layer of protection for the network."

"At least I made it through the week. I was terrified."

My parents suddenly walked in and gave me a hug.

"It sounds like you did great!" my dad said, finally letting me go.

"You could hear it all the way to your office?"

"We were listening in the hallway," my mom admitted. "I just wish they'd say your name properly. Didn't you talk to them, Del?"

"Mom, don't worry about it." I was upset enough about the mispronunciation; I didn't need my mom picking at the wound. I picked up my idea notebook. "I have to write down the judges' notes before I forget."

Del packed up her stuff. I'd see her again on Monday. As soon as she left, I called Auntie Cher. I couldn't tell her the results, but I needed her knowledge. I hadn't talked to her all week as I couldn't have her help me with the recipe. The rules were very clear, but there was nothing against studying between judging and the mystery ingredient reveal. Chef Kwan was right. Fusion was more than dumping one ethnic dish on top of another.

Chapter Nine

Tortang Talong with Giniling, or eggplant omelette with ground pork, is a common peasant dish in the Philippines. I added more eggs and replaced the ground pork with some bacon-y goodness, then baked it for a fluffy texture. Voila, it's a frittata! Great for brunch, lunch, or merienda (light meal).

Frittata Talong with Bacon Crumble

2 slices thick-cut bacon, chopped fine
2 tbsp water
1 Chinese or Japanese eggplant (the long kind)
1 tbsp soy sauce
1 tbsp rice vinegar
1 Thai chilli, seeded and minced or ½ tsp or more
   chilli flakes (optional)
2 cloves garlic, minced
4 eggs, beaten
2 green onions, chopped, divided

Add chopped bacon and water to a cold 10-inch non-stick and oven-safe frying pan.

Fry bacon at medium heat until slightly crispy, approximately 6–9 minutes, depending on the thickness of the bacon.

While bacon is cooking, slice the eggplant crosswise into 1-centimetre disks. Discard the stem and end.

Mix soy sauce, vinegar, garlic, and optional chilli in a bowl.

Add eggplant. Mix until eggplant is coated. Let marinade a few minutes while cooking bacon.

Once cooked, push all of the bacon to one side of the pan.

Using tongs, add eggplant slices in a single layer in pan to cook in the bacon fat.

Transfer bacon crumbles to the bowl with remaining soy, vinegar, and garlic.

Fry eggplant, 2 minutes each side.

Turn on oven broiler to high.

Pour beaten eggs on top of eggplant. Spread crumbled bacon with soy sauce evenly on top of eggs.

Sprinkle half the green onion on top of the eggs, save the other half for garnish.

Turn off stove.

Place pan under broiler for 60–90 seconds until the top of the eggs appears dry.

Place pan back on stovetop. Let stand for 2 minutes.

Use a silicone spatula to loosen frittata from pan. Slide onto a platter.

Garnish with green onions and cut into slices.

Check back to my recipe on Triple-S Sawsawan to really amp up the salty-sour flavours.

Winnipeg

"Tortang Talong with Giniling," Auntie Cher announced, placing a wide white platter in front of me. The upper stems of two eggplants stuck out at the top of the weirdly shaped egg concoction, but the eggplant itself was squished flat with scrambled egg and minced pork holding it together. "Eggplant omelette with ground meat.

"And this," she pointed to a much smaller plate, "is Pritong Talong, fried eggplant with soy and garlic."

"To be dipped in sawsawan," I said, pointing to the little bowl. "Vinegar and soy. What's the red stuff?"

"Thai chilli."

"What's with all the eggplant?"

"They were on sale." She opened her rice cooker and added a scoop to my wide and shallow bowl. "If you ever make anything like this, use Japanese eggplant. Chinese eggplants will work too but they're not as spongy. They're both long and thin and roast quickly. And stop the giggling. The emoji gave eggplants a bad rap."

I was over at Auntie Cher's house for brunch, well a late lunch by now. It was already two pm, but Auntie Cher was at the restaurant until three am last night. They no longer served brunch, and she had a few hours before she had to go back to the restaurant for that night's dinner service.

The eggplants were roasted until the skin was blistered. We peeled the skins off with satisfaction to reveal the silky flesh. We flattened the eggplants with the back of a wooden spoon, leaving the stems intact. After frying up some ground pork, seasoned with garlic and soy sauce of course, we removed the pork and added the eggplant to the hot pan, poured eggs over top. Auntie Cher used the technique of lifting the omelette and allowing the liquid egg to seep underneath. Once most of the egg was cooked, we re-added the pork as a topping. She carefully flipped the omelette over while holding the pan with both hands. I'd never been able to master the technique.

The result was a hearty omelette, loaded with soft eggplant and salty pork.

"This is delicious!" I said, my mouth full. I poured more of the sawsawan over my slice of eggplant. "I love the spice of the chillies."

"Filipino food isn't normally spicy, but I like to bring the heat once in a while."

Auntie Cher watched me eat my second helping. She smiled.

"Do you miss cooking Filipino food?" I asked.

"Yeah, I miss watching people eat Filipino food."

"Why don't you make it at the restaurant?"

She shook her head. "I've added Filipino elements to our dishes. I've made lumpia, longanisa, and liempo, but I call them Garlic Pork Spring Roll, or Sweet Cured Chorizo, or Banana Glazed Pork Belly. So yeah, I sneak in some Pinoy representation onto the menu.

"For more than a decade, I've seen TV shows and videos and read articles claiming that Filipino food is the 'next big thing', but it never happened. Even the great Anthony Bourdain, RIP, decreed that Filipino food was supposed to be the next Thai or Vietnamese or Korean, but it never hit those heights. It's considered obscure peasant food that your co-worker can bring to a potluck but not worth paying for when it appears on a restaurant menu.

"I'm sorry, but I get ranty when it comes to this topic."

I finished my plate, licking the last grain of rice soaked with vinegar and soy off my spoon.

"If your mission is to make Filipino food more accessible, then shouldn't you use their actual names?" I asked. "You have the hottest restaurant in the city, one of the most popular in the country. Whatever you make, people will order. Let customers know what they're getting into. As a chef, aren't you the one responsible for what food will be trendy?"

"You're too smart for your own good, Sar." She took my empty plate. "One of my first jobs as a line cook, I worked in a Filipino restaurant. I had just started culinary school. I thought I was such hot shit.

"It was an older business, an older building. There was a smell in the air, old oil clinging to the yellow plaster walls, a staleness that seeped into the carpets and cracked vinyl booths. Everyone spoke

Filipino. I knew enough to get by. The owner and head cook—we called her Ate, the respectful term for older sister—she hated me.

"I was always trying to make the dishes fancy. I'd add a couple of carrot pieces in the shape of a flower or green onion curls on top of the rice. *Just put the rice on the plate!*" She imitated the clipped Filipino accent in a sharp, angry voice. "My plating training was imbedded in my hands; I couldn't help myself.

"I was fired after a couple of months. My mom was so mad. She knew the owners. They gave me the job because the owners felt bad for us. They knew my dad. He was a regular in their restaurant; it was close to work. *How does my daughter not know how to make rice?!*"

Auntie Cher's imitation of my grandmother's accent was in a slightly deeper voice, with a stress on the word daughter, pronounced DOW-ter. I hadn't heard my grandmother's voice in so long that I had almost forgotten the tone. DOW-ter. I suddenly remembered that she pronounced my name SHAH-rah. I didn't mind though.

"Shah-rah!" she said when we visited her in BC when I was six. "These are your cousins, Mina and Manda, and this pogi little boy is your cousin, Christo. Say hello to your Manang Shahrah!"

She pronounced it COWsin. She also yelled when she spoke. Or maybe it wasn't yelling, but she spoke very loudly.

"What does Manang mean?" I asked my aunt as she rinsed the dishes off. She passed them to me to load them into the dishwasher.

"It means 'older sister'. It's a term of respect, like Ate, but Ate is Tagalog, the main dialect of the Philippines. Manang is Ilocano, a dialect spoken in the north. Why?"

"When I was little, Lola said I had to call my older cousins Manang. And my younger cousin had to call me Manang."

"Both my parents were from Luzon, northern Philippines. They spoke both Ilocano and Tagalog. When I was very little, I had to call Grace Manang, but she would have none of it after she was seven."

"And what can you speak?" I asked.

"Enough Tagalog to hold a conversation. It's what most Filipinos in Winnipeg speak. Some Ilocano."

"Why do you speak Filipino, but my mom doesn't?"

My aunt closed the dishwasher door.

"I had more exposure than she did."

"What does that mean?"

Auntie Cher looked out the kitchen window that I knew faced the neighbour's exterior wall. I kept my eyes on her. I wasn't going to let her avoid the question. I had never noticed these things before but now they were beginning to bother me, like a nagging itch. She sighed, as if resigning herself to the inevitable. She turned her gaze back to me.

"She wasn't interested."

"What does THAT mean?"

"She didn't have Filipino friends. I did."

"Why?"

"Why don't you have Filipino friends?"

"I dunno. It just happened that way."

"Exactly. Sometimes that's just how life goes. Shit happens."

My aunt took my hands in hers. We stood eye to eye. I surpassed her in height by a mere couple of centimetres when I was fourteen, but even when I was little, she had treated me like an equal. She was one of my best friends.

"My mom never talks about growing up. Was it so bad?"

"No, no, no. Not bad," she assured me. "She chooses not to remember."

"But why?"

"Not my story to tell."

My aunt pressed a glass container into my hands. I peered through the clear lid. It was full of sliced rectangles of fried eggplant. The bottom of the container was wet with brown soy sauce.

"My mom told me this used to be one of Grace's favourite dishes." she said. "Ask her to remember."

"I will. Thank you."

I tucked the container under my arm carefully, as if it held all the questions that were just starting as embers inside of me. If my mom opened the lid to release the scent of soy, vinegar, and garlic, would the answers be freed as well?

Thirty-nine years ago
Winnipeg

Grace sat down at the desk, her black hair tied in pigtails that swung as she plopped down into her seat to eat lunch. She pulled out a margarine container that didn't contain margarine. When she opened the lid, she smiled to herself at the briny mixture of soy sauce and sour vinegar that accompanied almost everything she ate. She peered inside to see today's savoury surprise. The container was loaded with rice topped with brown rectangles and scrambled egg.

A tall boy peered over the eight-year-old girl's shoulder and wrinkled his nose in disgust. He was in grade three. He pinched his nose with the hand that wasn't holding a metal lunch box with a cartoon superhero across the front.

"Ugh, Grace brought more gross stuff for lunch!"

"Did she bring butter again?" a girl across the room yelled.

"She never brings butter," the tall boy answered. "Her parents are poor, so her mom takes out the containers from the garbage and uses that for her lunch."

A few of the kids laughed. The little girl looked over at the other Filipino kid in the room. He tucked his margarine container back into his backpack and pulled out an apple to eat. He usually brought rice and luncheon meat. Rice and ground beef. Rice and noodles. He never brought anything with a pungent smell, nothing that brought attention. She put the lid back on her container.

Their elementary school was small. Most kids walked home

to mothers that would have a warm lunch waiting, but the kids whose parents worked or those that lived too far to make the trek there and back had to eat lunch at school. The little kids, grades one to three, were in one room, while the big kids, grades four to six, were assigned to another room down the hall. The teachers had lunch in their staffroom by the office. Once in a while a teacher would pop their head into the students' lunchrooms, but for the most part the kids were left to their own devices.

The tall boy continued to tower over Grace as she cowered at her desk. He put down his lunch box in front of her on the desktop and undid the clasp. When the lid popped, it knocked her carton of milk to the floor. Luckily, she hadn't opened it yet. She didn't pick it up. The boy opened a thermos with the same cartoon character wrapped around his lunch tin. He took a swig of juice or Kool-Aid, the red liquid shiny above his upper lip. He closed the lid tightly and placed it back into the lunch box.

He pulled out a square orange plastic container, a sucking *shup* sound coming out as he opened the lid. He pulled out the white triangle of a sandwich with the crusts cut off and took a bite. He was still chewing as he leaned over.

"Why do you always bring stinky food?" the tall boy asked.

His mouth made wet smacking noises as he chewed. He was close enough she could smell the peanut butter squishing between his teeth. She shrunk down in her chair, worried he would speak so loudly he'd spit on her, but she knew better than to turn her head away.

"It's what my mom makes me."

"It's gross." He finally swallowed.

She touched the rim of the margarine container, checking one more time to make sure it was closed. She reached into her bag and pulled out a banana with dark spots all over the yellowed skin after being banged around loosely against books, pencils, and a carton of milk. She unpeeled the banana slowly and ate the bruised fruit quietly as the boy straightened up.

He took another bite of his sandwich and placed it back into its square plastic box. He dropped the orange container into his lunch box, not closing it properly, the sandwich halves tumbling out. As if he didn't notice, he slammed the lid of his lunch box and snapped the clasp closed, leaving a smudge of peanut butter across the front. He leaned down and picked up her milk carton, slamming it onto her desk. The corner of the carton wrinkled slightly. She was worried it would drip. He leaned over again.

"Don't bring that shit to school again," he said. Some kids gasped at the eight-year-old's cuss world. "The smell makes me want to throw up."

He stood straight and picked up his lunch bag. With the other hand, he pulled on her left pigtail hard. She yelped from the sharp pain on her scalp, but she knew not to cry. The pigtail was now lower than the one on the other side of her head, a smear of peanut butter and jelly on the end.

Her hair was asymmetrical for the rest of the day.

Grace's mom came to pick her and her younger brother Christoffer up from school at three-thirty, her two-year-old sister Cherish in an umbrella stroller.

"What happened to your hair, Anak?" her mother asked, referring to her as her dear child.

"It got caught in a door," Grace lied.

She held her little sister's hand as she walked. Christoffer ran ahead as he always did, picking up a branch from the ground and hitting it against trees as they passed. The half-day of kindergarten never exhausted his boisterous energy.

"Mom," she asked. "Can I bring something different to school for lunch?"

"You didn't like the tortang giniling?" her mom asked.

Last night they had pritong talong, fried eggplant, for dinner, along with a minced pork omelette and a potful of rice. The omelette was so good, there was only enough leftovers for their father's lunch. Her mom gave her plain scrambled egg to go with the eggplant. And rice. There was always rice.

"I don't want to bring rice to school anymore."

"Why is that?" her mother asked.

"Yeah, why?" Christoffer repeated, running back to them. "Rice is the best."

"I don't like the smell," Grace said. "It makes my stuff stinky."

"Rice doesn't have a smell," her brother said.

"It always smells bad! Everything I get for lunch smells bad."

"What is it that you want to bring to school?" her mother asked.

"I want normal food," Grace said, tears stinging her eyes. She wiped them away with the back of her hand. Something inside was being torn away from her. She could feel something changing, but she didn't know how to react to the gnawing pain in her stomach. She reacted the only way she could understand. Anger. "I don't like being the weird kid! I just want to be like everyone else! I don't want stinky Filipino food anymore!"

Her mother stopped walking, gripping the handles of the umbrella stroller, as if the words had weakened her. Little Cherish turned in her seat, wondering why they had stopped. Christoffer continued to hit a branch against a tree, fighting an imaginary battle. Grace stared up at her mother in defiance and rage, tears now flowing freely, but the pain in her stomach engulfed her, fuelled by the hunger from skipping lunch.

She began to scream, a hollow, hungry scream that made a neighbour peer out her front window. Christoffer stopped mid-battle. Grace closed her mouth and threw her book bag on the ground. The margarine container tumbled out and spilled its pungent contents onto the sidewalk. The little girl turned and ran down the block, her crooked pigtails bouncing with each step.

Winnipeg

"And the first *Cyber Chef* contestant to leave the competition is…"

I sat on the edge of the couch, my parents on either side. I didn't know Li or Geoff well, but I still felt a kinship with them. I knew what they were going through. I understood the pressure. We were competitors but also comrades, if that makes sense.

"Li."

The thirteen-year-old boy hung his head. After watching the clips, Sarah had to agree with the decision. Li's family had an Orange Sesame Chicken dish on their restaurant's menu. He thought he could adapt the recipe to incorporate the chicken tenders, however even with deep frying, the thin breading on the chicken could not withstand the heavy, sticky sauce. The fresh mandarin slices and toasted sesame seeds could not save the appearance. The vibrant sauce was far superior to any Western Chinese food the judges had tried previously; however it overpowered the droopy chicken tenders, rendering the dish lifeless.

"If we ever go to Calgary, can we visit Li's restaurant?" I asked.

Our family hadn't left the province since the beginning of the pandemic. With the virus variants and so many cases related to travel, the province required anyone visiting or returning to Manitoba to isolate for fourteen days. It made travel less feasible. I knew it could be another year before we would be able to go anywhere with ease.

"Of course," my dad answered. "Once we get the chance, we'll visit all of your new friends."

I got up to go to the kitchen, hungry again after watching an hour of videos with amazing dishes. I opened the refrigerator and grabbed one of the takeout containers holding the leftovers from dinner. My parents had ordered Greek, and we still had a couple skewers of lamb souvlaki. I pulled a piece of meat off the bamboo stick and opened a container of tzatziki for dipping. I closed both packages and stacked them neatly on the shelf. I was about to close the door, but my mother was behind me.

"I wouldn't mind a snack," she said, pulling out the white Styrofoam container.

At the beginning of the pandemic, every time we got takeout or delivery, my parents would dump everything out of the packaging into big bowls or our own containers. Then they would sanitize like their lives depended on it, which I guess at the time they thought they did. Now we were much more lax and whenever we ordered in, they'd just leave the containers as is. She reached into the refrigerator to pull out another container with rice and pita.

"What's this?" she asked, holding a lidded glass container.

"Oh, I forgot. Auntie Cher sent me home with leftovers. She said it used to be your favourite."

My mom lifted the lid slightly and peered inside. A shocked look spread across her face as the scent of vinegar hit her nose. The container landed on the tiled floor with a crash, the pieces of fried eggplant and shattered glass sent sprawling. Drops of soy-vinegar splattered up onto my grey socks and blue leggings. The smell filled the room.

"I'm so sorry, Sar." She grabbed a roll of paper towels from the kitchen counter. "Are you cut?"

"No, I'm okay," I said. I bent down to pick up large chunks of glass and the plastic lid. I opened the cabinet under the sink to throw glass into the garbage.

"No, Sar. I got it. Go change." She took the lid out of my hand and tossed it into the sink. She picked up the eggplant with a paper towel, like she was trying to avoid touching it. "Be careful where you step. Rinse out your clothes before they stain."

"Yeah, sure."

As I turned down the hall, I remembered I was supposed to ask my mom why she couldn't speak any Filipino. I was going to walk back into the kitchen, but I heard soft sobs. I peeked around the doorway. The kitchen appeared empty, but I could see my mother's shadow near the island where she was sitting on the floor leaning against a cabinet.

I turned to go back to my room. The questions were no longer important.

Chapter Ten

Ube is purple yam. I know, yam in a drink? What?! But it's sweet and earthy and rich. And it's PURPLE! Don't you want a purple hot chocolate?

Ube White Hot Chocolate

1 cup ube puree*

3 cups milk, divided in half (can sub with almond milk)

3 ounces white chocolate (finely chopped bar chocolate preferred, but ¼ cup white chocolate chips will work)

¼ cup white sugar

1 tsp vanilla extract

Garnish: whipped cream, white chocolate shavings

*Frozen ube is readily available in Asian grocery stores. Thaw overnight in the package. You can sub with 1 cup diced fresh ube—just cover with water and boil with enough water for 12-15 minutes until soft then puree in a food processor or with an immersion blender and follow the recipe in the same manner.

Heat milk in a deep saucepan on medium until scalding.

Turn heat down to low and stir in ube puree. Use an immersion blender to mix thoroughly and ensure a smooth consistency.

Add white chocolate, blend again with immersion blender.

Add sugar and vanilla, stir gently for 3 minutes.

Turn off heat and pour into mugs.

Garnish with whipped cream and white chocolate shavings
if you're feeling extra.

Winnipeg

"Li," Cindy said. "I never saw that coming."

The next day during our seven forty-five Monday morning video chat, all of us were quiet, the reality of having lost one of our own heavy on our minds. I wondered if the adult contestants from other seasons felt this way when one of their fellow competitors had been knocked off. Were they regretful? Were they relieved? Were they sad they didn't get the chance to know someone who could have been a potential friend? Did it feel real?

I looked at the grid of pictures, the program interface fitting five boxes on the screen instead of six. The symmetry of the gallery was gone. Chuck and Jenna would be joining us soon. Our numbers would still be uneven.

"You guys, I'm not sorry," Geoff said, breaking the silence. "Somebody had to go. Better him than me."

"You made a buffalo chicken wrap," Cindy shot back. "It was the most basic thing you possibly could have made."

"It was a habanero butter chicken wrap with aviyal vegetables," Geoff said, the arrogance now on overdrive.

"Why are you even making butter chicken?" Cindy asked. "You're not even Indian."

"You don't know that."

"I'm pretty sure, White Boy."

"Well, I'm not Indian like you."

"What the hell is that supposed to mean?"

"You're Indian."

"I'm Métis. And you can't use that word."

"Fine. What does it matter what you are or what I am—"

"You're not East Indian." If Cindy was standing, she would

have had her hands on her hips. "You have no right to appropri-ate another culture's food."

"Seriously? I'm not allowed to cook food that I like?" Geoff said indignantly. "If we can't share different recipes, what the hell are we doing here? You think anyone that's not Métis shouldn't be allowed to attempt your sad flatbread taco?"

"Bannock taco!"

"Whatever."

"It's shitty that *you* get to make whatever *you* want."

"What's that supposed to mean?"

"It means that half of us would never get the chance to put up a pathetic attempt at butter chicken."

"Excuse me, excuse me," Kendra said. She was the oldest of us at seventeen, but only older than Cindy's seventeen by a couple of months. Geoff's fifteen-year-old temperament bordered on a tan-trum. "We need to be calm. Yes, we are competitors, but we must get along. We must be, how you say it, civil."

The awkward silence returned, but only for a few seconds.

"Can we say a prayer for Li?" Harriet asked in a meek voice. "I just want his family to stay safe."

"He's not even Christian," Cindy said. "I don't think any of us are. Well, obviously Sarah is. Maybe Geoff."

"Uh," I started. "Actually, I'm not—"

Another box popped onto the screen, the other video windows automatically adjusting for size and shuffling us to different posi-tions in the gallery of boxes, slightly left or right.

"Good morning everyone!" Jenna said in her cheery voice. All of our microphones were suddenly set to mute. "I hope you all slept well last night."

We nodded or shrugged, unable to answer verbally. Chuck logged on immediately after. He seemed grouchy, but I wasn't sure if he even had cheerful in his repertoire.

"Morning." He yawned. I yawned on instinct, as did Kendra and Geoff.

"We can keep this short and sweet today," Jenna continued. "This week's mystery ingredients—"

Did she mean ingredients, plural? I thought.

"—are loaded with protein. They are flavourful and hearty and often the base of an amazing breakfast. This week's mystery ingredients are... bacon and eggs! Organic and free-range bacon and eggs are available at Pangea Trading..."

As Jenna began to give her spiel about the brand, my mind whirled. I saw the pieces come together in my mind—eggs, bacon, what else? Soy, garlic, vinegar... I remembered the heartiness of the late brunch I had at my aunt's house. Omelette. *Tortang.* Meat. *Giniling.* I raised my hand, physically and virtually, for the first time excited to be the one to speak first.

"Yes, Sarah." Jenna beamed her pretty smile.

"I know exactly what I'm going to make."

Toronto

"I'm shocked they got rid of Li," Leng said to her mother over lunch. "You couldn't do anything about it?"

Poppy reached across the table to squeeze her daughter's hand.

"I have a hand in every facet of the show, but I have no influence over the judges. Unlike other shows, our results are real."

Poppy was also disappointed about the decision, but she wanted *Cyber Chef* to maintain its integrity. In all of the seasons, she had never even spoken to any of the judges. Sure, the judges were sometimes given notes from the producers to keep an eye on certain concerns, usually to ensure that the sponsored products were featured prominently, but other than that, there was no influence. No one was going to accuse her of fixing the competition.

"Who am I going to root for now?" Leng asked, ripping one of the croissants she had made that morning in half. She was back onto baking, falling in love with the process of laminating dough, the culinary technique of folding dough over and over to create layers separated by luscious butter for tender flaky croissants.

"Whomever you want," Poppy said. "Who do you like?"

"I like Sarah. I like her fusion vibe."

Poppy smiled. She wasn't surprised that Leng was cheering for the only other Asian candidate on the show. After all, she wanted her daughter to see herself in media and television. She wanted other kids like her to have role models. Poppy wanted to even out the playing field. This was her gift of equity to her daughter, to so many daughters.

"I like Sarah too."

"Cool. I think I've read her blog before. *Fusion on a Plate.* Her recipes seemed familiar."

"You should make me something."

"Yeah, I'll check what ingredients I need."

"Order from Pangea. I have a discount."

Poppy reached for a second croissant. They may need to bake another batch.

Winnipeg

Lena

r u mad at me

no y

wut did u do

i thot ur mad coz i said u shudnt fix ur name on cc

i thot ud tell them 2 fix it anyway

u said cmon!!!!!!!!

i thot ud say sumthin

u always do

SRSLY????????????????

seeeee??????

ur maaaaaaad

im not mad

i swear

but u never call me or j

been super busy w cc

can i try wut ur making

NO!!!!

i signed a nda

wuts that

non disclosure agreement

me n rents had to sign 2 get on cc

all shows do it

wut happens if u disclose stuff

we gotta pay

$$$$$$$$$$$$$$$$$$$$$$

Reeeeelllllyyy?????!!!!

wut if i come over l8r

and we just hang out

ya dats cool

j around

hes working

he wants dem wheels

k

come after 7

well sit on the deck

and u still cook me sumthin

not from cc

just sumthin good

ya of course

sumthin sweet

im not a resto

ur my resto

jk ima make something special 4u

wear purple

"Sar," Del called out. "Get off your phone. They're ready."

I had just turned off the heat on the ube puree. This recipe took three tries. I had originally wanted to make an ube dalgona with a meringue cloud on top of milk, but it fell flat once I added the yam mixture. I eventually thinned it out with milk and ended up with something closer to hot chocolate. Two more adjustments later I ended up with ube white hot chocolate. I was used to making changes on the fly.

"Coming."

"Welcome back, Cyber Chefs!" Jenna's voice rang out as I sat down. "The judges have come to a decision!"

This judging session was different from the last. My heart was beating fast with hope. My recipe was solid. Combining Tortang Talong with bacon was a no-brainer. When I first tested the recipe, I was shocked with how well the eggplant served as flavour sponges.

"The winner of this week's challenge will receive a new panini grill from Counter Culture Couture."

She went on a spiel about the features of the grill. We already had a panini press, so I wasn't as interested. I wasn't even that excited about the show's grand prizes, a twenty-five thousand dollar package consisting of a five thousand dollar travel voucher (that we won't be able to use for another year or so), a five thousand dollar delivery service voucher (with mostly chain restaurants), a five thousand dollar gift card to Pangea (which would be spent in a matter of months), and ten thousand dollars cash (which my parents would make me stick in an account).

What I really wanted was the title of Cyber Chef. It wasn't about the fame, sort of. The subscriptions to my blog had tripled since the show started. I had so many new followers and new comments on my Instagram posts that I had to turn off my notifications or my phone would be buzzing all day. Del had recommended I remove the email link from my website and communicate through private DM to avoid creepers and trolls. I was recognized at Pangea again, this time by a lady in line behind me. I was bombarded by questions from my classmates, none of which I could answer. My mom asked if I could take the rest of the month's classes online.

The longer I was on the show, the more well-known I would become. The winner would have their blog featured on the *Cyber Chef* website, under the Champion section. I could share my recipes on a scale I could never have imagined before. The world would know my food, my baba's food.

I had been thinking of my grandmothers a lot lately. Baba had died, but her food lived on through me. I was learning my lola's recipes, incorporating them into what I presented on the show. I wondered if they would have gotten along. They met briefly at my bat mitzvah four years ago, but I don't even know if they spoke. If they talked about food, maybe they would have swapped recipes.

"The winner is…" Jenna paused. I held my breath. "Harriet with her bacon-infused shakshouka!"

I smiled and clapped quietly, even though my microphone was muted. She was a strong competitor, but I had no idea this quiet little Christian girl from Nova Scotia could come up with such a complex recipe. I had a shakshouka recipe on my blog using quinoa to add substance to the baked tomato stew with eggs. The addition of bacon to the Middle Eastern dish bordered on sacrilegious, but as a lover of all things fusion, I applauded her for the sheer bravado.

Automatically my mind wandered over how I would add Filipino elements to shakshouka. Maybe eggplant. Maybe salted duck egg. Maybe sardinas, canned Filipino sardines in stewed tomato sauce, often served with eggs.

"And now we find out which of you will be in the bottom two."

I had almost forgotten this part. The judges were so complimentary of my dish, loving the salty tartness of the eggplant, the texture of the crumbled bacon. Even Chef Kwan said she enjoyed the contrast in flavours and colour, the aubergine of the eggplant, the red chillies, the green onion, and the organic egg with its bright yellow yolky scramble as the backdrop.

"You have a learned chef inside of you," she said. "Your technique shows discipline and knowledge of flavour profile. I'm shocked you are only sixteen. Bravo."

I utterly beamed and was near speechless until Chuck literally snapped his fingers to prompt my response.

"Thank you so much, Chef. It's such an honour to hear this from you."

"You're welcome." She gave a small smile, seemingly surprised I referred to her in the manner of a member of a kitchen staff. My aunt, as well as television, had taught me the lingo.

"We hate to do this," the baker judge, Robyn, said almost regrettably. "But the bottom two are Geoff and Cindy."

I inhaled sharply but silently, everyone's video reflecting the same face before we were all kicked out of the chat. I was glad Lena was coming over. I welcomed the distraction. A voice in my head said, *it better be Geoff,* but I refused to entertain the thought any further. One day, that could be me.

Chapter Eleven

Matzah Balls

About 1 cup of matzah meal	3 matzahs, finely ground in food processor
1 tsp baking powder	
3 tbsp schmaltz	chicken fat, can sub with oil
3 tbsp broth	
3 eggs, beaten	
2 pinches of salt	a pinch for the recipe
	a pinch to throw over your shoulder
Mix together	all ingredients
Put in fridge for about an hour	wet your hands before rolling!
Roll into balls but not too big	approx 2 tbsp per ball, makes 12–15 balls
Put balls in refrigerator	on a cookie sheet or plate for 30 minutes
Boil a big pot of water	fill a large pot ¾ full of water
Carefully add balls to pot	Use a slotted spoon
Lower heat	drop heat to medium
Cover pot slightly	put lid on askew,
	leave a space for steam
Cook for 30 minutes	
Add to soup when ready to serve	heat balls in soup for at least 5 minutes
Enjoy	I miss you Baba

Eleven years ago
Winnipeg

A little girl walked into the lunchroom, her perfectly symmetrical dark brown pigtails swinging with each step. She looked around at the sea of faces. She recognized none. It was her first day at the new school. Her uniform was still a little scratchy, and she wasn't used to wearing tights.

A blond girl from her class waved her over. Oh good. She didn't want to eat alone on her first day. The girl in pigtails sat down at the long table. Another girl with thick dark brown hair sat down next to her. Another girl joined them. Her hair was the same colour and texture, but shorter.

"I'm Gabi," the blond-haired girl introduced herself. "This is Talia and Devra."

"Shalom," the girl in pigtails replied. "Ani Sarah."

The girls giggled.

"We don't have to talk in Hebrew when we're not in class," Devra said.

Sarah opened her thermos. A wonderful smell wafted out. It was still warm. Her baba had come over to the house early that morning and dropped off a huge container of the comforting soup. Matzah balls were her favourite.

"Where are you from, Sarah?" Talia asked.

"Here," Sarah answered.

"No," Talia said. "Where are you really from?"

"I used to go to Greenway School."

The girls looked at her, confused. They went back to eating their lunch. Gabi unwrapped a sandwich. Talia pulled at the lid of a glass container.

"Was that your dad who dropped you off this morning?" asked Devra.

"Yeah, why?"

"You don't look like him. Do you look like your mom?"

Sarah started to feel uncomfortable. "I kind of look like her."

"Where is your mom from?" Devra pressed.

"Here."

"No, really."

"She was born here."

The three girls stared at her. Sarah shifted in her seat. They started to eat their lunch again. She ate her lunch quickly. The soup didn't warm her like she hoped. When the bell rang, she packed her things quickly into her bag and went to class.

They went to the school library. After their teacher read a lovely story about a little boy and a wool coat made by his mother, each student was told to pick a book from the Hebrew section and sit at a table to read to themselves for a few minutes. She saw that Gabi, Talia, and Devra were sitting at one table. They were talking to each other and giggling.

She turned to another table where a boy and girl sat. She'd noticed throughout the day that no one seemed to talk to them. She walked over and sat down.

"Shalom," the little girl said. She had blond hair and a spatter of freckles across her nose.

"Shalom," Sarah answered.

The pudgy boy looked up and smiled. He looked down again at his book quickly.

"I'm Sarah."

"Shmi Lena." The girl had a slight accent. Sarah learned later Lena had come from Russia by way of Israel last year.

"Jaden," the boy said, not looking up from his book. She learned later that his family had come from Argentina a few months before.

The next day, Sarah wordlessly sat down next to Lena and Jaden for lunch. After she finished her matzah ball soup, drinking every last drop of the comforting broth, she put down a cookie in front of each of her two tablemates, a triangular cookie with raspberry jam, hamantashen. Her baba had dropped them off that morning. She was prepping for the Jewish holiday of Purim in a week. It was a tradition to share treats with friends.

"Todah," Lena said, picking up the cookie.

Jaden reached out a tenuous hand and picked up the cookie. He took a nibble and smiled.

Sarah sat with Lena and Jaden for lunch the next day, and the next day after that. And the next and the next, until the three were inseparable.

Toronto

"This is bullshit."

"Cindy," her media manager cautioned. "You can't say that to the judges."

"But that's what this is!"

"Don't be a sore loser—"

"Shut up, Geoff!"

Cindy was trying to stay calm. Mara, her media manager, knelt down beside her, just out of the camera's reach and took her hand. Cindy was trying hard not to cry.

"Cindy," Jenna said, in a soft yet somehow still sickly sweet voice. "You know the judges' comments are not meant to hurt you."

"Cindy," Robyn, the baker, said softly. "You are an incredible cook. We loved your flavours, but I think you know that we needed to see more range. Your dish was creative and delicious—Blueberry and Bacon Bannock Benedict was a creative idea, but you used fry bread in last week's recipe, and we wanted to see something new."

"Cindy," Chuck said. They all kept saying her name. Was this some sort of battle technique to wear her down? "You need to calm down," Chuck said, slowing down the words *calm* and *down*, as if saying them slower would allow the weight to seep in further. Her anger returned like cream boiling over the edge of a pot, burning on the element below. If this went on any longer she would catch fire.

"You're the reason I'm getting thrown off the show!"

"Cindy—"

"Stop saying my name!" Tears threatened to fall down her cheeks. "I did everything you asked and they're still kicking me off."

"Everything you asked?" Chef Kwan said. "What does that mean?"

"Mara," Chuck said, alarmed. "I'm cutting the judges feed."

"But wait—" Chef Kwan and the other judges, as well as Geoff's video boxes were gone, leaving only Chuck, whose face now took up the majority of the screen.

"That could have been a disaster," he said, his voice pointed with anger. "Mara, why aren't you doing your job?"

"I'm doing my best, Chuck," Mara said, now upright and fully in the shot next to Cindy. "She's a seventeen-year-old girl. Cut her some slack."

"Why did you let her turn in the same recipe as last week?"

"It's a completely different dish!" Mara defended. "A taco is different from eggs benedict. One is lunch and one is breakfast."

"But some variety. That's all we want. She should have seen this coming."

"She did her best, especially given the limitations you set on her."

"Then her best wasn't good enough and she should accept the judge's decision without having a meltdown."

It was too much for Cindy to bear.

"I'm right here." The tears flowed down her cheeks, her voice cracking. "Stop talking about me like I'm not here."

"I'm sorry, Cindy. I let you down."

"No, Mara, you did nothing wrong. I should have just googled a recipe and changed the instructions."

Mara whispered something in Cindy's ear. She nodded in return. Mara then stood up and walked off frame and out of camera rage. She let go of Cindy's hand, giving it one last squeeze. Cindy took a breath and wiped a tear away with the back of her sleeve.

"It's not fair," she said, her voice a little calmer. "All I wanted to do was share what I love to cook and what I love to eat, but you—" She pointed at the screen, her fingertip touching the image of Chuck's face. He couldn't even see it, as the camera was higher than her hand. She put her hand down.

"You told me I had to cook from my 'Indigenous culture'." Cindy used air quotes around the words. "My grandparents were raised in a residential school. Our culture was ripped away from us. What 'culture' was I supposed to share? All I have is my grandfather's bannock recipe. That's all I have left and you're saying it's not good enough."

"I never said that." Chuck's voice was icy. "The judges' decision is final."

"I have so much more to give!" she said. "I wanted to show you more. You wanted me to honour my heritage. I wanted to honour my grandfather."

"Listen," Chuck said, much calmer. He took off his headset and leaned closer to his laptop. "I lost my grandparents in the Holocaust. My great-aunt was able to save my mother and snuck her into Holland. They pretended to be Polish for years until there was almost nothing Jewish left.

"I never met my baba, but my aunt passed down her kugel recipe to my mother when she was old enough to cook. It's basically the same as any kugel recipe you can get off the internet, but it was hers. My mom fell in love with a Jewish man when she came to Canada and had to learn about our culture from scratch, starting with that recipe. She taught it to my wife who makes it almost every holiday."

They stared at each other's image, two people who understood each other's multigenerational trauma.

"It's been so hard," Cindy said, a new wave of tears coming, but this time without anger. "I was hoping I would do better in the competition. We moved to Toronto because my dad got a really good job. My mom too, but last year both of them were laid off because of the pandemic. My dad got to go back after a couple of months, but my mom got COVID. It took so long for her to get better, but she's always so tired now. She can't go back to work.

"I was working as a server, but with the most recent lockdown, there's no money coming in. There's the government money, but it's not enough. You know what rent is like in Toronto. It's drowning us. I was hoping I could do better on the show so I could help my family." She took a deep breath. "But I understand. Sometimes your best isn't good enough."

They were quiet for a moment.

"Cindy, do you think you could say goodbye to the judges?"

She took a breath. "Yeah, I can do that."

Mara set up the feed again. Chuck picked up his headphones. Geoff and the judges reappeared on the screen. They looked concerned.

"Everything okay kid?" Gary said, awkwardly jovial.

"I'm good. I'm sorry I blew up earlier."

She looked down, defeated.

"Don't be sorry," said Gary lightly. "I blow up at people all the time. That's why I'm a comedian and not a politician. Although if I was in the US, that would make me a politician."

Cindy chuckled. She took a deep breath and looked directly into the lens, her intense brown eyes boring into her laptop's camera.

"Thank you for having me. It was an honour to be on the show."

"No, Cindy," Robyn said gently. "It was an honour to make your grandfather's recipe."

Her screen went dark. Cindy then stood up and headed down the hall to the bedroom where her mother was resting. She was propped up on pillows and was watching television. Her mother picked up the remote and muted the TV.

"How did it go?"

Cindy climbed into the bed and gave her mother a huge hug.

Toronto

From: Popp SMD (poppsmd@email.com)
Sent: April 24, 2021 10:26 PM
To: Cindy D (cinfulcharmes@email.ca)
Subject: Consolation Prize

Cindy,
Thank you for your contribution to *Cyber Chef: Next Gen*. As a contestant, you brought tradition and spirit to the competition.

Please click on the links in the attached PDF's to redeem your consolation prize for your participation on *Cyber Chef*. As per the terms of the non-disclosure agreement signed by you and your parents, you are not to discuss with anyone the nature of the consolation prize including the amount, the vendors, or the date received.

Thank you for sharing your food.

Sincerely,
Poppy St Martin-Dubois

PS. My daughter and I enjoyed making the Bannock Benedict. We love the combination of wild blueberries, poached eggs, and bacon. Delicious!

Cindy opened the attachment with two different website links. She clicked on the first. It was a virtual gift card for five hundred dollars to a pizza place only blocks from her apartment. The second was redeemable at a nearby grocery store worth one thousand dollars, not Pangea Trading, the sponsor of the show, but for a generic big box grocery store where the money would last four months instead of four weeks. She cried out in joy and ran to tell her mom.

Winnipeg

"Geoff goes home, right?" Lena said, bouncing on her knees in anticipation. "Tell me he goes home."

"I told you, I don't know," I replied. "I find out at the same time you do."

"He a jerk IRL?" Jay asked.

"NDA," I said, my answer to most of their questions.

Jay and Lena came over to watch the show, however we were out on the veranda with my laptop open on the glass patio table. We each sat in deck chairs, wrapped up in blankets. All week I had been attending school through distance learning. My parents could see the isolation wearing on me. Last year they saw firsthand how the loneliness pulled me into depression a few months into the pandemic when the city had shut down. It was my guidance counsellor's idea to reach out to my friends virtually. Although I contacted my friends from school, Lena and Jay were the only ones to reach back.

I could feel the stress wash over me again after only a week of learning remotely. I wasn't getting out of pyjamas each day. I took classes in my bed. It was a lot of reading and typing and watching videos. I didn't interact with anyone. *Cyber Chef* was my outlet for interaction. I talked to Del and Chuck and the other contestants. I spent the rest of my time shopping and cooking. We were lucky in Manitoba. Other provinces had locked down fully due to the third wave, although I could tell we weren't far behind. However, Chuck had said next week I would have to do all my shopping online, just like the other contestants. The playing field had to remain level.

I realized I wanted to share these moments with my friends. I ached to tell them about the backstage drama. I wanted to tell them it was so much harder than I thought it would be. I wanted to show them all the new stuff I got. For now, I would have to be satisfied with having them by my side, two metres away.

We were only halfway through the episode. They had shown my segment first, creating the Tortang Talong with Bacon Giniling. I promised I would make it for them sometime. Kendra's Corn and Bacon Pie dazzled us and Harriet's Bacon-infusion Shakshouka was inspiring. Geoff's Cloud Eggs made us roll our eyes. This trend was so three years ago.

"You still haven't talked to them about your name?" Lena asked.

"NDA."

I reached into the bowl of furikake popcorn, my fingers slick with browned sesame butter. I may have added too much this time. We each had individual bowls of popcorn, something my mother insisted upon.

Footage played of Cindy climbing into her mother's bed and giving her a hug.

"It's been so hard," Cindy said in a voiceover, her voice cracking slightly. "We moved to Toronto because my dad got a really good job. My mom too, but last year both of them were laid off because of the pandemic. My dad got to go back after a couple of months, but my mom got COVID. It took so long for her to get better, but she's always so tired now. She can't go back to work.

"I was working as a server, but with the most recent lockdown, there's no money coming in. I was hoping I could do better on the show so I could help my family."

Although Cindy was my direct competition, my heart went out to her. Toronto was expensive, comparable to New York in density, price, and diversity. I couldn't imagine living somewhere where a condo would cost the same as our four-bedroom house.

They showed the video of her Bacon Benny over Bannock with Wild Blueberry Compote. She described the preparation with finesse, but she repeated the bannock recipe that she had featured the week before, including the same story of how the recipe was passed down to her. The story was told during a voice over as she mixed, but her tone was different, harsher, angry, although she was completely justified.

"My grandparents were raised in a residential school. Our culture was ripped away from us. All I have is my grandfather's bannock recipe."

When they announced the bottom two, I sat up straighter. My friends leaned forward in their seats, awaiting the judges' comments.

"Geoff, I've seen Cloud Eggs on social media, but I was always intimidated to make them on my own," said Robyn. "They always seemed unattainable, like something created for a picture but not for consumption."

"It was so fancy," Gary said. "They were like marshmallow fluff with bacon bits. I know that's not the most appetizing description, but it's the only way I can describe the texture."

A photo appeared of his version of the whipped egg whites dotted with red, nesting a barely cooked yolk. I had to admit the result was stunning. There was a reason the trend had caught so many foodies' attention... three years ago.

"Cloud Eggs were a 2017 trend," Chef Kwan said coldly. They were older than I thought. "Generally, they're pretty and they taste okay. I do like the cayenne with the bacon. The effect on the eggs adds a flavour and visual pop. But still, a trend that borders on basic."

"Ouch," Lena exclaimed. On a show geared towards foodies, even she knew that was one of the harshest criticisms the judge could lay.

"Cindy," Gary started. "Blueberries, eggs, and bacon, who knew?"

"Is this the same bannock recipe from last week?" Robyn asked.

"Yes," she answered, apprehensive. "My grandfather's recipe."

"It is an excellent bannock recipe."

"Thank you."

"But your dish is rather… simplistic," Robyn said carefully.

I heard Lena gasp. Jay traced his finger through the furikake seasoning in the bottom of his bowl and stuck his finger in his mouth.

"Fried bannock, a couple slices of bacon, poached egg, and blueberry compote," she listed. "You lifted our expectations after last week's Bannock Taco recipe; we expected the same level of complexity."

A video of blueberry sauce being ladled carefully over poached eggs appeared on the screen, then a knife being held by an unseen hand poked into the egg underneath the mound of fruit compote and a trickle of bright yellow egg yolk oozed out over the bacon and bannock underneath.

"It was a solid dish," Chef Kwan said. "But it was barely a recipe. The bannock was great, but we already knew that from last week. Poached eggs are poached eggs—"

"Even I know how to poach an egg." Gary said proudly.

Chef Kwan pursed her lips at the interruption.

"Fried bacon is fried bacon," she continued. "There was nothing unique to the preparation of either. The blueberry compote on the eggs was lovely, especially the addition of maple syrup. My restaurant has a blueberry barbecue sauce. Fruit and meat are an exceptional combination, but was this exceptional enough?"

"Thank you, Cindy," Jenna said kindly. "We'll hear from the judges after the break."

We debated back and forth between us as we muted the commercials in the background.

"It has to be Geoff. B-A-S-I-C. Even the judges see through him," I said.

"But Cindy made bannock two weeks in a row," Lena countered. "They don't like repeats on *Cyber Chef*."

"But it's her grandfather's recipe!" I defended.

"And this is a recipe competition,"

I turned to Jay. "Who do you think is going home?"

Jay looked up and scrunched his mouth to the side in thought.

"Whatever they liked least."

Ugh. So very Jay.

"Welcome back!" Jenna returned with a smile. "The judges have made their decision."

Cindy and Geoff's faces were centred on the screen. Robyn's face appeared between them.

"The next *Cyber Chef* contestant to leave the competition is..."

Instinctively, my friends and I reached out to hold each other's hands. I knew my mom would be mad, but she wasn't there. I didn't care. We could sanitize our hands afterwards.

"Cindy," Robyn said softly. Her eyes dropped downward, defeated. She took a deep breath and looked up again, intensity boring through the lens and out of the small screen.

"You are an incredible cook," Robyn continued. "We loved your flavours, but I think you know that we needed to see more range. Your dish was creative and full of flavour—Blueberry and Bacon Bannock Benedict was an interesting idea, but you used fry bread in last week's recipe, and we wanted to see something new."

"Thank you for having me," Cindy said with class. "It was an honour to be on the show."

"No, Cindy," Robyn said gently. "It was an honour to make your grandfather's recipe."

Geoff's picture moved to the bottom left corner of the screen and joined the photos of all the other contestants, including me.

An X appeared over Li's photo and Cindy's. Their photos faded to the background and the four remaining contestant's faces were in a symmetrical box like windowpanes.

As Jenna's voice prattled on, asking for the audience to join them next week, I could suddenly feel the walls of the box closing down on me like plates of a panini press.

Chapter Twelve

Lugaw is the Filipino version of congee, a savoury rice porridge heavy on the ginger and garlic.

Rice, ~~Cauliflower~~, and Quinoa Lugaw

5 cups low salt chicken broth (boxed or homemade, can also sub with veggie broth)

1 cup leftover white rice (cooked rice, refrigerated at least 12 hours)

¼ cup quinoa, rinsed

3 cloves garlic, minced

2 tsp grated ginger

~~2 tsp soy sauce~~ *2 tsp patis (fish sauce)*

~~¾ cup cauliflower rice (raw cauliflower pulverized in a food processor)~~

Garnish: Sesame oil, chopped green onion

Add broth, rice, quinoa, garlic, and ginger to a large pot, break up any chunks of rice.

Bring to a boil then drop heat to medium low.

Stir every few minutes. *Scrape the bottom!!!*

Continue to cook until mixture is the consistency of thin porridge (15–20 minutes).

Mix in ~~soy sauce.~~ *Change to patis*

~~Mix in cauliflower rice. Cook another three minutes.~~

Taste, add more ~~soy~~ *Patis!* if more seasoning required.

Serve in bowls. Garnish with drops of sesame oil and chopped green onion.

Winnipeg

"Rice!" Jenna said enthusiastically, as if announcing the winning number in the lottery.

Immediately, my spirits soared. Rice is a staple in the majority of the world's cuisine. It was the pasta, bread, and potatoes of Asian gastronomy.

"We want you to bring rice from the background to the foreground, from the sidelines to the centre," she explained. "We want you to bring your own cultural spin on this universal carb."

Suddenly I realized I trapped myself in a corner. My aunt had taught me how to make plain white rice. She taught me how to make garlic fried rice. She taught me how to make Java Rice, the most flavourful of the three, but I had already placed the recipe on my blog before the competition.

I knew how to make sushi rice, but I already made that for the show a couple of weeks ago. Maybe a rice pudding, I could add quinoa—

"I'm thinking a rice pudding. I can add a healthy spin by adding steel-cut oats," Harriet said, as if she had plucked the idea from my brain. "There's a farm where my family has a grain-share, and they have the most wonderfully hearty oats."

That idea was out. What to do, what to do, maybe a fried rice of some sort—

"Ma mère makes a Confetti Rice recipe," Kendra said. "It is a colourful Caribbean rice that is fried with spices. There is coconut, ananas, ah pineapple, capsaicin. It is very spicy."

"Ooh," Jenna cooed. "That sounds amazing!"

Another idea gone. What was that dish we ordered at dim sum a few months ago? It was wrapped in banana leaves. And there was meat in it—

"My favourite dim sum item is that glutinous sticky rice with pork," Geoff gushed. "Ugh, it's soooo satisfying to unwrap the banana leaf and release the steam. Yum!"

Crap! My mind quickly took inventory of the recipes on my blog. There had to be something—

"Sarah," Jenna coaxed. "What about you? How do you plan on elevating rice?"

"Congee," I blurted out. "Filipino congee. It's basically rice porridge. Super comforting. It's perfect for Winnipeg weather." I glanced up at the window quickly. "It's only four degrees here so I could use some comfort."

"It's minus eleven here in Nunavut so I would love some of your Filipino Congee to warm me up!"

"Great job, guys!" Chuck said, unusually chipper. "You're starting to get the hang of this!" He had been so quiet I had almost forgotten he was on the call. The last time I had heard him speak was our last session with the judges. That felt ages ago.

"You seemed a little thrown off by the mystery ingredient," Del commented as she was packing up. "I would've thought rice would be easy for you."

"That's just it, too much choice," I lied. "I got a little overwhelmed."

After Del left, I picked up my phone and did some research before logging into my online class. I had made congee before, a pale porridge made with broth and day-old rice. On my blog, I had added cauliflower rice as a healthy way to cut into the carb ratio while keeping the pale colour. I knew there was a Filipino version, I just couldn't remember what it was called.

Different options came up: Arroz Caldo which had boiled chicken on the bone; Goto which was made with beef broth and tripe; Lugaw was the closest to congee with broth, ginger, and heaps of garlic. I could take my congee recipe and adapt it. Easy peasy.

While online, I mused about Cindy. What would she have made? I would have loved to have seen a recipe using wild rice, a staple of some Indigenous cuisine. I had made a wild rice fruit salad for my blog using seasonal fruits.

I pulled up her site *I Can with Pots and Pans.* I scrolled through her archives that went back four years. Her recipes focused on stretching foods to fit a budget, using seasonal or frozen produce with canned or jarred goods to make dishes that were tasty, healthy, and filling. Spicy chilli using jarred salsa. Perogy casserole with frozen veggies and homemade velouté. She even had her own version of congee using instant ramen, leftover rice, and leftover vegetables. She had almost five thousand followers on her Instagram.

Her grandfather's bannock was her very first post. She mentioned his recipe a year later when she described how to make fry bread. After almost a hundred different meals, snacks, and desserts, she posted a few more recipes using bannock in different ways: bannock wrapped around hot dogs and cooked over a fire, Bannock Strawberry Shortbread, Bannock Chicken Pot Pie. All of those recipes were dated a few weeks before the premiere of *Cyber Chef: Next Gen.*

I closed her site. We had a lot in common after all.

Twenty years ago
Winnipeg

Cher ladled steamy lugaw into six bowls. She wiped away stray drops of porridge that had gotten on the sides. She pinched crispy-fried garlic from a ramekin and sprinkled it just off center of each bowl, then added another pinch of meticulously cut green onion curls. She added three drops of sriracha near the top, then dragged the tip of a toothpick across the three dots to join them with thin lines. Her recent graduation from culinary school would be lost on her family, but the soigné plating was for her enjoyment, not theirs.

She checked the oven where she was baking escabeche—whole tilapia with sweet and sour vegetables. She had made it as part of her final exam, which she had passed with flying colours.

Cher brought out the bowls and set them out for her mother, her sister Grace and her fiancé, Aaron, and her brother Christoffer and his girlfriend, Mimi, whom no one acknowledged was clearly pregnant. Cherish would have brought the person she was seeing, but it wasn't that serious, sort of. She wasn't sure. She was too busy with work and school to figure it out.

"Have you made your wedding plans, Grace?" her mother asked.

"We've been engaged a week, Mom," she replied with disdain, the natural voice she used when addressing their mother.

"If you want to book St. Edwards, you have to book very far in advance."

Grace looked at Aaron, pleading for help.

"We have lots of time to talk about wedding plans. We don't have to discuss this now," Aaron said, hoping it was enough to wave the subject away. He looked across the table at Cher as she took her seat. "This is excellent, Cher, and beautiful too. Oh, congrats, by the way, on graduating. We're proud of you."

"Thanks, I appreciate it."

"Hey," Mimi said, after she had picked out all the green onion curls. She had placed them in her napkin. Cher made sure to avert her eyes from the bundle next to her bowl. "Does this mean you become the chef at your restaurant?"

"It doesn't really work that way," Cher said. "I'm still a sous-chef, but I've only been there for a couple of years."

"Oh, so you're a chef already," she said. "What was the point in going to school for it?"

"There's different levels of being a chef," Cher explained patiently. "Sous-chef is like a deputy chef. The next step would be Chef de Cuisine, which is the head chef. Sometimes there's an executive chef, but this is usually for big kitchens, often for chains. They're more managerial. They create recipes but they don't usually cook."

"Ohhhhh." Mimi spread out the word but clearly didn't understand what was just explained. "Soooo, what now?"

"I have plans."

"Are you going to open your own restaurant?"

"Maybe someday," Cher said, trying to close off the conversation with one of the most annoying people she had ever met. "There's a lot of steps to go through before anyone should own a restaurant. I still have a lot to learn."

"Are you going back to school?"

"No, not quite."

"Ahh!" her mother said, bringing the attention back to her. "Christoffer has some news." Cher and Grace turned towards him, expecting to finally hear about what was so incredibly obvious. Their mother proudly announced, "He is going back to school for engineering!"

Grace and Cher exchanged a look. Aaron appeared to be biting his lip to withhold a smile.

"Engineering technologist, Nay," Christoffer said sheepishly. Nay, which rhymed with eye, was short for Nanay, or Mother, but Cher and Grace had stopped calling their mother Nay when they were kids. Of course darling Christoffer still called her that. "I'm not going to be an engineer."

"Oh, but I am so proud of you!" their mother beamed.

"I haven't even done anything yet," he said, exasperated.

Christoffer was always the favourite of the three siblings, especially after their father passed away. They all knew that, but he felt the burden of his mother's disproportionate affection. When their father died over a decade before, he felt the wave of unconditional love shift onto him. Their mom always seemed mad or disappointed in his sisters, but they had become used to the negativity and they bonded as they faded into the background. The pedestal their mother had built for him made him feel precariously uncomfortable and sometimes alone.

"But you are going to do so much, Balong."

Cher and Grace rolled their eyes in unison. Balong meant 'young boy'. Although Cher was the youngest, Christoffer would always be the baby,

"So, Grace," Christoffer deflected. "If you're not getting married in a church, are you getting married in a synagogue?" Grace's eyes appeared to shoot fire across the table.

"Of course she is getting married in a church!" their mother insisted. "She has to be married in the House of God!"

Grace gripped her spoon so hard it would have snapped in half if it wasn't metal. Aaron leaned over to whisper to her, but her jawline remained tight.

"Actually, Mom, we're not getting married in a church or a synagogue," Grace said. "We want an outdoor ceremony."

"Oh, my dear, it is not a Catholic ceremony if you do it outside," their mother lectured. "It has to be in a church. Aaron is not Catholic, but I have been told that you can go to classes and they will let you get married. If you want, you can make a small ceremony at the church and then make a big ceremony outside for all your guests. That is what your tita Lydia did last year with your cousin."

"No, Mom." Grace put the spoon down. "We're having a Jewish ceremony, and just a Jewish ceremony." She glanced at Aaron and took a deep breath. "I converted to Judaism about a month ago."

"WHAT?!"

Their mother's spoon dropped out of her hand and clattered in the half-empty bowl of lugaw, splattering what was left all over her blue floral-patterned blouse. She grabbed a napkin, trying to wipe off the globs of wet rice only to smear them further.

"Why would you abandon everything I have taught you?"

"It's not about you, Mom!" Grace said furiously. "This is about me and Aaron!"

"Honey, maybe we should discuss—"

"Stay out of this, Aaron," Grace snapped. "This is between me and my mom."

Cher caught Aaron's eye, and they both suppressed a laugh. This felt like a sitcom. She stood up and started to clear the bowls. No one was going to finish their lugaw tonight. Aaron picked up his empty bowl and Grace's barely touched porridge.

"Welcome to the family, Aaron," Cher said, once they were in the kitchen.

"Grace and your mom are so much alike, it's not even funny," he said, dumping out the full bowl. "If we talked it out instead of yelling, I think this wouldn't have gone so badly."

"Are you kidding? This is your best-case scenario. Yes, there's a lot of fire and drama, but it'll burn out. You'll see."

"Or it could rage out of control."

Cher pulled the fish out of the oven and transferred it onto a platter, arranging the sweet and sour julienned vegetables over top. Her sister and her mom were still arguing. Something about going to hell; she wasn't sure who was saying what at this point. She would bring the fish out while Aaron carried the white rice and sesame green beans.

"...Why don't you ask Christoffer if he's getting married in a church?"

Oh no, thought Cher. *Don't get Chris involved.*

"Hey, we're not even thinking of—"

"Oh really, Chris?" Grace was standing. "Because your girlfriend is clearly four or five months pregnant and mom would probably want you married in a church before the baby is born."

Silence.

"I look five months pregnant?" Mimi started to cry. "But it's only been three!"

"Baby, she didn't mean it like that!" Christoffer assured her. He turned his wrath on his older sister. "Why are you taking this out on us?"

"Because I'm sick of you being perfect!"

"And I'm sick of you wrecking this family!"

Cher could see the invisible blaze spreading across the table. It would soon engulf them all.

"I swear you come here just to pick a fight! And look," he pointed at their mother, "You're making Nanay cry."

"This is what it feels like to disappoint your mother!" Grace yelled. "We've been in that club for a very long time, Christoffer."

"Don't drag me into this, Grace." Cher begged.

"Why?" Christoffer said. "Are you afraid that mom's going to find out that you're leaving Winnipeg to live in hostels around the world?"

"She already knows that, Chris. Nice try."

His face got red. "Well, does she know that you're going on the trip with your GIRLFRIEND?"

Silence.

For the second time in the last five minutes.

They all slowly turned to look at their mother, who stood up.

"I'm going to be a grandmother?"

A bright smile spread across her face, and she began to weep. Cher couldn't remember when her mother had last looked so radiant, maybe the times she watched them dance Tinikling or that one time when their father had come home to announce he had been promoted to foreman. Their mother went to Mimi to pull her up in an embrace. Christoffer held them both.

Cher went back into the kitchen, poured the leftover lugaw into a margarine container she found in the cabinet, and placed it in the refrigerator. She then picked up her purse and left the house.

Winnipeg

"Sarah and Harriet."

Jenna's voice didn't sound as chipper as it normally did. The windows of the other contestants blinked away, leaving Harriet and

I with the judges, Jenna, and Chuck. My heart fell to the bottom of my gut. I felt scared. I wanted a hug from my mom.

"Sarah, do you need a second?" Chuck asked, reading my mind. "Maybe some water or something?"

"No, no, no, I'm fine." My voice cracked and my mouth dried out. "Maybe some water."

Del passed me my water bottle.

"We're going to keep filming. Just let me know if you need a break," Chuck said, almost fatherly. I nodded. "You good, Harriet?"

"Good to go!" she said, almost too excitedly.

"Sarah, the judges would like to start with you," Jenna segued. "Sarah."

"Gary."

"Yeah, like I said before, I really dug the flavour of this dish," Gary said. "It was an easy recipe, but I have to admit, I might have screwed it up. I, uh, a lot of it burned at the bottom of my pot. Anybody else have that problem?"

FOLLOW THE INSTRUCTIONS. I could hear my friends saying.

"Some of it stuck to the bottom of my pot too," Robyn admitted.

"Wait, what?" I said, dumbstruck. "Didn't you scrape the bottom of the pot as you cooked?"

"That wasn't in the instructions," Gary said.

Oh no, I thought. *ADD IT TO THE RECIPE.* I would have shouted at the screen as a viewer.

"And it was kinda busy, ya know?"

"I have to agree with Gary," Robyn said.

"Wow, twice in one shot. That's a first."

"Possibly not the last," she chuckled. "I don't think the cauliflower rice was necessary. Sure, it's a healthy addition, but it feels like an afterthought. The cauliflower is so flavour neutral, it just seems to serve as filler."

"I agree with all of the above," Chef Kwan started. I sat up straighter. Though I would never say so out loud, as a professional chef, her critique held the most weight for me. "I had one issue with the flavour. I've eaten and made many different versions of rice porridge—congee, jook, arroz caldo, etc.

"The Filipino version has always been very flavour-forward. Your recipe had the right amounts of ginger, and was perfectly garlic-heavy, however the use of soy sauce, and the small amount of it, didn't bring me the umami I was expecting. The traditional use of patis, or Ngoc Cham, or fish sauce for the English speakers, would have been a more effective choice.

"If your lugaw punched me in the face with the saltiness that comfort food should bring, I wouldn't have cared that there's rice, quinoa, cauliflower, or whatever you wanted to dump in, because it would have brought me to my knees with flavour. That's one of the things I appreciate in Filipino cuisine, the salt factor. Unfortunately, your dish didn't bring that."

"Thank you, Chef," I said meekly, trying to maintain composure. A box of Kleenex sat close by. "Thank you all. I will be sure to keep your critiques in mind."

I sat silently as they critiqued Harriet's Chai Rice Pudding. Even though my microphone was on mute, my image stayed on the screen. Although I know the footage would be edited so only Harriet's image would appear in front of the judges, I kept my eyes focused forward.

"You okay, Sar?" Del asked.

"I'm fine."

"It was good feedback. They really liked your dish. A couple of tweaks and it would have been perfect."

"I guess."

"Sar," she leaned forward. "I really liked it. I would probably make it at home. A lot of people will."

I turned to her. "Thanks."

"Thank you, judges, for your feedback," Jenna said. "And we will hear the results when we return."

"Okay," said Chuck. "Here is where we will slot in a couple of commercials. We're going to keep filming. Are you both okay? Do you need a break?"

Chuck was oddly coddling. I almost preferred it when he was sharp and critical. I started to wonder what happened last week. Or maybe this was what he was like during the final judging? Finally displaying sensitivity as one of us was going, or I guess staying, home.

"Go ahead, Jenna."

"Welcome back to *Cyber Chef: Next Gen!*" Jenna brought back her cheer. "The judges have made their decision."

Gary dropped the hammer this time. "The next *Cyber Chef* contestant to leave the competition is… Harriet."

I exhaled.

"As we said, we love your healthier spin on rice pudding, but it was too cinnamon heavy and missing the other key spices. It lacked authenticity but was an excellent first attempt. I hope you do consider revising the recipe with more research and consultation with someone more familiar with chai masala spice."

"I'll definitely take that advice. Thank you for the opportunity."

"Congratulations, Sarah," Jenna said. Chuck and the other judges repeated the sentiment.

"I'm so sorry, Harriet," I offered.

"I saw it coming." She smiled. "I'll pray for you."

After disconnecting, my parents came into the room and enveloped me in a big hug.

"You did great, honey," my father said, kissing me on the forehead. "And the lugaw was delicious, better than your aunt's."

"You've had Auntie Cher's lugaw?"

"A long, long time ago, but it was very memorable."

"Cher texted me. She wants to know how you did this week," said my mom.

"You didn't tell her, did you?"

"Of course not. NDA."

"Can I stop by the restaurant? I don't want to stay home. I feel antsy."

"I could drop her off," Del said. "Mosaic, right? It's close to where I live."

"Mom?"

"Yes, just call us when you want to be picked up."

I rummaged through the refrigerator for the container of lugaw I had saved for my aunt. I tested the recipe twice this week and ended up making A LOT. I had sent some home with Del and my dad had been taking it to work for lunch. My mom tasted it but wasn't diving in nearly as much as me and my dad. Maybe she thought it had too much going on, just like the judges.

I instructed Del to drop me off at the back door. I sent a quick text to my aunt. It was only four pm, and the restaurant didn't open its doors until five thirty. I invited Del to come in with me.

"I've been here before," Del said. "Good food. Good variety. But I have to upload all of today's footage before six."

"You sure? I'd love to introduce you to my aunt. We can be quick."

"Another time, I promise."

I took the back door, which was propped open with a can. One of the staff was leaning against a wall, smoking. I held my breath as I passed by. He nodded, and I gave a wave. As I walked into the kitchen, all the cooks said hi. I had been a regular visitor to Mosaic's kitchen since it opened six years ago. One of the prep cooks pointed to the office. I nudged the slightly open door with my elbow.

"I have lugaw for you." I put the container down on the desk.

"Oh, yum. Don't tell me, the mystery ingredient was rice."

"I can't say."

"How'd you do?"

"I can't say that either."

"Whatever happens, I am the proudest aunt ever. Come."

She took my hand and led me to a table in the dining room. She stopped the kitchen manager as she passed.

"Ask Nadia to make some Morel Purses and Ravioli Uovo special for me and my niece."

"Not Tio?"

"It's just a snack for us. Tell her it's a test."

"Yes, Chef."

"Nadia is new-ish," Auntie Cher said as we sat down. I took off my mask. "She recently graduated with her Red Seal. We've been having her prep and make the staff meal. She gets to experiment a little, but she's too slow to work on the line. Very creative though. These morel purses she came up with are out of this world."

"Are you thinking of putting them on the menu?"

"Our morels are foraged. We can only use a few at a time and we want them seen. Usually unsightly stuff goes into a dumpling, ground meat or minced vegetables. That's what's in these purses, morel stems."

"Hey, I have a question," I said. "What do you use as the salty part in your lugaw? Soy sauce?"

"I use patis, fish sauce. I know I've been pushing soy on you a lot, but it's the easiest to source for a recipe, although fish sauce is pretty much available in every grocery store nowadays. I prefer patis in brothy stuff because it doesn't lose its pungency. I probably should have covered that earlier. I am so sorry if that cost you the competition."

"No, no. There's so much to cover. I can't expect you to teach me everything."

"Patis is really good in Ginatang, coconut broth. We can make that the next time you come over."

"I'd like that. I wish I grew up with some of this food."

"Yeah, well, cooking was never your mom's thing. It's good that Aaron cooks."

"But you don't even bring this food to our house. Other than pancit, eggrolls, and pork skewers, I don't know anything about Filipino food. It sucks."

"Grace isn't a fan." Auntie Cher shrugged her shoulders. "She's never liked Filipino food. Ever. She figured out how to make peanut butter sandwiches and how to microwave a frozen pizza when she was a kid."

"I thought you said she didn't cook."

"Oh, honey. That is not cooking. She made her own lunches and when she got older, she would only eat rice and stir-fries most of the time, usually the frozen kind with the veggies, meat, and seasoning in a pouch. She'd eat pancit once in a while, but my mom only made it on special occasions. My mother taught me to cook, and I ended up cooking for Grace by the time I was nine."

"Wow. Mom usually likes my cooking, but she barely tried my lugaw. Everyone else seemed to like it. Dad can't get enough."

Auntie Cher smiled to herself, a laugh hovering on her lips.

"What is it?"

"Just thinking of the last time I made lugaw for the family. It was a memorable night."

"That's what my dad said."

A petite server set down a stone disc that held three deep fried wonton bundles with a green onion tied at the top. Three green dots of sauce radiated away. These must be the morel purses. Two stone bowls were set in front of us with a clear broth at the bottom and a single large ravioli floating in the middle, a small pile of green and purple microgreens perched on top. I was about to take a picture, but my aunt held up a hand to stop me.

"What made the night so memorable?" I asked.

"I was pissed off at the time it happened, but now I realize it was ridiculously melodramatic."

"Tell me."

Auntie Cher poked into the ravioli with a tine of a fork and soft egg yolk oozed out beautifully into the broth. I took a quick snap.

"Please?" I asked. I scooped up a spoonful of broth, a ribbon of custardy yellow pooled in the center. The flavour was like a savoury custard.

"Alright. I'll tell you about the worst... dinner party... ever..."

Chapter Thirteen

This is one of the most bougie dishes I have ever made. Yes, it's a lot of instructions, but so worth it! This is THE appetizer if you want to cook to impress. If the directions seem intimidating, the TLDR are: Freeze yolks, cook filling, stuff wontons, deep fry, serve.

Crispy Wontons with Longa & Uovo
8 unbroken egg yolks, frozen (instructions below)
1 tsp oil
2 small longanisa sausages or 1 large longanisa sausage,
    meat removed from casing
1 clove garlic, minced
1 tsp minced ginger
1 tsp soy sauce
1 tsp rice vinegar
1 tsp sriracha (optional)
1 package wonton wrappers, thawed
2 + 1 tbsp egg whites, separated
1 tsp water
High temperature oil for deep frying (peanut, sunflower,
    avocado)
Kosher salt
Chopped green onions or cilantro leaves for garnish

Freeze yolks:
At least four hours before or the night prior, prep the egg yolks.

Separate eggs, using your hand, a spoon, the eggshell, or the empty water bottle technique (Google it!)

As you separate each egg, carefully place each individual unbroken yolk spaced apart on a parchment or silicone lined cookie sheet. If the yolk breaks, wipe it up and separate a new yolk.

Save three egg whites for later.

Place the cookie sheet in the freezer. Ensure the sheet is level.

Freeze the yolks for at least four hours or overnight.

Make the filling:
Preheat a non-stick pan on medium. Add one teaspoon of oil.

Add longanisa meat to pan. Using the edge of the spoon or spatula, mash out any lumps or chop pieces smaller until meat is an even consistency.

Add garlic and ginger.

Sauté on medium until sausage is lightly brown (which can be difficult to tell since the meat is usually red) approximately five minutes.

Turn off heat. Remove meat from pan and put into a bowl.

Add vinegar, soy sauce, and optional sriracha. Mix well.

Mix in two tablespoons of egg white into the longanisa mixture. Set aside.

Stuff wontons:
In a ramekin or small bowl, mix one tablespoon egg white with one teaspoon of water.

Remove yolks from freezer. Peel the yolks from the parchment paper or silicone sheet. Trim any frozen egg white from the yolk with a sharp knife.

Cut open the thawed wonton package. Peel off two wonton wrappers and place on a cutting board or a plate. Keep the remaining wonton wrappers covered with a damp tea towel when not in use. Stuff only one wonton at a time.

Using your finger or a pastry brush, dampen one edge of a wonton wrapper with egg white.

Place the second wrapper on top, matching the edges. Press down on the wet edge to seal.

Open the top wonton like the cover of a book with the sealed edge down.

Add a teaspoon of longanisa meat in the middle of the bottom wonton, about the size and shape of an egg yolk.

Place a frozen egg yolk on top of the longanisa. Press down to flatten the meat.

Brush egg white on the bottom longanisa wrapper around the meat, outwards towards the edges.

Close the wonton 'book' by covering the egg and meat with the top wonton.

Press to seal the outer corners. Then seal the edge opposite the 'spine' of the wonton book.

Carefully pick up the wonton and seal the open ends. Around the egg yolk and meat, try to push out as much air as possible. Turn the wonton in your hand to ensure all edges are sealed.

You should end up with a square package with the meat and egg tightly secured in the middle.

Repeat process to make seven more wontons.

You can freeze the wontons at this point if you want to save for another day.

Fry wontons:
Fill a medium-sized heavy-bottomed pot half-way with a high temperature oil for deep frying. Heat on medium.

Do NOT use an airfryer. Trust me.

Prep a cooling area by placing a wire rack over a cookie sheet.

Heat oil to 350 degrees. Use a thermometer or toss pieces of wonton wrapper into the oil. If they start bubbling, then you're at the right temperature.

Fry one wonton at a time. Carefully slide a wonton into the oil, egg-side down. Count ten seconds to set the shape, then using tongs, turn the wonton over.

Then fry the wonton meat-side down until golden, thirty to forty-five seconds. (Longer if frozen.)

Using tongs, turn wonton over again to finish cooking the egg-side down for fifteen seconds or until lightly golden.

Transfer to a wire rack to cool.

Repeat process with the remaining seven wontons.

Serve immediately, garnished with green onions or cilantro. If you want a condiment, use a chilli sauce, spicy mayo, sweet & sour, salsa, or my Triple-S Sawsawan.

Winnipeg
"That looks amazing, Sar!" my mom exclaimed. "It's restaurant worthy!"

I had just plated the crispy wonton in the middle of a plate, on top of a swipe of sriracha mayo. I added a drizzle of my Triple-S

Sawsawan on top of the wonton, allowing a drip off to the side for some esthetic imperfection. I added a few cilantro leaves for garnish then took a few shots with my phone as Del hovered over me with her camera hoisted on her shoulder.

"Just wait," I said.

I grabbed a knife and fork and cut into the wonton. The yolk oozed out as I had expected, flowing out onto the plate with bits of longanisa tumbling out afterwards. It mixed with the pink sriracha mayo and the sawsawan, creating a swirl of sauce at the bottom of the plate. I cut away a quarter of the wonton and held it by the crispy corner, dragging it through the bright yellow yolk mixed with the sauces and popped it into my mouth. Salty, sour, garlic, with creamy barely cooked yolk as the dominant sauce. It was exquisite, just like the Ravioli Uovo my aunt had introduced me to a few days before but combined with the satisfying crisps of the fried wonton purses and relentless spikes of strong flavours to pique the palate.

It was as if the new dishes from Mosaic were perfectly timed to the announcement of sausage as this week's mystery ingredient. I couldn't wait to tell my aunt.

"Do you want to try it?" I asked my mom.

"What kind of sausage is it?"

"Longanisa."

"Oh, I don't know. Don't waste your taste test on me," she said. "What about you, Del? Do you want to try it?"

"I've already had two whole wontons," Del said, pulling her face away from the camera. "Aaron's also had two."

"This is my third batch," I explained. "I froze a couple for Auntie Cher and to make for Lena and Jay later this week, after the episode airs. I just finished frying the last two."

"I'm supposed to be impartial, but I have to admit this is one of the best things I've ever eaten," Del said, returning to the camera. She closed in on the wontons cooling on the rack.

"Do you want to taste it?" I pushed the plate towards my mother. She stared at it blankly. "Please?"

She sighed. "Alright, one taste."

My mom cut another quarter of the wonton and held it by the corner as I had, dragging it through the yolk that had begun to dry and crust. She nibbled gingerly on the wonton, then put it down. She looked at it for a second. I couldn't place the look on her face; her eyes were almost regretful.

"It's tasty, yes," she said. "But not my thing. It is breathtaking to look at, especially with that yolk."

I felt a lump in my throat. I pulled back the plate.

"Mom, why do you hate Filipino food so much?"

"I don't hate Filipino food, Sar."

"If I put merguez, or Italian sausage, or even bratwurst, would you have liked it?"

"I find the longanisa very sweet."

"That's why I added soy sauce and vinegar," I said. I could hear my voice rising. "The flavours are balanced. It's the most balanced dish I've ever made!"

"I don't like the salty/sour combination," she reasoned, her voice calm. "I don't pick on you for your dislike of dill."

"That's crap, Mom!" I said, my face now flush with anger. "I made Lai's Larb recipe from the last season of *Cyber Chef* and it's loaded with fish sauce and lime and you gushed over it. I also made Nessa's Chicken n Waffles with chipotle marmalade honey TWICE, because you liked it so much. You love pad thai, lemon pepper wings, hot and sour soup. You LOVE salty sour.

"Ever since I started learning how to make Filipino food, you've been avoiding eating what I cook. Why?" I asked desperately. "Why do you hate my cooking all of a sudden? Why do you hate Filipino food?"

Hot, angry tears ran down my face. I grabbed the green striped cloth napkin off the table that I was using as a prop for the background. I wiped my face, but my eyes still burned. Tears still lingered along my bottom eyelids. I could feel my mascara running. I knew there would be dark circles. My foundation would be smudged, revealing the acne outbreak on my cheek caused from wearing a mask.

"Sar, I don't hate Filipino food," she said gently. "And I certainly don't hate your cooking."

"But you hate being Filipino."

The words tumbled out of my mouth before I could stop them. They lay on the floor, writhing between us.

"I don't hate being Filipino. How can you ever think that?"

"You hate Lola."

"Did Cher say that?"

"She didn't have to."

"What did she tell you?"

"Things that you would never tell me."

"What did she say?"

I stared at my mother, unblinking. Truth was, Auntie Cher didn't tell me anything. Not really. No one told me anything. I was sealed shut and ready to burst. All I needed was the tip of a knife. I looked over at the jagged edges of what was left of the wonton. That was all it took.

Click.

I turned to the left and realized Del was still in the room. She was closing her camera case on the countertop.

"I should go," she said.

"Yes, you should leave," my mother said coldly.

"No," I said. "We still have work to do."

"I have the last shot we needed. I'll email you." She started to step out of the room.

"Del, wait," I said. "I'll come with you."

"Where are you going?" my mother said angrily.

"Out!"

"You have to clean this mess up!"

"I will clean it later!"

"You are not taking her anywhere, Del."

"Then I will WALK!" I screamed.

I brushed past Del, picking up my phone and bag off the counter, and left through the back door, running.

Four years ago
Winnipeg

"Sarah did good, right?" Gloria Abad said to her son-in-law, Aaron.

They stood at one of the buffet stations in the synagogue's banquet room. They loaded party sandwiches onto white plates, selecting from tuna salad, salmon, egg, and cream cheese with cucumber. No meat choices as the building was designated kosher and dairy couldn't be served with meat, but Aaron explained that fish was allowed.

"Yes, she did wonderfully," Aaron replied, taking another salmon sandwich. "We are very proud."

"Is the Hebrew a lot of work?" Gloria asked.

"Sarah attended a private Hebrew immersion school, but learning to read the Torah and lead the service takes a lot of practice," Aaron explained. "She's been working with the rabbis for just over a year."

"Oh, she is such a smart girl. She is very dedicated to her studies."

Aaron took Gloria's elbow gingerly and led her to the next buffet station where a blond server stood wearing black pants, a white shirt, a black vest, and white gloves. The young man offered a piece of baked salmon with lemon slices and capers on top. She lifted her plate to accept the serving of fish and two latkes and nodded in thanks.

"Sarah helped to pick out the menu," Aaron said. "She insisted she wanted no dill."

He gestured to the six buffet stations down the centre of what would be set up as a dance floor that night, three sets of tables on each side, a mirror of the other. One pair offered a selection of salads and buns; one offered party sandwiches, a tray of olives, and raw vegetables and dip; another table offered baked salmon and potato pancakes. Most of the children and teenagers congregated on one end of the room, where they were offered cheese or veggie pizzas. The opposite end of the room would display several cakes and tortes, but was not yet set up for service.

"Everything looks very delicious."

"She picked out her favourites," Aaron said. "The selections were limited here at the synagogue, but she had complete say over tonight's dinner menu."

Gloria couldn't believe this incredible array of food for lunch, while an elegant sit-down dinner was scheduled for later that night. Jewish people certainly loved food, but she had to admit that Filipinos loved food as well. A typical Filipino house party with friends and family would have tables covered with platters piled high with pork, chicken, beef, fish, egg rolls, and several types of noodles.

It struck her that Sarah wouldn't be familiar with a Filipino house party. Though almost ten percent of the population of Winnipeg was of Filipino descent (with Tagalog surpassing French as the second most spoken language—she loved to bring up that statistic to her friends) other than Cherish and Grace, none of that population were their family.

When her son, Christoffer and his wife Mimi moved out to Penticton, BC, Gloria was more than happy to join them to help raise her twin granddaughters and eventual grandson. She had three cousins in Vancouver who had several children and even more grandchildren who called her Lola Glo. They visited Vancouver often. It wasn't far. Moving closer to extended family had done wonders for her social life and general happiness. She didn't miss Winnipeg's bitter winters. Grace and Cherish had also made it clear she had nothing left in Winnipeg.

Aaron led Gloria to the table where Christoffer and Mimi had already started on their loaded plates. The sixteen-year-old twins were on their phones, two plates of untouched pizza and salad in front of them.

"Hey, girls," Aaron said gently as he pulled out a chair for Gloria. "I don't want to interrupt or anything, but phones aren't allowed in the synagogue on Shabbat, uh, Fridays and Saturdays."

They rolled their eyes in sync at their uncle and put their phones face-down on the table.

"Mina, Manda!" their mother admonished. "Put your phones away. Don't get Uncle in trouble. And apologize."

"Yeah, listen to your mom," Christoffer said between bites.

"Sorry, Uncle Aaron," they said in unison in a sing-song voice.

"Oh, that's not necessary."

The two girls shot daggers at their mother. She reflected the look, and they each grabbed their plates and stabbed into their salads with a fork.

"Where's Christo?" Aaron asked, nodding at the empty seat with the empty plate in front of it. The girls nodded at their nine-year-old brother running around with a little boy with brown curly hair and deep dimples in his cheek. They squealed as they ran by. Mimi glanced at Aaron, as if asking for approval.

"I'm glad Christo made a friend."

Gloria watched Sarah across the room with her friends. The twelve-year-old girl was happy and smiling, her laughter echoing across the large space. She wore an elegant pink knee-length pencil skirt dress with short, fitted sleeves and a boat neckline, delicate pearls around her neck. If she wore white lace gloves and oversized sunglasses, she would look like an Asian Jackie Onassis. She wore a pink kippah pinned to the crown of her head, her long dark hair cascading down her back, curled at the ends.

Like most *mestiza* girls with mixed heritage, Sarah was a beauty. She had the colouring of Snow White with pale creamy skin and rich dark brown tresses, a hair colour she knew her daughter, Grace, bought for herself in a salon. Sarah had high cheekbones and the mildly pointed nose that most Filipinos desired and sometimes paid for. Though they were almond-shaped, her eyes had the coveted double-eyelid.

"Do you like the room you're staying in?" Aaron asked, taking a seat and putting down his loaded plate.

"Oh yes, it's very nice," Gloria lied.

"We wanted to make sure you were comfortable, and the room has a beautiful view."

"Yes, it is lovely."

Gloria thought it was a disgrace—pardon the pun—that Grace didn't invite her to stay with them. It's Filipino tradition to have your family stay with you, especially your mother. They had a four-bedroom house. Surely they could have invited her, but of course, Grace spit in the eye of Filipino tradition.

She probably would have turned them down anyway.

Gloria did enjoy the luxurious king-sized bed and whirlpool bathtub. The mattress felt like a cloud compared to the hand-me-down queen that she had in her bedroom in Penticton. Christoffer and Mimi only got one hotel room for the whole family. When Gloria saw that her grandson was banished to a cot crowded in the corner, she insisted he share the large room with her. She made it sound like she was doing them a favour but in fact, she wasn't used to being alone and enjoyed his company. Instead of the cot, she let him sleep on the pull-out couch.

"Aaron!" A loud, boisterous woman with big hair and harsh makeup approached the table and squeezed Aaron's cheeks. "Mazeltov! Sarah has quite the keppie on her. So smart! You and Grace must just be kvelling!" She turned to the family. "You must be Grace's family. I am Sadie. I am Aaron's aunt. I live in Toronto. And it is just a joy to see Sarah so beautiful and grown up."

While Aaron introduced his aunt, she held out her hand to Gloria, who sat closest for a handshake. Her fingers were covered in rings and her wrist jangling with bracelets. The girls stared in awe of this whirlwind of a woman.

"Aaron, darling." She took his hand, pulling him up. "You have to come say hi to your uncle Morley. He's using a walker so I am not going to make him schlep all the way over here. Be a mensch and come say hello. Nice meeting you all!" She waved goodbye with a sparkly hand.

"That was so weird," Mina said.

"Like a total stereotype," Manda chimed in.

"Girls," Gloria said. "Don't be rude. The people here are very nice."

The girls picked at their salads, as Christoffer and Mimi stood up to get a second helping.

"Lola, is Uncle Aaron's family rich?" Mina leaned over and asked. "Mom and Dad said no but they are clearly lying."

"Oh, sweetheart. They are not rich. Uncle Aaron works very hard."

"He's, like, a doctor, right?" Manda asked. "Which means he's rich."

"No, he works for a laboratory."

"So he's a rich scientist."

"No, he works in the office, but they are very comfortable."

"What does Auntie Grace do for a living?" Mina asked, abandoning her salad. Her sister followed suit.

"I don't know."

"Why not?"

"She never told me."

"How do you know what Uncle Aaron does?"

"He talks to me. He sends me emails and pictures. Sometimes he calls me."

"That's so weird." Mina shook her head.

Gloria gazed back at Sarah and her friends.

"Why don't you go hang out with your cousin?" Gloria suggested. "Her friends are nice."

"Ugh, no," Manda said, rolling her eyes and leaning back. "They all look snobby."

"You don't know that," Gloria said, defending a granddaughter she only knew through smiling photos. "She is a very nice girl and has very nice friends."

"Why doesn't she have any Filipino friends? Why didn't she invite our BC cousins?"

Gloria already knew they had been sent an invitation, but those members of the family barely knew Sarah, or Grace, for that matter. They weren't going to make the expensive trip from the coast to the prairies for a virtual stranger. Christoffer decided they would drive to Winnipeg, with Mimi and the girls taking turns driving. It was a long two full days, thirteen hours to Calgary and then another thirteen to Winnipeg. Gloria sat at the back of the van quietly, mesmerized by the view of rolling oil pumps and vast canola fields passing by, her grandchildren staring at their electronic devices the entire drive.

"It's weird being the only brown people in a room," Mina said sulkily.

"That family looks brown-ish. I think they're Latino." Manda pointed to a Hispanic-looking family that appeared to fit in fine. Their son seemed to be one of Sarah's close friends.

Christoffer and Mimi returned plates loaded with desserts. The torte table seemed to be open.

"Girls, they have Schmoo," Christoffer said excitedly.

"What's Schmoo?" Mina asked, almost annoyed.

"I dunno, what's Schmoo with you?" he laughed boisterously at his own joke. Mimi patted him on the back as he began to cough. "But seriously, it's cake with caramel and pecans and whipped cream. It's heaven in torte form. God, I forgot how much I missed Winnipeg food. We need to get perogies and honey dill sauce before we leave, not together of course."

Mina and Manda looked at each other.

"We have to use the bathroom."

They stood up in unison, subtly grabbing their phones.

Gloria looked at the table where Grace sat. Cherish sat next to her, wearing a fitted suit and her hair slicked back. She looked debonair. Can a girl look debonair? They were sitting with Aaron's family. Grace was talking to them animatedly, waving her hands to emphasize her words. She was passionate and full of fire. Cher was laid-back. They both looked happy.

Gloria would have liked to at least have visited their home. Aaron told her Sarah was interested in cooking, that his mother was teaching her. Gloria would have liked to have made dinner for them one night; she would have taught Sarah her technique for cooking rice. She would have liked to have made turon. Or maybe lugaw or tortang talong. She thought it could have been a way they could have connected.

Instead, she watched her granddaughter laugh from across the room as she ate baked salmon with lemon and capers.

Chapter Fourteen

This recipe was a happy accident. I had a whole lot of leftover wonton wrappers and longanisa sausage after working on another recipe. And it was a cold day. Why not have some sinigang tamarind soup?

Tamarind Soup with Sweet Chorizo Wontons
Wontons:
½ cup sweet chorizo sausage (longanisa), meat removed
    from wrapper
1 clove garlic, minced
1 tsp minced ginger
1 bird eye chili, seeded and minced (optional)
1 tsp soy sauce
1 egg white
1 tsp water
Frozen wonton wrappers, thawed

Chicken broth:
6 cups low sodium chicken broth
1 tsp sugar
2 tsp soy sauce
2 tbsp tamarind soup powder (sinigang)
1 cup thinly sliced bok choy
1 cup thinly sliced carrot discs
3 green onions, chopped

Wontons:

Mix longanisa meat, garlic, ginger, chilli, and soy sauce in a bowl.

Mix water and egg white in a small bowl.

Place a wonton wrapper on a cutting board or plate.

Cover remaining wontons with a damp towel to keep them from drying out.

Add rounded tsp of sausage filling to the centre of a wonton wrapper.

Brush egg white on the wonton around the filling outwards towards the edges.

Gather up the corners and edges and seal the wonton to create a little sac. Try to squeeze out as much air as possible. Or you can be fancy and fold the wonton in either of the traditional styles (Google it!) such as a folded triangle with joined corners, or in a rectangle with pinched corners. Whichever shape you choose, try to get out as much air as you can.

Repeat with the rest of the sausage meat.

Tamarind Soup:

Bring broth to a boil. Add sugar, soy sauce, and tamarind soup powder.

Add carrots. Cook for 5 minutes.

Add bok choy and wontons. Cook 8 minutes. 10 if frozen.

Taste broth. Add seasoning if required; add water if too salty.

Remove from heat. Ladle into bowls. Top with green onion.

Winnipeg

"You okay?" Jay asked.

"Yeah," I nodded.

I sat at a picnic table at a nearby park. My phone was on a table, propped up against my purse as I talked to Jay on video chat.

It was just past six so the structure at the end of the path had thinned out with little kids, but a couple of teenagers hung out by the swings. There were still a couple hours left of daylight and I was sensible enough to know not to stay out in a public park after dark. I just needed time to calm down, and Jay was always a calming influence. With his conservation of words, he was also the most sensible out of all of my friends.

When I called, he was in the middle of a video game, but he saved quickly and focused his attention on me like a good friend. I was no longer crying, but I still felt shaky inside, and my chest ached with guilt. I had explained to Jay the things I had said to my mom, how the accusations burst out of my mouth like yolk from a poached egg.

He looked up thoughtfully, trying to think of the right words. "Why ask now?"

I stopped to think. Why now, indeed. I was in my fourth week of the competition. These questions had sat within me as idle curiosity for years, but after being immersed in Filipino culture for almost two months, the questions floated to the surface like cooked wontons.

"I've been spending a lot of time with my aunt, trying to cook Filipino food," I said. "I'm hearing all of these stories about my grandmother and my mom, and it hit me: I don't know anything about my mom's side of the family. I don't know anything about my grandmother."

He looked up to think again, as if his wisdom could only be accessed in the higher region of his brain. "Why now?" he asked again.

"What do you mean?"

"Why Filipino food? You've never cared before."

"Well, that's not true. I love Filipino food."

"Before *Cyber Chef*?"

"I like pancit and egg rolls."

"Everyone likes pancit and egg rolls."

It was my turn to think. Before *Cyber Chef*, did I even eat Filipino food? During one of our coaching sessions, Auntie Cher had revealed to me she had given me liempo as a toddler, in spite of my mother's wishes. We laughed it off, agreeing she was good at playing the role of the fun aunt. I should have asked her why my mother didn't want me to eat liempo in the first place. I should have asked my mom what she thought would happen.

"I love Filipino food now."

"Why?"

"It tastes good. It has good flavour." I paused to think for a moment. "It's balanced and not complicated but still complex. It's peasant food at its best. It's not pretentious, even though I plate it in a very pretentious way. It's salt, vinegar, and garlic. It's simple, but in your face at the same time. It's comforting and filling."

I thought about the research I had conducted, the articles I read, the videos I watched, all in preparation for the show.

"Every region has its own recipes. Every family has its own recipes. My aunt says it's hard to get Filipino food to be mainstream because no one wants to pay for something their grandmother makes better and would probably serve them for free.

"Supposedly my grandmother makes incredible food and I've never had it, just my aunt's fancy version that's been filtered through culinary school and years of working in a restaurant. I don't think my grandmother had six little bowls in front of her for perfectly measured mise en place. She probably didn't care about plating or colour palette or proportions. Her recipes were probably a pinch of this and a dash of that, like every grandmother's recipe.

"I don't even know my grandmother. I can't even remember what she looks like unless I see my cousins' Instagram first. They have lots of photos with her. I already lost one grandmother. I have one left and I barely know her."

I was crying again. Jay was silent on the other side of the screen. He knew to just leave me be for a moment. He waited patiently as my sobs turned into sniffles. My face had started to grow cold as the mid-May evening gave in to single digit temperatures.

"I'm sorry, Jay."

"No apologies necessary," he said. "Talk to your mom. Ask her questions, specific questions. Ask her what you really want to know."

I wiped away my tears with the back of my hand.

"Thanks, Jay."

"All good."

I hung up and put my phone in my bag. I recognized my dad's car idling at the edge of the park. He probably looked up the location of my phone through GPS. I wasn't mad. I needed to be found eventually.

Two years ago
Vancouver

"...And introducing our debutants, Caramina Loren and Amanda Lynn Rosario Abad!"

The three hundred guests filling the banquet room rose to their feet as the eighteen-year-old twin girls stepped in through an elaborate balloon arch and walked towards the middle of the dance floor. They waved to their guests, the tiny jewels embedded in their gel manicures sparkling in the bright lights.

A couple of years ago, the twins were on the fence when their parents asked them if they wanted a debut—a traditional Filipino coming-of-age party to celebrate turning eighteen, similar to a Spanish quinceanera where the daughter is introduced as an adult to the world.

After attending a few debuts for friends and family, they fell in love with the elaborate party with multiple changes of ballgowns and dresses. They were also excited about the cotillion dance, where they would choose their closest girl and boy friends to perform a traditional ballroom dance requiring months of preparation. They also prepped for the newer tradition of performing a modern dance with hip hop choreography.

They now stood in the middle of the dance floor wearing pink high-heeled strappy sandals and matching pink and white off-the-shoulder ballgowns, one with pink trim and white bodice and the other with white trim and pink bodice. The skirts splayed outwards from scratchy petticoats. Their identical crystal tiaras twinkled as they walked under the numerous lights. A professional photographer bounced from one spot to another to get the best angle while friends and family held their phones out to upload to social media using their selected hashtag #minaandmandasdebut.

The music changed, and they looked over to their mother, who gave them the cue to leave the dance floor. They had taken many pictures earlier in the day, wearing the elegant ballgowns, but their feet hurt and their legs itched. Their cheeks hurt from smiling. They shuffled off the dance floor and headed to the room that served as the staging area. The first thing they did was kick off the shoes that added ten inches to their small frames.

"Would mom kill us if we switched to flip-flops now?" Mina asked.

"Maybe we can leave them under the table."

They started to unzip from the dresses and exhaled. The two girls were slim to begin with, but the dresses were unforgiving with their built-in corsets and wired boning.

"*Bilisan mo,* hurry up, girls!" their mother said as she slipped into the room.

"Knock first, Mom!" Manda yelled. "What if we were naked in here?"

"You don't have time to be naked. They're starting to serve dinner."

They quickly slipped into their dinner attire, pink and white off-the-shoulder cocktail dresses with shorter tulle ballerina skirts. The first had a pink bodice with white sequins and the other had a white bodice with pink sequins. Someone knocked at the door softly. They pulled out their pink and white flip-flops from a bag when their mother's back was turned.

"Lola!" the girls hugged their grandmother from each side.

"You were two beautiful princesses on the dance floor."

"Thank you, Lola."

Gloria had had a debut in the Philippines just before her oldest sister immigrated to Canada. Her dresses were nowhere this fancy, but she had a tiara, handed down to the oldest girl in the family. It was a blessing she had left it behind with one of her sisters. She would never have been able to choose which girl to give it to. Or worse yet, she didn't have the heart to have it taken apart to create two. She couldn't believe the granddaughters she raised were already eighteen.

"Have you talked to your cousin Sarah, yet?"

"No, we haven't gotten the chance," Mina answered.

"You should say hello before you sit with your friends."

"But we're really hungry. We haven't eaten since breakfast."

"At my debut," their mother chimed in. "I didn't eat the entire day. My dress fit better that way."

"That's called an eating disorder, Mom," Manda remarked.

"Please talk to your cousin," Lola begged.

"It would be nice for you to get to know your cousin better," their mother said softly. "My friends were my cousins when I was growing up, even when they moved away."

"And maybe you can ask her to… hang out with you later," Lola suggested.

"Ew, no. She's fourteen." Mina wrinkled her nose. "Why can't Christo hang out with her?"

"He's a boy. That's not the same!" Lola said. "And all he does is play on his video games. And you should be nice. Your uncle

Aaron's mother, Sarah's grandmother, passed away last month. That is why he did not come to Vancouver."

"Oh," the girls said in sombre unison. They looked at each other, their own grandmother's mortality suddenly in their face. They nodded to Lola.

"Is that why they didn't stay at our house?" their mother asked.

They knew their father had extended the invitation for Auntie Grace's family to stay with them. They were ready to give up their rooms for a week and sleep on an air mattress in their brother's room, but Auntie Grace and Sarah stayed in a hotel instead. Their father offered their bedroom to another family member, a distant uncle from Hawaii.

"Your Auntie Grace likes hotels," Lola answered. The girls shrugged in response.

The girls walked into the ballroom again, but without the fanfare of the earlier entrance. They were wearing flip-flops. Lola was sandwiched in between them, her arms linked in theirs. She gently led the girls to the right where Sarah and her mother were seated at a table with seven other people. The girls recognized the guests as each of their parents' bosses. None of them were Filipino.

Auntie Grace was talking to one of the men animatedly. Sarah sat quietly, turning over the leaves of the Caesar salad with her fork.

"Sarah," Lola started. The girl stood up and gave her grandmother a compulsory hug. "I am so sorry about your baba. I know that you were very close."

"Thank you, Lola," she answered flatly.

"And you too, Grace." Grace stood up and accepted a quick hug from her mother. "Please give my condolences to Aaron."

"Yes, of course." Grace turned to the twins. "Thank you for having us. You are both so grown up from the last time I saw you."

"Thank you for coming, Auntie Grace," Mina said. The twins hugged her politely. "We're sorry for your loss."

"Say hi to Uncle Aaron for us," Manda said. "Sarah, we're sorry for your loss too."

The fourteen-year-old hugged the twins politely. Their cousin had grown. They would have matched her height if they were still wearing their heels.

"You know, after dinner, you can hang out with us for a bit," Mina offered. Manda looked at her sister and nodded.

"Maybe," Sarah said non-committal, and they knew she wouldn't take them up on the offer. It had been too long. There was too much distance. Too much time had passed.

Lola saw the gulf between them, as wide as the one between her and her daughter.

"Enjoy your dinner."

There was nothing left to say.

Winnipeg

"That smells good," my mom said, leaning in the kitchen doorway.

I looked up from my bowl of soup. My dad stood up and pulled out a chair for my mom. She sat down to the bowl I had already ladled out for her ten minutes ago. It was no longer steaming, but it was warmer than tepid.

My dad hadn't said a word about our argument as he drove me home. The kitchen was exactly how I had left it. I quickly cleaned it up, throwing out the mangled wonton which had already served its purpose. The two leftover wontons that I had left to cool on the rack were gone. Maybe Del had taken them home or my dad scarfed them down, the latter the most likely.

I rinsed off the dishes and stuck them in the dishwasher. I put away all the ingredients I had left out, throwing away anything that wasn't salvageable. Then I pulled out the ingredients for the dinner I had planned out in my head earlier in the day.

I had been making wontons with leftovers throughout the past two days of trying to master an uovo recipe, so I just had to make the broth, which was easy since it was mostly pre-made ingredients—broth, soup mix, sugar, soy. I chopped up vegetables while the broth came to a boil. Dinner was ready within thirty minutes.

"What is it?" my mom asked. It made me feel like I was the mother to a picky-eating child.

"Tamarind Soup with Sweet Chorizo Wontons."

"Sounds amazing."

"It tastes amazing," my dad replied.

She gingerly took a spoonful and sipped at the warmish broth, trying to avoid slurping. Her shoulders relaxed. I knew Hot and Sour Soup, which had a similar flavour profile, was one of her favourite dishes.

She perched a wonton on her spoon and ate it whole, not having to worry about getting burned by hot filling inside. She nodded in approval.

"This is delicious," she said.

"It's always delicious," my father added, pouring her a glass of white wine.

"Thank you," I responded.

We ate the rest of our dinner without speaking, a Tragically Hip album playing in the background, the lead singer's haunting voice switching between melancholy notes and poignant storytelling. After my father had seconds, and my mother finished the last wonton and the rest of the bok choy, I stood up to clear the table.

"I can help you, Sarah," my mom said, grasping my arm as I tried to take her bowl.

"There's not much to clean up," I said. "I put everything in the dishwasher."

"We should talk."

"I'm expecting an email from Del," I said, wrenching my arm away. I picked up her bowl and cutlery. "We have editing to do.

The video is due by ten. And besides, I don't know if you'll want to talk to me."

"Why?"

"Because I just fed you longanisa wontons in sinigang broth. Surprise. You just ate Filipino food."

I left her empty bowl on the counter and headed straight to my room.

Chapter Fifteen

Dearest Sarah,

Here is my lox and bagel recipe, just like you asked. I've taught all my children how to make lox bagels this way, even your mother. When we go to your friend's Bar Mitzvah next week, I'm going to test you on this!

A sesame seed bagel is the best kind. Sesame seeds have a flavour to them. Poppy seeds taste like nothing and can leave black crumbs on your clothes, and who wants that?

Load enough schmear on your knife to spread it all over both sides of the bagel at once. Do not go back for more schmear! You'll get crumbs on the cream cheese and that's inconsiderate for everyone else, especially if you made the mistake of getting poppy seed.

Look at the slices of tomato. They should be thin. Find the widest slice and put it right in the middle of the bagel. If they're small, you may need a second slice. Put them on each side, overlapping in the centre. Don't take more. That would be greedy.

Layer three slices of lox. Fold the lox on top of the tomato like the ruffles of a dress. Each piece of lox should cover a third of the bagel, not a third of the tomato. It should hang over the bagel's edge, like the brim of a hat.

If there's capers, add them. I know you don't like dill, my dear, but you are missing out. A couple sprigs of dill make for an amazing lox bagel.

Top it all off with a few slices of cucumber. It adds a really nice fresh bite.

If they have freshly ground pepper, add a couple turns. If it's in a shaker, don't bother, especially if you already have capers.

Top it all off with the other half of the bagel. I hope you remembered to spread schmear on the top half! If you did forget, leave it be. Do not go back for more schmear.

And there you have it. Lox and Bagel. Easy peasy, creamy cheesey.

With all my love,
Baba

Winnipeg

"And that's why I don't like Filipino food."

"Mom," I said, flicking away the tears that had gathered in the corner of my eyes. I leaned over to hug her. "That's so sad. I'm so sorry that happened to you."

After brushing my teeth and splashing water on my face, I'd returned to my room to find my mom sitting on my bed. She patted the space next to her and told me a story of a bully who stood over her desk and screamed at her for bringing pritong talong to school.

When I pulled away, I looked at her in a new light. I saw a seven-year-old girl with eyes the same shape as mine, who wore her black hair in pigtails crusted with dried food.

"And when your lola saw the peanut butter and jelly in my hair, she yelled at me for not being careful around the other kids. She took me to the bathroom and washed the ends of my hair in the sink. She kept yelling, 'You can't let the kids think you are dirty! You can't let them think that about us!'"

When my mom imitated her mother's voice, she didn't use an accent like my aunt. I wondered if my mom could do the accent at all. I knew I couldn't. I've tried. I hadn't heard it enough to capture the subtleties other than pronouncing the F's as P's.

"And you never ate Filipino food after that?"

"I traded my lunch sometimes," she admitted. "You could do that in those days. I sometimes just ate the banana she always gave me. After a couple of weeks of seeing me come home with uneaten food, my father insisted she start making things I would eat. I got sandwiches, mac n cheese, canned pasta and soup, processed cheese and crackers. Sometimes my mother would add a small container of white rice as filler to an insubstantial meal, but I rarely dove in.

"By the time I was twelve, I got into better sandwiches, fancier pasta, soups and salads. I could make these things on my own because I could just throw things together easily and not have to read a recipe or wait long for something to cook."

I smiled hearing her talking about food, knowing that her cooking prowess hadn't improved much since she was a preteen. My father and I were the main cooks of the household, influenced by Baba's love of cooking.

"But Auntie Cher eats Filipino food," I pointed out. "She even knows how to cook it. She makes Lola's recipes."

"She didn't have the disdain that I did. Cher and Christoffer still got leftovers for lunch."

"Lola made a different lunch for Uncle and Auntie? That must have been hard."

She was quiet for a moment. "Yeah, I guess it was." She noticed the time. "You have to finish your video. I've kept you long enough."

She started to stand up.

"But Mom—"

I had so many questions, but I had no idea what they were. I wasn't prepared for the story she'd placed in front of me. There was more that we had to talk about, more that needed to be said, but she was standing, looking at me, feeling satisfied that the handful of rare memories she'd shared were enough.

"Thank you for telling me this, Mom."

She leaned down to hug me.

"I'm glad you now know." She pulled away. "I promise you, I will try the next Filipino dish. Maybe I'll like it. I will give it a chance. Okay?"

"Okay." I nodded.

Maybe it is enough.

For now.

Twenty-one years ago
Minneapolis
CRACK!

Grace squeezed Aaron's hand as she remembered last night's wedding ceremony. She thought of how the sound of the glass breaking had echoed across the sanctuary as the groom and bride both stomped down on the suede pouch placed at their feet.

"Mazel tov!" yelled the room.

In unison, the guests clapped their hands and started to sing a universal song that had never been formally taught to them but passed down through generations of simchas and celebrations.

Siman Tov u'Mazel Tov. Mazel Tov u'Siman Tov. Siman Tov u'Mazel Tov. Mazel Tov u'Siman Tov...

He had handed her a handkerchief. She was not an emotional person. Scratch that, she was very emotional, but not in a way that caused her to cry at random events, except for weddings. Weddings were her weakness.

He had turned to her. "I love you, you know that?"

"Of course, I do." Grace smiled as she gave her usual reply.

They had driven to Minneapolis for Aaron's cousin's wedding, a three-day event that began with an elegant cocktail party for out-of-town guests, friends, and family on Saturday night, then the lovely wedding ceremony on Sunday afternoon followed by an opulent reception in the evening, and finally today's come-and-go brunch in the hotel's largest meeting room. The casual brunch was mainly for out-of-town guests to grab a meal or snack before heading to the airport, but most of the family would show up to say their last goodbyes.

There were also informal get-togethers for each evening. Since they arrived, all of Aaron's cousins of legal age would gather in their hotel room each night to drink beer and reminisce about when they were kids.

"Aaron, Grace!"

They turned to see Aaron's cousins gesturing for the couple to join them at a table in the corner. They sauntered over and put down their loaded plates of bagels, lox, schmear, pickles, and crudité. Grace thought to herself that Aaron's mother must have been pleased there were capers on the relish tray. How that woman loved capers. Grace looked around. Aaron's parents must have been there earlier.

As they sat down, one of Aaron's cousins said, "It's a good thing there's no prosciutto!"

The cousins, including Aaron and Grace, erupted in laughter.

"I thought the couple kept kosher," commented a girl that had accompanied Aaron's cousin Ben.

"That's what's so funny." Aaron turned to the girl and the other newer significant other at the table who also didn't know the story behind the inside joke. "Ben was visiting my family in Winnipeg and Uncle Jake decided it would be funny to tell him the tongue sandwiches were actually prosciutto…"

Grace had heard the story several times before, but she never tired of hearing it. They had visited Aaron's extended family in Minneapolis several times over the past four years since they had started dating–his younger cousin's bar mitzvah, his uncle's wedding, his great aunt's funeral, and other road trips for no reason at all. All his life, his extended family had come to visit Winnipeg or to get together at his parents' cabin in the Whiteshell. Though they lived eight hours away, through many frequent visits, Aaron was close to his Minneapolis cousins and aunts and uncles. In fact, he was close to all of his family, including those that lived in Calgary, Toronto, New York, Dallas, and Detroit.

Grace envied Aaron's relationship with his family. She had family in British Columbia but barely knew them. Heck, she barely knew her mother and brother.

"Uh, oh. Auntie Sadie's coming."

All the cousins, including Grace, started to focus intently on their food. She started to spread cream cheese over her poppy seed bagel. Black dots fell onto the plate and tablecloth.

"Oh, look at you here all together!" Auntie Sadie exclaimed. She looked at all of them and finally zeroed in on Aaron, who swallowed his bagel and egg salad too quickly. "Aaron, you are so grown up! How old are you now?"

"I'm still twenty-eight, same age as when you asked me two days ago."

"Aaron, sweetie. You have some schmutz on your face! Let me get that for you."

She licked her finger and started to wipe it off his cheek. The cousins suppressed their laughter, but Grace accidentally let out a small snort.

"And Gracie!" Auntie Sadie refocused her attention. "My beautiful Gracie! What a shayna punim!"

She pinched Grace's cheek and added the obligatory twist. Grace held her breath. The cousins were shaking from holding in their laughter. She had gone through this rite of passage three years ago, when she had first met Auntie Sadie. After rubbing her cheek to bring back the blood flow, the cousins had welcomed her as one of their own. She felt loved in that moment in a way she had never felt before. And a part of her felt robbed that she never had this feeling in her own family.

"The two of you have been together how long?"

"Four years, Auntie Sadie."

"Oh my, so long!" She threw her hands up. "Has Aaron proposed to you yet?"

"Uhhhh…"

"We haven't even talked about it," Aaron answered.

"Aaron!" Auntie Sadie said in a shocked tone. "How could you? Why haven't you proposed to this shayna maidel?"

"Uhhhh…"

"Auntie Sadie, I have to get more lox." Aaron's cousin Ben stood up. "I want to share some news with you. It took a couple of tries but I got into law school."

"Benjamin!" Auntie Sadie beamed at him. "Mazel tov!" She walked over to pinch his cheeks, both cheeks. She turned back to Aaron quickly, wagging her finger at him. "I am not done with you yet, Aaron Elijah Dayan."

The cousins stared at their food awkwardly as Auntie Sadie and their saviour Ben walked away from the table. One cousin looked up at Aaron.

"Have you told Grace the story about when Ellie was seven and we told her that matzah balls were cut off matzah cows before they were turned into brisket?"

The table erupted in laughter once again. And yes, Grace had heard the story before.

After the brunch, Aaron and Grace rode the elevator in silence back to their hotel room.

"I love you, you know that?"

"Of course, I do," she answered flatly, watching the numbers tick upwards.

Silence as the doors opened.

"My family loves you so much."

"And I love them."

Grace was lost in thought as they walked down the hallway. She thought about family. She thought about Aaron's family, how she had started to think of them as her own. The sound of their footsteps was lost in the carpeted floor. The click and high-pitched beep of the door unlocking felt loud in the quiet. Aaron held the door open. She walked in and sat in a bucket chair in the corner to take off her shoes. Her feet were still sore from dancing the night before.

"I've talked about it with my parents."

"Talked about what?"

"Proposing to you."

She turned to look at him, no words forthcoming. She wanted to hear what he had to say. She wouldn't beg.

"There are... concerns."

She looked out the window. "Because I'm Filipino?"

"No, of course not," he said, dismissing the idea immediately. "How can you possibly think that? Auntie Sadie is married to a Black man and today Ellie married someone Japanese. My uncle Bart has been with a Korean woman for six years. It has nothing to do with race."

"Then what is it?"

"You're not Jewish."

"Ellie's new husband isn't Jewish."

"No, he's not, but that's not the issue." He sat down on the bed. She turned back towards him. She wanted him to look her in the eyes. "Judaism is inherited through the mother," he explained. "My mother is Jewish; therefore I am Jewish. Ellie is Jewish; therefore her children will be Jewish. It doesn't matter the religion or ethnicity of her husband.

"My parents want the family line to continue. My sister is still in high school, so she's not even thinking about who she's going to marry one day. She's not thinking of what her kids are going to be.

"My family loves you," he reiterated. "But they would prefer if I marry someone—"

"Who isn't a shiksha," Grace shot at him, spouting the derogatory term for a non-Jewish girl.

"Don't say that. That's not what you are."

"That is what I am."

She closed her eyes for a moment and took a breath. She opened them again and turned to him.

"This is all about religion?"

"Being Jewish is far more than religion. It's a culture. It's a shared history. It's... encompassing."

"So you're saying I can't become a part of that?"

"Well, of course. You can always convert, but I could never ask you—"

"I'll do it."

"But Grace—"

"Aaron," she said gently. She stood up and sat next to him on the bed. "I haven't stepped foot in a church since my parents forced me to get confirmed when I was thirteen. I barely have any 'culture'. I know nothing about being Filipino except for living in this skin that I was born with. I barely have any family, and I love your family. I love your family so much and I love that I know that they love me."

Tears ran down her face, the rare tears that flowed when she ached inside. She usually dealt with her pain through anger, but she felt desperate and raw in this moment, which was how she knew this was what she really wanted, what she needed. He handed her his handkerchief, the same one she used at yesterday's wedding ceremony.

"I love you. This is what I want."

"If you convert," Aaron's eyes had begun to moisten. "It can't be for me."

"This will be for me, Aaron," she promised. She took his hands. "I have nothing else."

They wrapped their arms around each other and wept, the handkerchief slipping to the floor.

Chapter Sixteen

This soup will wrap its arms around you and let you cry into its shoulder. It's filling and comforting and even better than ice cream out of the tub. My lola's recipe uses hot dogs and macaroni but I wanted to try making a grown-up version. The quail eggs are from her recipe though. And they really do make the soup.

Sopas—Filipino Chicken Noodle Soup
1 tsp butter
2 litres chicken broth, unsalted
2 tsp salt (omit if using salted broth)
1 boneless chicken breast
2 cloves garlic, minced
½ cup chopped shallots
1 medium carrot, diced
1 stalk celery, sliced thin on the diagonal
1 cup sliced fennel, sliced same size as the celery
¾ cup orzo
1 can quail eggs, drained
1 cup sliced farmers sausage
1 ½ cups of water
1 can evaporated milk
Fennel fronds for garnish

Heat pot, add oil or butter, add shallots, carrots, celery and fennel. Sauté for 1 minute. Remove vegetables from pot.

Add broth to pot, crank heat to high and bring to a boil.

Add chicken breast and garlic. Drop heat to medium and cook 10 minutes.

Remove chicken breast from broth and allow to cool.

Bring broth back to a boil. Add orzo, cooked vegetables, and sausage. Drop heat to medium and cook for 6 minutes. Add 1 cup water or more if too much liquid has evaporated.

In the meantime, shred chicken breast meat.

Add shredded chicken, quail eggs, and evaporated milk. Stir. Heat another minute.

Taste and season with salt and pepper.

Ladle into bowls and garnish with fennel fronds.

Winnipeg

"Hot dogs in soup?" I asked. "What am I, twelve?"

"Sweetie," Auntie Cher said, putting her hand on my shoulder. "All Filipinos are twelve-year-olds at heart."

I smelled the bowl of soup she placed in front of me, the vapour wafting upwards from the thin creamy broth. I dipped my spoon in and slurped slightly, the savoury aroma coating my mouth and my insides with comfort. The flavours were chicken and saltiness, no underlying herbs like sage or rosemary, as in a complex soup. The macaroni and vegetables were soft and tender, the translucent onions having given up their valuable aroma. And the hot dogs added pops of satisfying salt.

"It's like, simple, but so good."

I scooped up another spoonful, this time making sure I got a quail egg, which was about the size of a grape tomato. When my aunt opened the can of quail eggs, she revealed these firm orbs of pre-cooked, pre-shelled mini-eggs that she promised were essential to the sopas. She said that you could buy fresh quail eggs, but they were very difficult to crack open and even harder to shell. When I bit into the firm white orb, the hard-boiled yolk burst out, creamy and luscious, the texture of custard. My eyes opened wide.

"Quail eggs were my mother's secret ingredient," Auntie Cher insisted. "They're not traditional, but this is what made my mom's sopas extra special and set it apart from your standard chicken noodle soup."

"Do you think my mom would like this?" I asked between mouthfuls.

"Grace loved eating this as a kid, even as a teenager. It was one of her favourites."

"Really?" I asked, perplexed. "But I thought my mom 'wasn't into' Filipino food?"

"That's the trick. My mother called it 'Macaroni Hot Dog Soup', but she didn't add the quail eggs in Grace's bowl," she revealed. "Nay would hide them in the bottom of everyone else's bowl, like a secret surprise. It became a game to me and Christoffer. My mother and father would openly eat their eggs but for us it was a special treat."

"Quail eggs aren't exclusively Filipino."

"I know that, and you know that, but when Grace was a kid, she thought that any exotic food that she didn't hear about on TV or see in another kid's lunch was Filipino. In fact, she thought tofu was Filipino until she tried it at a friend's house when they ordered Chinese."

"I talked to her," I admitted. "She told me what happened when she was seven, when she was bullied because of her lunch. She says she's going to try and be more open about eating Filipino food."

Auntie Cher put her spoon down and dabbed a napkin to her lips.

"My father told me about that, but I was bullied about my lunch. I was bullied about the container. I was bullied for wearing my brother's hand-me-downs and having short hair." She leaned towards me. "A lot of kids were picked on for what they brought to school—the kid with pesto, the kid with chickpea curry, the kid with a ham and pickle sandwich."

"What are you saying?"

"Sometimes it's not about the food."

I looked at her thoughtfully as I swallowed my last bite. The questions finally formed in my mind.

"If I ask you some questions, will you tell me the truth?"

"Of course, unless it's not my story to tell."

"Then I want to know about you."

"Fine, shoot."

"Why do you and Uncle Christoffer understand Filipino?"

She held my gaze. "We were exposed to Filipino through our parents and their friends."

More questions formed in my mind. I finally knew what to ask.

"Lola and Lolo had Filipino friends?"

"A few."

"Where are they now?"

"A few moved away. One or two died. Some lost touch. Some just disappeared after Tatay died or when I came out. That happens. Then Nanay moved away. I haven't kept in touch with any that are left."

"Did they have kids?"

"Most of them, yes."

"Were you friends with their kids?"

"Yes, a lot of them, but same deal. We just drifted apart. We're now just Facebook-level friends."

"And you had Filipino friends in school?"

"A few. Most of Christoffer's friends were Filipino, mostly because we did Filipino folk dance for a couple of years."

"And do you have Filipino friends now?"

"Yeah, of course. I'm in the restaurant industry, and I live in Winnipeg. It's practically Little Manila in some parts of the city."

"And do you hang out a lot?"

"As much as you can hang out with anyone during a pandemic."

"And my mom had no Filipino friends?"

"You'll have to ask your mom."

I pursed my lips together. I already knew the answer.

I had no Filipino friends. Other than Auntie Cher, we had no other Filipino family in town. Since I was six, I've attended a private Jewish school where there were no Filipino kids. Most of the activities I participated in were done through school or the synagogue. I remember attending a few painting and pottery classes through the art gallery. There were other Filipino kids, but it wasn't an environment where you got to talk a lot during class. Same with swimming lessons. And I was never into sports.

My mother made the choice.

For herself.

And for me.

Toronto

"Whoever wins this week's challenge will not only win the incredible prize of a Deluxe Edition Tabletop Outdoor Smoker and Grill by Wooden Coal, but will also… Oh, wait. I'm so sorry, I screwed up the name of the company. It should have been Wood and Coal," Jenna admitted. "Can I start again?"

"Of course, Jenna," Chuck said. "Whenever you're ready."

It's too wordy. Who wrote this? Poppy thought as she watched the raw footage from this week's *Cyber Chef*. She found Jenna to be somewhat syrupy at times, but Poppy had to admit her voice was kind and sincere and everyone needed kindness and sincerity nowadays. Marlee had made the right call. She watched as Jenna took another two tries at the run-on sentence.

Poppy looked at the faces of the remaining contestants. Kendra looked nervous. Sarah was doing that weird thing with her mouth. *At least we can edit that out,* she thought. Geoff looked bored. *He better not be looking at his phone,* she thought. *You need to get on with this, Jenna.*

"Can I change around some of this?" Jenna asked. "It's really wordy."

Chuck sighed. "Sure, Jenna. Whatever you need."

"Good."

She wrote something down on a piece of paper, no, a post-it, Poppy realized as her hand came into view. Jenna reached over and seemed to stick the note on the second screen that served as a teleprompter. *Come on, Jenna.* Poppy leaned forward in her seat in anticipation.

"This week's prize is a Deluxe Edition Tabletop Outdoor Smoker by Wood and Coal," Jenna said without any issues. "The winner will also be guaranteed a spot in the *Cyber Chef: Next Gen* finals."

"Good job," Poppy said out loud to her otherwise empty office.

"This week's winner is…" Jenna smiled. "Sarah for her Crispy Wontons with Longa and Uovo!"

Sarah's eyes opened wide, and she let out a scream of joy. She then covered her mouth with both hands to stifle the sounds.

"I'm so sorry." She sounded breathless. The teen bounced in her seat as if she were trying to keep herself tied to the chair. "Thank you so much! I'm so excited! And I'm honoured. Thank you. And thank you Kendra, and Geoff, and Chef Kwan, and Chef Robyn, and Gary, and Chuck, and—"

"Let the judges talk, Sarah," Chuck said. "And don't mention my name. I'm not here."

Poppy was surprised he didn't snap at her, but she knew he was trying hard to be nice. She knew he wasn't used to being around teenagers. He better get used to it. He announced last week that he and his wife were having a baby.

"Sarah," Chef Kwan's voice instantly appeared to sober the girl. "Not only did your dish display a knowledge of technique that would rival any classically trained chef, but your dish was also accessible due to its simplicity and well thought out instructions."

"Thank you, Chef. Your comments mean everything to me."

"No, thank you. I will likely make this dish again."

The girl clasped her hands together and squealed again. Her feed was cut off.

"Okay, enough of that." That was the Chuck Poppy knew and respected. "Jenna, continue."

"Kendra, Geoff, by default, you two are our bottom two contestants. One of you will be leaving *Cyber Chef: Next Gen*."

To Poppy's surprise, Geoff looked like he was going to cry. She was worried he would blow up, like Cindy did. She could see that he was saying something. From the shape of his mouth, it looked like he was whining. She realized his feed was muted.

"Geoff, I'm not turning on your mic until you calm down," Chuck said.

He pressed his lips together and nodded. The microphone icon went from white to red.

"I was just asking why. Why?"

"This is why I don't take you off mute," Chuck said, cutting off Geoff's words with a touch of a button. "Let the judges talk. You've been in the bottom two a couple of times now. You should be used to this."

Geoff crossed his arms. He looked up to his unseen media manager. He appeared to sigh and sat straighter with his arms more relaxed. He mouthed the word *fine*.

"Kendra, Geoff," Robyn said gently. "Your dishes were excellent, however, when there are only three people left in a competition such as this, somebody has to end up in the bottom two."

"If you don't win, you lose," Gary said. "It's something my dad said to me all the time. He still says it to me. Hey, both of your dishes were solid. In my eyes, you're both winners, but in this case, one of you won just a little bit more than the other."

"Kendra," Chef Kwan said. "Using merguez sausage in your Jamaican patties was a clever move. The flavour was vibrant and awoke my taste buds. The dish was authentic; however, as one of my colleagues commented, the presentation was simple. Gary incorrectly compared it to a spicy Pizza Pop, but he clearly isn't familiar with the cuisine."

"I admit it," Gary said. "I know nothing about Jamaican food, but these past few weeks you've opened my eyes. I'm a patty fan now."

"Thank you for sharing your family recipe for the crust," Robyn said. "J'étais très impressionnée."

"Merci beaucoup. Thank you very much. I appreciate the feedback."

Classy and mature, Poppy thought. Too bad her French accent was so strong. At least they didn't have to subtitle her. It is one of Canada's official languages after all.

"Geoff!" Gary said, jovially. "Was it hard to compete against these fine ladies?"

"No, Gary," Chuck cautioned. "Start again."

"Yeah, Boss." Gary visibly shook himself. "Geoff!"

"Yes, Gary," Geoff replied.

"You did great. Your dish was great. I liked the play on words, Mash-in-Bangers. I thought it was fun. I loved the idea of creating a giant sausage filled with mashed potatoes. Unfortunately, as you know, mine fell apart, but I think I made the most of it by creating my Mash-in-a-Banger Volcano."

Poppy pictured a cut to the ludicrous image of a brown pile of sausage with mashed potatoes 'erupting' through the centre. She would normally be furious with how the judge repurposed the finished dish, but after reviewing the instructions for the recipe, she agreed they were difficult to follow.

"My recipe clearly required a higher level of cooking technique," Geoff said arrogantly.

As much as she abhorred his smugness, she knew it made for great television. The producers had no say in how the judges made their decisions, however she secretly cheered as he continued week after week. She relished the reactions on social media.

#CCNGGeoffSucks

#CyberChefTeamAntiGeoff

#ShutUpGeoff

"Your attitude needs a higher level of technique," Gary shot back.

Poppy loved the comeback but knew it would be edited out. A grown man arguing with an immature fifteen-year-old often backfires.

"You had the flavours," Chef Kwan said. "It tasted like Bangers and Mash, but crafted in the most complicated way possible. Why would anyone choose to make your recipe when the original is as simple as cook a sausage and put it on mashed potatoes?"

"Because it looks cool," Geoff replied. "Poach an egg in a fried wonton and you call it gourmet. I shove potatoes in a sausage and it's too complicated. Please."

"I'm sure you can see the difference," Chef Kwan said, maintaining her cool.

"Yeah, I think we've heard enough," Gary said.

"Yeah, I think it's pretty obvious," Geoff said.

"Geoff!" Chuck said through clenched teeth. "You need to allow Gary to say the words."

"Yeah, fine."

Gary looked uncomfortable, but he steeled himself, almost emulating Kwan's cool demeanor. "The next contestant to leave *Cyber Chef: Next Gen* is… Geoff."

"Be classy, Geoff," Chuck warned.

"Thank you for this opportunity. If I had darker skin, I'm sure I would have done a lot better—"

His lips kept moving, but no sound came out, his microphone clearly muted. Geoff looked up at his media manager. They appeared to be yelling at each other. He stood up. The video feed snapped to black. Everyone remaining on the call seemed shaken up.

"You okay, Kendra?" Chuck asked.

Her eyes looked almost tired. "I have become accustomed to it."

"That's unfortunate, but congratulations nonetheless. Well done."

"Merci."

Poppy stopped the video. She was furious. She sent a text to Chuck.

Chuck

You will keep all footage.

Air it as is.

Chapter Seventeen

Matzah Brei

Five sheets matzah	break into quarters
Boiling water	4 cups
2 or 3 eggs	3 eggs
Pinch salt	½ tsp
Oil	2 tsp, can sub with butter
Black pepper	three turns of pepper grinder
Add matzah to bowl.	big bowl
Soak in boiling water.	5 minutes
Strain out water.	use colander
Dump wet matzah into bowl.	
Add eggs and salt.	beat eggs first
Mix.	gently!
Pre-heat pan on medium.	non-stick pan!!!
Add oil to pan.	butter tastes better
Dump matzah in pan.	spread across bottom of pan
Stir in pan until it stops sizzling.	break up clumps, use silicone spatula
Don't dry it out!	I won't!
Add black pepper	This is what makes it baba's recipe
Serve with jam.	Or almond butter and maple syrup. Yum!

Winnipeg

"What does this mean, Sarah?" my mother asked.

"I don't know."

The announcement that I was a finalist had interrupted my plans to talk to my mom, really talk to her. My family insisted we go out for dinner. I was floating and didn't want to bring rain down with my questions. I had hoped to talk with her today, but when I woke up this morning, I received a cryptic email from FaD.

From: FAD Channel Canada (info@fadchannelcanada.ca)
Sent: May 16, 2021 7:42 AM
To: Sarah Dayan-Abad (sarah.da@email.ca)
Subject: Cyber Chef: Next Gen – Episode S3E5

Ms. Dayan-Abad,

Tonight's episode of *Cyber Chef: Next Gen* will feature footage that had been recorded on Saturday, May 15, 2021, during the Judges' Decision. The producers have opted to air the footage in its entirety without editing.

Please refer to the following Terms and Conditions to which you agreed when you had first applied to *Cyber Chef: Next Gen*:

46.2a) Any opinions expressed by a contestant belong to the contestant alone.

46.2b) *Cyber Chef: Next Gen, Cyber Chef,* Food and Drink Channel, Home & Life Canada and their international subsidiaries, and any paid sponsors of the above companies and organizations cannot be held accountable for the opinions or actions of a contestant.

Food and Drink Channel, Home & Life Canada supports diversity through equitable hiring and casting as well as multifaceted programming and content. We will not tolerate racism or discrimination of any kind, nor do we choose to sweep it under the rug. In this light, we hope that you will understand our decision to air this footage as it had been recorded.

If you require mental health support after watching tonight's episode, you can access Home & Life Canada's Employee and Family Support Program until May 30, 2021. Please view the attached PDF for details.

Any questions or concerns about this matter can be sent in writing to your assigned media manager. Food and Drink Channel and Home & Life Canada may respond through our legal department.

Sincerely,
Poppy St. Martin-Dubois
Executive Producer, *Cyber Chef: Next Gen*
Vice President Talent Acquisition and Development
Food and Drink Channel – Canada

"Did something happen on the call yesterday?" my mom asked.
"If it did, it happened after my feed was cut."
"Maybe Del would know?"
"Good idea."

Del

> fad sent me a weird email

> did something happen on the call after i left

> ?

Twenty minutes went by. I started making breakfast. Hmmmm… matzah brei. Most people only eat matzah during Passover, but our family eats matzah brei, a sort of stir-fried French toast, all year round, usually on happy occasions, like today. Or at least it was happy before I read the email. Now I'm just confused.

Del

Can't talk about it.

You'll have to watch the show.

I will be coming over tonight to watch with you.

why

?

Just doing what I'm told.

then come over early for dinner

530

im making thai

Sounds good.

"Del is coming over for dinner and she's staying to watch the show with us tonight."

"She's watching the show with us?" my dad asked. "Does this have to do with the email you were sent?"

"Probably, but she couldn't tell me anything."

"A lot of secrets at FaD."

I turned back to making breakfast. Instead of my usual almond butter and maple syrup, I topped my bowl of matzah brei with straight lines of cubed mango, sliced avocado, freshly sliced pineapple tidbits, and a drizzle of condensed milk. I left a third of the fried matzah plain and exposed. I was inspired by the smoothie bowls I had seen on Instagram. After a quick snap, I sat down and dug in. My dad had his usual dollop of strawberry jam. My mother usually did the same, but she stared longingly at my creation.

"Is there more avocado?" she asked.

"Yeah, do you want some?"

She stood up and retrieved the other avocado half that I didn't use, spooned it out of the shell and dropped it in the middle of her bowl of matzah brei. She then plopped down a spoonful of the condensed milk without any thought for plating. She gave it a good mix and sat down with her bowl of pale green mush.

"When I was little, one of the treats my dad used to make was what he called Filipino Ice Cream," she explained.

My dad looked up from his bowl. I stopped chewing. She never talked about her father.

"He would scoop out the avocado, mash it in a bowl with condensed milk and put it back into the avocado shells. It wasn't even cold, but he still called it ice cream." She looked up wistfully. "I haven't thought of that in a long time. Did Cher tell you about that? Is that how you thought about putting these flavours together?"

"No, she told me a good combo was mango and condensed milk. I thought adding the green avo would make for a better pic."

My parents laughed. I laughed too. I mixed up my bowl of fruit and matzah and dug in.

The day passed slowly as I waited for *Cyber Chef* to air. I had things to do. I had lots of homework. This was my only chance to catch up because I knew I would be busy in the next two weeks to prepare for the last three recipes and videos.

The second-to-last show was always a recap show that cobbled together clips, interviews, and additional footage. I always thought they added the extra episode to build momentum but now I knew it was to give contestants time to research and create the recipes, as well as to give judges the time to make all the dishes.

The last challenge was recipes for a three-course meal surrounding a theme we would be given on Monday morning. There would be no mystery ingredient, but I liked having the central idea for a dish handed to me. It kept me tied to the ground. With too much freedom, I worried I would be a kite without a string and twist in the wind without guidance.

I also remembered I had a group text to send.

Lena, Jay

> sorry guys

> u cant come over to watch tonight

> something came up

> its rly confusing

> cant talk about it

Lena: oh no

were you kicked off

im sooooooooo sorreeeeee

> i cant say if i get kicked off

Jay: allgood

u need us we hre

Lena: ya of course

jjj u alwys no wut 2 say

thanks guys

Right after dinner, we took our places in the den to watch *Cyber Chef.* My parents and I sat on the couch. Del explained she had to set up a camera while we watched the show to capture reaction shots. My mother was at first uncomfortable with this, but Del had been following us around the house for weeks working on extra footage that would likely appear during the recap show. She assured us it would be like one of those times.

"Is this because of the email Sar received?"

"I can't say," Del said, placing headphones over her ears.

The episode started off like normal. It had more interviews, but there were fewer contestants. Something had to fill the time. Geoff was obnoxious. Kendra was sincere. I was always portrayed as a know-it-all.

"Ravioli ouvo is a gourmet dish renowned for its delicacy and technique." I watched myself say in an interview to the camera. "I just had this recently at a local restaurant and I fell in love with the way the yolk joined with the broth. I also had wonton purses at the same place and I loved the crispiness of the deep fried stuffed dumplings. I knew I had to incorporate both elements in my dish somehow, but I had to make it easy to prepare, hence the frozen egg yolk."

Ugh, did I say 'hence'? I covered my face with my hands. My friends saw that. And now Del has me on camera being embarrassed about saying something embarrassing. *Who talks like that?*

Kendra was always at ease in her videos. I loved her accent. My French was comme ci comme ça, but I loved how she would add some French words and translate herself.

"The Jamaican patties normalement sont faits de boeuf aux épices. Ahh… normally made with, ah, beef with spices."

She was only seventeen, but she appeared worldly. #selfgoals

When my name was announced as this week's winner, I squealed. My parents already knew, but I was still excited to hear the words out loud. Jenna then announced we would hear more from the judges after the commercial break. When the show returned, a black screen with the following words faded in one sentence at a time.

Tonight's episode of *Cyber Chef: Next Gen* will feature raw unedited footage recorded on Saturday, May 15, 2021, during the Judges' Decision.

The producers have opted to air the raw footage in its entirety without editing.

The additional person you will see on screen is Chuck Segal, the Digital Director of *Cyber Chef: Next Gen*.

All opinions expressed by contestants belong to the contestant alone and do not reflect the opinions of the Food and Drink Channel, Home & Life Canada, and their sponsors.

"Whoa."

My mother sat to my left. My father sat to my right. I took one of their hands in each of mine, like I did as a little girl watching the scary part of a movie.

The shot opened up on a grainy recording of our video call. All three judges, Jenna, Kendra, Geoff, and Chuck, appeared in separate boxes. The feed appeared slightly blurry when expanded on our 4K television. I had a new appreciation for the second camera that recorded each person's side of the screen for a better-quality shot. The sound had a tinny quality with a slight echo. I suddenly appreciated that they record our sound at a higher quality while concurrently filming.

As Robyn spoke gently to Kendra and Geoff, I felt bad for both of them. There were three of us left. It could have been any of us. If we had gone with the random toss of a coin, the odds would have put me in the bottom two.

I was amazed that my dish had beat Kendra's, however I had to smugly admit to myself that my presentation far exceeded hers. I imagined hers had much more exuberant flavours. I cringed as I saw Gary's plating of Geoff's dish. It verged on sabotage, but if the instructions were as complicated as the judges explained, then maybe the only way to save the dish was for Gary to remain in character as the prankster.

"My recipe clearly required a higher level of cooking technique." Geoff rolled his eyes obnoxiously.

"Your attitude needs a higher level of technique," Gary snapped. I was taken aback to hear the clapback. What else is going to happen?

"You had the flavours," Chef Kwan said coolly to deescalate the situation. "It tasted like Bangers and Mash but crafted in the most complicated way possible. Why would anyone choose to make your recipe when the original is as simple as cook a sausage and put it on mashed potatoes?"

"Because it looks cool," said Geoff arrogantly. "Poach an egg in a fried wonton and you call it gourmet. I shove potatoes in a sausage and it's too complicated. Please."

I let out a tiny gasp. Clearly that was a dig at my dish. Was this what I was being warned about?

"Yeah, I think we've heard enough," Gary said.

"Yeah, I think it's pretty obvious." Geoff looked annoyed.

"Geoff!" Chuck interrupted, silent until now. "You need to allow Gary to say the words."

"Yeah, fine."

"The next contestant to leave *Cyber Chef: Next Gen* is… Geoff."

"Be classy, Geoff," Chuck spoke again.

"Thank you for this opportunity," Geoff said, his voice soaked in insincerity. "If I had darker skin, I'm sure I would have done a lot better—"

Both my mother and I sat up straighter in our seats, audible gasps coming from our slack-jawed mouths.

Geoff appeared to be muted as he continued to rant. He looked like he was yelling at someone off-screen, likely his media manager. He looked angry. He stood up. His video cut out, and the images rearranged themselves to fit the screen without his presence.

Awkward silence was made even more awkward by being aired on television.

"You okay, Kendra?" Chuck asked with genuine concern.

"I have become accustomed to it," she answered with poise. She looked like the only one not shaken up by the comment.

"That's unfortunate," Chuck commented. "But congratulations nonetheless. Well done."

"Merci," she answered.

Jenna's face returned to the screen, perfectly edited for high definition. I could now see the whites of her teeth.

"Join us next week on *Cyber Chef: Next Gen*."

The credits started to roll. My mom turned off the TV. She turned to me, still holding my hand.

"Are you okay, Sarah?"

"Yeah, of course," I answered. "I don't care what he says about my dish. I know it was amazing. That's why I won this week."

"No," my mom furrowed her brow and leaned her head forward. "Are you okay after what that boy said at the end?"

"Oh, yeah," I said, realizing what she was getting at. "I feel really bad for Kendra. I hope she's okay. I wish I could text her, but they didn't want us contacting each other during the competition. Maybe that's why Del was so secretive earlier—"

"No, honey," my mom pressed on. "You know Geoff directed that comment at you too."

I blinked. Oh. Right.

My father put his hand on my shoulder.

"I'm so sorry you had to hear that, and on national television too."

My mother hugged me. My father hugged me too.

I sat still. I didn't know what to feel.

Twenty hours earlier

Winnipeg

"That's not right, Chuck."

Del had her ear buds in and paced across her apartment, her phone in her hand.

"I didn't have to tell you in advance," Chuck said calmly. "I wanted to give you a heads up."

"Why, because I'm Black?"

"Because your contestant isn't White. It's not about you, Del. Geoff has no clue who you are."

"Sarah will be fine. It's Geoff who I'm worrying about."

"Why would you be concerned about a racist piece of—"

"Publicly humiliating a fifteen-year-old child is not how you fight racism!" she yelled. "Airing footage on primetime of an arrogant kid who doesn't understand what he's saying is going to traumatize him, not teach him a lesson."

"Don't worry about the kid," Chuck said. "He and his parents are being handled."

"Oh, they're being 'handled'," Del said in a mocking tone. "In other words, FaD's lawyers are ensuring they don't sue, but that's what the iron-clad contract is for, isn't it?"

"Everyone is being cared for and protected."

"Don't think I don't understand what you're trying to do. Sure, the episode will get high ratings. You'll get a lot of buzz on Twitter and Facebook, maybe even a hashtag or two. All the White people who run this network can pat themselves on the back and say they're doing a great thing to expose a budding White supremacist. Meanwhile, you are exploiting a stupid teenager and painting two young women of colour into victims to fit your narrative. As if it isn't enough what this show has done to exploit these kids and their ethnicity."

"You aren't offended by what he said?"

"Of course I'm offended by what he said!" Del threw her hands up into the air in unseen exasperation. "But like Kendra said, we are accustomed to it. And it's not like it's a guy who's birdwatching and some White lady calls the police on him claiming assault. This is an angry and probably ignorantly racist kid who is trying to win a bunch of prizes on a cooking show. You could have shown the footage to his parents. You could have talked to him to tell him why he was wrong. Kendra could have told him why what he said was hurtful.

"You could have turned this into a real teachable moment, but instead you're turning it into a spectacle. This kid is going to become a poster child for White supremacy if you don't drive him into signing up to become a right-wing racist himself. There is no real reason to magnify this. It doesn't help us. There is so much worse that is said to us in this world, but no one cares until it makes them a dollar."

"That's not what this is, Del."

"Then what is it, Chuck?" She sat down, tired of pacing, tired of fighting, tired of decades of carrying the responsibility of having to be a decent human being. "Enlighten me."

A beat of silence passed.

"It wasn't my call," he admitted. "Poppy wanted it this way."

"Of course, Ms. White Saviour." Del rolled her eyes. "I heard she was nominated for a diversity award. I guess this stunt is her way of making room on her bookshelf."

"It's already done."

She sighed. The fight was draining from her. Yelling at Chuck was literally screaming at a wall.

"What should I tell Sarah?"

"Tell her nothing," Chuck instructed. "She'll get an email from the network tomorrow morning. There's one last thing."

"What?"

"We want you to be at the house to film footage of the family watching the episode."

She stood up again in her apartment. "What did I just say about exploiting these kids?"

"You've been in this business a long time, Del. You know how this goes."

"Yeah." She looked out the window to the dark street below. Her face reflected in the glass. "Reality TV, i.e., manufactured drama."

Chapter Eighteen

Halo-halo means mix-mix. This dessert/drink is usually served with crushed ice and a whole bunch of layered candied fruits, but that's so much work and I want some noooowwww. We're going to mix up some of my favourite flavours and serve them with ice. Easy peasy.

Melon Halo-Halo on the Rocks
A jar of macapuno, drained, syrup reserved
A jar of coco de nata (gelled coconut), drained, syrup reserved
A can of jackfruit, sliced thin, juice reserved
1 cup honeydew, diced the size of sugar cubes
1 cup cantaloupe, diced the size of sugar cubes
Ice cubes
1 can evaporated milk

Mix the syrups and juices together, refrigerate minimum one hour.

Add a layer of jackfruit, buko, honeydew, coco de nata, and cantaloupe to six tall glasses.

Divide syrup mixture evenly between each glass.

Add three or more ice cubes to each glass.

Top off each glass with evaporated milk.

(Take a pic now as the milk drapes over the ice)

Serve with a straw and spoon.

Mix before drinking/eating.

Winnipeg

Exactly thirty minutes after the show aired, Geoff posted a video on his Instagram.

"I sincerely apologize to Kendra and Sarah for my outburst during the video chat segment of *Cyber Chef: Next Gen*," he said, tears running down his face. "I was angry and lashed out in the worst possible way by blaming you for my fails. Your talent as cooks and your ability to create recipes are what got you into the finals. I know this, but I chose to focus on skin colour.

"I am sorry. I am not going to pretend that I am not a racist as my mind automatically directed my anger in this direction. I clearly have to look to myself and admit that I have a lot to learn. I am fifteen years old, but I can't use this as an excuse. No one of any age should use ignorance and immaturity as an excuse for discrimination. Good luck to Kendra and Sarah in the finals."

I believed him when he apologized, but I wasn't sure if I should accept. Social media made its own judgements. After the penultimate episode of the last season of *Cyber Chef*, all I saw on my feed were #CCTeamNessa or #CCTeamLai. And now all I saw were #Geoffisaracist or #Geoffiscancelled. Of course there was also #CCTeamdarkskin or #thedarkertheskinthebetterthefood.

Even after the apology, the outrage continued. People doubted his sincerity. People blamed his parents. People called him a White supremacist. People started to throw barbs at his sexuality. Right-wing accounts supported him and turned on the show. They turned around the show's hashtag #CCNG and started using #coloredchefsnextgen and a couple of other hashtags with the N word. I hated seeing that word trending.

I tried to mute the hashtags. I tried staying off of social media, but my phone blew up as friends and family texted to express their support or send me screenshots of the good, the bad, and the downright ugly. Out of all the texts I received, only Lena and Jay congratulated me for getting into the finals. Auntie Cher actually called, but I didn't want to talk to her. I finally had to shut my phone off. I worried about Kendra. I even worried about Geoff. I couldn't wait until the masses could focus on the next awful thing that would happen in order for people to move on.

"You sure you're okay, Sar?"

"I'm fine, Del," I yawned. "Sorry, I'm tired. I'll be fine for the video call."

Del had come over an hour earlier than usual. We would have gone over all the information for the finals last night, but she could tell I needed to be left alone.

"What do you think of all this?" I asked.

"Doesn't matter what I think," Del said as she unpacked her equipment with unusual stiffness.

"It matters to me."

"It shouldn't," she said. "What matters is what you think and what you feel."

"I don't know how to feel."

Del set up all the equipment and pulled up a chair next to mine as I sat in front of the laptop. The program was set up and ready to go, but she still had to enter the login information to direct where to pull the feed.

"Can I ask you a question?" Del asked delicately.

"Of course."

"And you'll be honest?"

I nodded.

"Do you consider yourself White or Filipino?"

"Jewish." I didn't even have to think.

"That wasn't my question." Her dark eyes bored into mine. I looked down, the intensity too concentrated for me to hold my gaze.

"But that's what I am," I insisted. I raised my eyes to meet hers to defend my stance. "My parents are Jewish. I was raised Jewish.

It's not just religion, it's my culture. I get all the jokes. I celebrate the holidays. I eat and cook all the food. I even speak some Yiddish. I had family that died in the Holocaust. Go back far enough, I had family that were chased out of Russia. It's in my blood. I carry it on my shoulders. I. Am. Jewish."

"I have no doubts about your Jewish ancestry," Del clarified. "What I want to know is if this makes you White."

"Not all Jews are White."

"But are you White?"

Why weren't my answers enough for her? Del has always been matter-of-fact and direct with me, but this was the most blunt she has ever been and I wasn't prepared. Was she really going to make me say it out loud?

I ran my tongue over my front teeth while I formed my words.

"My father is Ashkenazi Jew and my mother is Filipino," I said, placing the mathematical equation in front of us. "Which I guess means I'm half White and half Filipino."

"Fine," Del conceded. "Then are you half White first?"

I shrugged. *Why are you doing this?*

"I'll take a different tactic," Del said. "What am I?"

"I don't know how to answer that."

"When you first met me, did you think I was Black?"

"Well," I looked her up and down again. "You're half, right?"

"I'm actually one quarter Black. My mother was half Irish and half African-American. My father was half Anishinaabe and half Italian. My skin is dark, so people assume I'm Black, like a blanket term to cover it all."

"I knew right away you weren't a hundred percent Black," I said, although it came out more smugly than I had intended. "I knew you were of mixed race, like me."

She leaned towards me. "I will always be labelled as Black because of my skin colour and the texture of my hair. I have more

White in me than Black, but I will always be called Black. I will never get the privileges of being what is technically half White and instead get all the disadvantages of being all-Black."

"Well, that's not fair."

"No one called Obama half White."

I looked down at the floor.

"I'm sorry."

"Don't be. You need to know that you may not have the choice of what you are labelled. I think you've already learned that you can call yourself Jewish, but others will decide what you are." Del glanced over at the camera equipment hooked up to the laptop. She looked back at me and met my eyes. "You need to embrace what you are. More than what you feel, more than what you know. Embrace all of what you are, including what they think you are."

I looked up at her and nodded, starting to grasp what she was trying to say. Del had gone through so much more than I ever had. She's earned this wisdom. I had so much more to learn.

Del brought out her notebook and started to go over the details of the finals, mostly stuff I already knew, but she let me know *Cyber Chef* was doing something different for *Next Gen*.

"Whatever happens," she cautioned. "Don't squeal. Chuck hates it. It's like nails on a chalkboard to him. If you get the urge to scream or squeak, hold it in until afterwards."

"I promise I will control myself."

When we finally logged in to the meeting, everyone was already present. Del had warned me we weren't going to have the usual ten-minute pre-show hang out. It would be awkward with only two people, especially when we were direct competitors.

"We're not going to talk about what happened last night," Chuck said. "Your media managers will sort out any questions or concerns you might have. You should submit them in writing. If you require counselling, you should have already gotten that info. We'll also be doing some interviews based on what happened and we don't want you to be rehearsed. If you have anything to say, that will be the time to say it. Understood?"

Kendra and I both said yes. She looked so confident. I looked exhausted, but I couldn't afford to burn out now.

"Congratulations, Kendra and Sarah," Jenna started with a smile. "We hope you are ready for the upcoming recipe gauntlet."

Jenna briefly explained how the process would work. The appetizer tutorial was due on Thursday at noon. The main course was due on Monday at noon. The dessert course was due the next Thursday at noon. Judging of the three individual courses would be recorded early on Saturday. The final judgement would be streamed for live television for the last ten minutes of the finale on Sunday night.

"And we have a surprise for you both," Jenna announced. "We wanted you to have a mentor to guide you through the process, someone who has been through this before."

There was a pause.

"Just hold on," Chuck said. "I have to... there."

Suddenly, two familiar faces joined the group.

"We would like to welcome the finalists from *Cyber Chef*'s last season, Nessa and Lai!"

I opened my mouth to scream but closed it immediately, remembering Del's warning.

"Sarah, as last week's winner, you get to choose your mentor."

"Lai!" I said immediately. "I'm your biggest fan! I've tried all your recipes. This is truly an honour."

"The honour is mine," Lai said. "I can't wait to work with you, Sarah."

SAH-rah. She pronounced my name properly. I bit my lip and balled my hands into fists to tamper down my excitement.

"Kendra, that means you will be working with Nessa."

"C'est bon," Kendra said. "I am very happy to work with Nessa."

"Je parle français aussi!" Nessa replied. "J'ai hâte de travailler avec vous."

"Excellent!"

"Hey! Parlez l'Anglais s'il vous plait."

"Je suis désolée, I apologize, Chuck." Kendra said. "We can do that again if you want."

"No, it's fine. We'll edit," he said.

"Now that you have your mentors to help you succeed, we need to announce the theme for the finale. Your three-course meal must reflect the theme of... Culture!"

My mind was a total blank.

Five years ago
Winnipeg

"I got you, don't worry," Grace said to her eleven-year-old daughter, wiping the tears from Sarah's face. "I've always got your back."

"Okay, Mommy."

She rapped her knuckles on the door jamb of the classroom's open door. Sarah's grade five teacher looked up and smiled.

"Ms. Abad, Sarah." She waved them over. "Come in, come in. Please have a seat."

The pair walked into the classroom of the exclusive private school. Grace closed the door behind her. Hebrew posters lined the walls, many with pictures of Israel. The whiteboards had a combination of English and Hebrew notes. A couple of low book-shelves lined the walls underneath north-facing windows. A smart board sat to the right of the whiteboard, ready to be turned on to access the internet. The teacher had already taken two chairs and placed them in front of her desk in preparation for the meeting. Grace and Sarah sat down.

"I apologize for being a little late," Grace said. "Traffic."

"Yes, of course. The overpass is crowded during rush hour, but we still have twenty minutes before class starts." She clasped her hands in front of her. "How can I help you?"

"I wanted to talk about Sarah's social studies project." Grace placed the duo-tang in front of the teacher, flipping to the cover page where sixty-five percent was written in red ink. "This grade is unfair."

"Sarah," the teacher turned to the girl who suddenly sat straighter, "I would like you to tell me why you think this mark is unfair."

The girl screwed her mouth up in a strange way, trying to gather her words. She took a breath.

"I did everything you asked me to do," she said, choosing her words carefully. "The project was to research the history of my family and that's what I did."

Sarah solidified her courage and stood up. She opened her duo-tang and flipped through the pages as she spoke.

"I have recipes from my baba. I have copies of my grandparents' love letters." She turned the pages. "I have a copy of a letter from my great aunt who died in the Holocaust. There's a picture of a prayer shawl that's been in my family since the Pogrom in Russia. My cousin in Poland sent me the pic. I don't know what else I can do."

Grace sat back proudly after her daughter concluded her defence. Sarah sat down.

"Yes, Sarah, this is an excellent project," the teacher agreed. "Your research far exceeds my expectations for a student your age. However, your project is incomplete. You were supposed to have presented information on *both* sides of your family."

The teacher's eyes flicked left to meet Grace's for an instant. Grace's mama bear instinct immediately flared.

"Sarah identifies with her Jewish roots."

"Of course she does, but there is more to her family than the Jewish half."

"I'm Jewish as well."

"Yes, Ms. Abad. I am not doubting your connection to Judaism—"

"It's not a 'connection'. I am a Jewish woman, ergo my daughter is Jewish."

"Ms. Abad," the teacher put her palms up in the air in surrender, "I apologize. I did not mean to imply that Sarah is not Jewish. I only meant to say that she is more than Jewish, and I want to know about her family history, your family history."

Grace was on the verge of exploding.

"Are you telling me that you expect my daughter to perform twice as much work as the other students in your class because her parents are of mixed race?"

"No, no, that is not what I—"

"Have you demanded this from all your other students of mixed race?"

"Sarah is the only student—"

"Are you sure about that?" Grace demanded. "Out of a class of eighteen students, there are no other children that are a mix of Russian, Polish, German, Hungarian, Israeli, more?"

The teacher sat straighter in her chair.

"Some students have presented information on their different heritages. One is Polish and Hungarian, for instance. One student had a Hasidic grandparent from New York—"

"You admit that some of the students are from a mixed cultural bag, but you only know that because they told you so." Grace leaned forward, perching on the edge of her seat. "Did you ask every student that handed in a report what is the cultural background of both of their parents?"

"No, I didn't, I—"

"In other words, you don't know if every student in your class researched all of their family history, because *you don't know*," Grace said, her voice loud. "I can't hide my cultural background.

It is obvious that I am a Filipino woman, therefore you have put unfair expectations on my daughter due to her mother's race. You are treating her differently than the other students because of what you perceive to be her cultural background. That is the very definition of discrimination."

Grace finished her argument and sat back again. She looked over at Sarah, who stared down at the ground.

"You are correct, Ms. Abad," the teacher admitted, taking a harried breath. "I have treated Sarah differently and unfairly. I sincerely apologize. I certainly have to think about how I approach this project in the future. I will gladly review Sarah's project and reassess the grade.

"Sarah," the teacher turned to the girl, "I am so sorry. Please, I never meant any harm. My comments were from a place of curiosity and a desire to know more about you."

Sarah looked up at the teacher and shrugged. "It's fine." Grace nudged her gently. "I accept your apology."

"Thank you for being open to change," Grace said.

"No, thank you, Ms. Abad. I learned a lot today about diverse perspectives."

Grace gave Sarah a final hug before leaving the room. Sarah lumbered to her seat and sat down. The teacher opened the classroom door and a flood of students in dark uniforms started to stream in. Grace stepped aside.

She looked back at Sarah, who slouched in her seat. Sure, she was embarrassed of her mother now, but one day she would be grateful for seeing her stand up for what is right. Grace squared her shoulders and left the room, proud of her small victory.

Winnipeg

"How do you know how to pronounce my name?" I asked Lai the first chance I got.

"I watched the videos you posted on your blog pre-CC," she replied. "If I'm going to be your mentor, I wanted to learn all about you."

My heart did a jump finding out that she had checked out my blog. I did my best not to squeal. In my peripheral vision, I could see Del give me a thumbs up.

Our 'one-on-one' video call, which also included Chuck, was being recorded, as per everything in my life. Del had been following me around with a camera over her shoulder for the past day. She wanted footage of me eating with my family, walking up to school (even though I was distance learning), cooking dinner (regular dinner, not for the show), and talking to my friends on video (Lena was ultra-excited and Jay was super-chill). She needed more footage to send to the network for this week's clip show and she needed it before I got cooking.

My call with Lai was scheduled for Tuesday morning, which was supposed to give me a chance to think of what I wanted to do.

"For the show, we're sticking with the normal pronunciation," Chuck interrupted. "For consistency's sake."

I hadn't realized Chuck was aware of the discrepancy.

"Don't worry, Sarah." She continued to pronounce my name correctly. "My name is actually pronounced Lye, like an eye."

I smiled wide. "I suspected that was how it was said."

"Please get on with it," Chuck said, growing with impatience.

"Our DD was way ruder than yours. She had a whistle when we got too far off course."

"I'm sure I can source a whistle if that's what you require."

"No need, no need." Lai waved him away. She took a cleansing breath and pasted on a bright smile. "So, *SEHR*-rah," she said, stretching out the incorrect syllable. "Your theme for the finals is Culture, and I'm sure they don't mean yogurt. What do you have in mind for the three courses?"

"I'm kind of stuck," I admitted. "It was easier when I was given an ingredient. I feel like there's too many choices out there. I'm a little overwhelmed."

Lai relaxed her smile to one of compassion and understanding.

"I get it. You'd think that being boxed in would limit your potential, but in actuality the limits stimulate your creativity. The box is what forces us to think outside the box, if that makes any sense. Without boundaries, we don't know how to exceed them."

"Wow, that's exactly it," I agreed. "Without a starting point, I don't know where to start."

"Okay, enough of the Yoda stuff," Chuck commented. "Move on."

"Then let's give you a starting point. Appetizers," Lai said with authority. "Have you given any thought about how you want to start your journey?"

"I kind of want to make a soup. It's like a redemption for me," I said. "I did badly on my lugaw, rice porridge. I want to make up for it."

"I watched that episode. You didn't do badly. There was a slight misstep in the instructions. It happens."

"I think I can do better." I assessed my words. "No, I know I can do better."

"That's a good place to start. Tell me about your soup ideas."

"I was thinking of lomi or mami, two popular Filipino soups. Or maybe a wonton soup or hot and sour, maybe a sinigang with a tamarind broth. I think I can do a fusion dish with any of those."

"That's good," she commented. "Stick with your brand. Your blog is *Fusion on a Plate*. Do that. Put some fusion on a plate, or a bowl. Most importantly, be *authentic*. Be *you*."

Chuck made a motion, turning his hand, encouraging us to wrap up.

"That's great advice. Thank you so much, Lai," I said, pronouncing it the correct way.

Chuck sighed and wrote something down, probably notes for editing my dialogue.

"Good enough. We'll schedule another video call before you start your entrée recipe. Sarah," he said with the correct sound for the first syllable. "You'll have to start thinking about your main. I don't want a repeat of the same conversation."

"Yes, of course, Chuck."

"Thank you again, Lai." He rhymed her name with Day.

"Of course, we'll talk soon."

I logged off and was about to gush to Del about how awesome Lai was when my home phone started to ring. It surprised me because no one seemed to call our landline anymore. I made a mental note to remember to turn off the ringer, in case it ever rang while we were filming.

"That's going to be for you," Del said.

I looked at her quizzically as I stood up when the ringer suddenly stopped.

"Sar!" my mom called out from her office. "Phone!"

I picked up the cordless phone from its base. UNKNOWN NUMBER.

"Hello?"

"Hi, Sarah. It's Lai."

"Oh, hi!"

"I wanted to give you some advice, off-camera. Del gave me your number. I hope that's okay."

"Yeah," I said, glancing up at Del. She nodded and continued to put equipment away. "Of course."

"This is all off-the-record. I'm not supposed to be talking to you outside of the show, but we're friends now, right? We're just two friends talking."

"Yes, yes, we're friends!" I couldn't hide the giddiness in my voice.

"And friends are honest with each other, right?" she said.

"I… guess." Suddenly I was worried.

"It's nothing bad. It's a concern I have," she said, the compassion still apparent in her voice. "I told you, I looked through your blog, all of it. I love it, there's so much creativity. Your creations using your grandmother's recipes are my favourite.

"But I noticed a change in April. I think you know what I'm talking about."

"I added more Filipino recipes."

"You didn't add *more* Filipino recipes. You added Filipino recipes, period. I read your entire blog, going back two years. I think there is only one Filipino recipe, Melon Halo-Halo, but it was kind of generic, to be honest."

I was silent. I wasn't sure what to say, but technically she didn't ask me a question, so I didn't have to give her an answer.

"Did the CC producers tell you to post more Filipino recipes? You can be honest with me. I told you, this is off-the-record."

"Yeah," I said slowly. "They asked me to post some 'family recipes' on the blog before the show started. I knew what they were asking. I ended up adding more than that, plus the recipes I created for the competition."

"They're good recipes, they're clever. All your recipes are clever. For example," I could hear typing on a keyboard and the click of a mouse. "The Java Kimchi Fried Rice is brilliant, same with the Ube Hot Chocolate. Clever recipes.

"But a real recipe, one that will capture the judges and the audience, will represent *you*. Your cooking, your heart and soul. Your recipe should represent you and just you. *Fusion*, which is what you are, should be more than dumping a bunch of ingredients in a bowl then ladling them into a glass. Whatever recipe you come up with should be *authentic*."

I felt a lump in my throat. I know she was trying to help, but I wasn't fully catching whatever she was trying to tell me. It was like trying to capture a mist.

"I know this is confusing, but I know you can exceed your boundaries. The best way to do that is to look inwards."

"Okay, thanks."

"One last thing. Have you looked at Kendra's blog?"

"I skimmed through it."

"No, really look through it. I recommend you read her recipes, really try to understand her story, and I'm not talking about the paragraphs before the recipe and instructions. I want you to look at the recipes she shares and the overall story. You should know what you are up against."

"Alright, I will."

"Good. We'll talk soon."

As soon as she hung up, I looked up Kendra's blog. I scrolled back and looked at every recipe. It looked like she had started around the same time I had, about two years ago. All her recipes were from the Caribbean—the Bahamas, Jamaican, West Indies, Dominican, different islands. There were some repeats of dishes, but a different twist on each one—types of rice, doubles, rotis, patties, and more.

But more than a collection of dishes and ingredients, it was apparent how much she loved each dish. She would even repeat a recipe with a slight update because she was excited to try something new. Many of the recipes came from her parents, her grandparents, aunts, uncles, family friends. She wanted to share her love of her food, food that brought her happiness, comfort, and nostalgia.

Authenticity.

I realized what I had to do.

Chapter Nineteen

As I grew up, my ultimate comfort food was matzah balls. My baba (Yiddish for grandmother) would make them specifically for me. I recently learned that my lola (Filipino for grandmother) would make sopas (milky chicken noodle soup) for my mother and her siblings while growing up. It was their comfort food. I wanted to combine that love and warmth in one bowl.

Matzah Ball Sopas

Matzah Balls:
1 ½ matzah sheets, finely ground in food processor
½ tsp baking powder
1 tbsp melted butter (can sub with oil if you keep kosher)
1 tbsp broth
1 egg, beaten
½ tsp salt
Water for boiling

Sopas:
1 tsp oil or butter
½ cup diced onion
1 cup diced carrot
2 litres chicken broth, unsalted
2 tsp salt (omit if using salted broth)
1 boneless chicken breast
2 cloves garlic, minced
1 stalk celery, sliced thin on the diagonal

1 can quail eggs, drained

2 hot dog weiners, sliced thin on the diagonal

1 can evaporated milk (can sub with oat milk if you keep kosher)

Chopped green onion for garnish.

Make the matzah balls:

Mix all ingredients together to form a wet dough.

Put in fridge for 30 minutes.

(This is a good time to prepare the vegetables for the sopas.)

After removing matzah ball dough from fridge, wet hands and roll dough into small balls, approximately 1 rounded teaspoon per ball.

Put balls on a cookie sheet and put in refrigerator to set for 15 minutes

In a medium pot, fill ¾ full of water and bring to a boil.

Add matzah balls. Cover and drop heat to medium. Cook for 20 minutes.

Start the Sopas:

While matzah balls are cooking, heat a large pot on medium, add oil or butter, add onions and carrots.

Sauté for 1 minute. Do not allow them to brown; it's not that kind of soup.

Add broth to pot. Cover and crank heat to high to bring to a boil.

Add chicken breast and garlic. Drop heat to medium and cook 10 minutes.

Remove chicken breast from broth and allow to cool.

Add celery. Let cook another 3 minutes.

During this time, slice the chicken breast in half lengthwise and shred the meat.

Put everything together:

Add quail eggs, hot dogs, shredded chicken, and evaporated milk. Mix.

Transfer matzah balls from the medium pot to the sopas using a slotted spoon. Stir gently.

Simmer for 5 minutes on medium.

Taste soup and season with salt and pepper.

Ladle into bowls and top with green onions for garnish.

Winnipeg

"What do you think?"

"It's delicious, Sar. My mother used to make a soup that tasted like this. It takes me back to childhood, before things… got hard," my mom said wistfully. "Her version had macaroni and hot dogs. She put quail eggs in the soup too, but I didn't care for them then. My brother and sister seemed to love them. They thought they were secretive about hiding the eggs, but I knew they got some and I didn't."

The bowl of soup I had placed in front of her was dotted with orbs, matzah balls and quail eggs, both approximately the same size. My mom scooped up a spoonful with a quail egg, along with some carrot and celery. She bit into the egg and I could see from the satisfied pleasure that she had bitten into the yolk and the richness spread across her palate.

"I was wrong when I was a kid," she admitted. "The eggs are delicious."

"Creamy, right?"

"Yes, exactly."

"Thank you for trying it, Mom."

"Thank you for opening my eyes to try something new."

I looked up at Del, and she nodded. It was the last of the footage we needed for the clip show, as well as for the appetizer recipe video. She helped me tidy up the kitchen island.

"Do you have everything you need?" I asked her as I rinsed dishes.

"Are you sure you want me to go in this direction?"

"It'll say everything I want to say."

"Don't you want to talk to your parents first?"

"The recap show is supposed to tell my story," I insisted. "This is my story. I want everyone to know."

"You got it, boss."

"Thanks, Del."

Toronto

"Chuck, what is this?" Poppy asked.

"This is the footage the media manager sent me," Chuck said in defence, his face appearing puffy and red on her screen. "She won't send me more. I'm trying to go through the footage we have and piece something else together—"

"Is this true?"

"What do you mean?"

"Did we side-step her Jewish identity?"

"W-wait, what?" Chuck stammered. "That's not what we did. Nothing like that."

"Then tell me what we did," Poppy said, anger on the edge of her voice. "Because I have a video that says otherwise."

She pressed play on a video Marlee had emailed her and shared it in-screen. It was a clip of raw footage of an interview with one of the finalists, Sarah Something-Something, the Filipino girl. She scolded herself for thinking of the girl that way. She turned up the volume for Chuck to hear over the speakerphone.

"Um, my name is actually pronounced SAH-rah. It's the Hebrew pronunciation," the girl said carefully. "I'm actually half-Ashkenazi Jew and half-Filipino. My mother is Filipino. My father is Eastern European Jewish. I probably should have said something earlier. I don't know, I just, I wasn't sure how to correct it, or even if I should. I went with the flow because it was easier. That's what I've done my whole life, but not in the way you'd think.

"I was raised Jewish. I have Jewish friends. I went to a Jewish school. Almost all the activities I've participated in were through school or through the Jewish community centre. I have very little Filipino family in town, only my mom and my aunt. My grandmother on my mother's side moved to BC before I was born.

"I mainly connected with my father's family, because that's the family that was here while I was growing up. Every Friday, we would hold Shabbat meals, Friday evenings, usually at Baba's house, sometimes at my parents' house. My aunts or uncles and their families would come. It was huge.

"When I was little, Baba taught me how to cook. For my Bat Mitzvah, she gave me her box of recipe cards. It's my most prized possession, this bright orange plastic box. It's like a treasure chest to me."

The shot widened. Sarah held the box in her hands and flipped it open.

"I made little notes in pencil on each of the cards, just ways to improve the recipes. I liked seeing my writing next to hers, like we'd always be together. She also bought me a stack of blank cards so I could write down my own recipes. I always gave her suggestions. I liked to try new things. She would encourage me to write down my ideas, combining Indian flavours with latkes, adding mascarpone to a kugel. She taught me how to craft a recipe, how to figure out the proportions and ratios."

A hand passed her a tissue. She dabbed at her eyes. She ran her tongue in front of her teeth. Poppy remembered being annoyed at the movement. Now she found it humanizing.

"Thanks. Um, she passed away two years ago. Stroke. She didn't go right away, but she wasn't here. Not really. A month later, she was gone. At least I got to say goodbye.

"We stopped holding Shabbat dinner after that. I mean, we tried doing it at my aunt's house—my dad's sister—but she couldn't handle cooking for that many people. Me and my dad tried—my mom doesn't cook—but it's hard to cook a big Friday night dinner when he had work and I had school. After a few months, we stopped trying.

"But I missed Baba so much. I had a box full of her recipes and I had no Shabbat table to cook for. That's when my aunt, my mom's sister who also helped me learn to cook—she's a chef—she suggested I start a blog. When coming up with the name, I wanted to call it Baba's Shabbat Table, but my aunt said that would limit what I could post. My family doesn't keep kosher, and I liked to cook pork and shellfish and milk with meat, so I didn't want to offend any Jewish readers looking for new Shabbat meals.

"My aunt and I talked about fusion cooking—combining food from different cultures to create something new and innovative. And I thought—I'm from two different cultures. The blog will be me. Hence, *Fusion on a Plate* was born.

"But I look back and now I think I was wrong. Fusion cooking is supposed to be the integration of two dishes, but that's not what I am. I'm lopsided. I'm Jewish, like really Jewish, but I feel like I've ignored my Filipino side. There's so much I don't know, so much I want to learn. And I have learned. Right before the show, I was encouraged to have more Filipino recipes on my blog. I had every culinary culture represented, but not Filipino. My aunt gave me a crash course on Filipino cooking, and I applied everything I knew about fusion food. And then when *Cyber Chef: Next Gen* started, I was encouraged to make Filipino food for my dishes.

"I'm sorry. I feel like I've lied. I'm sorry for covering up my Jewish roots. I don't blame the show. I think they were trying to be diverse by pushing me to explore my Filipino side. In a way, I actually thank them. I learned about my family and myself.

"But I'm done with that now. I want to share me, the real me, all of me. I am fusion and I will prove it."

Poppy hit stop.

"How did Marlee get that footage?" Chuck asked suspiciously.

"Sarah gave Marlee's email address to her media manager. She said she wanted whoever was in charge to see it. Marlee watched it and decided to send it to me."

"Well, that's unfortunate."

"Did we push her to create only Filipino dishes?"

"No?" Chuck said, his voice brimming with uncertainty. "Maybe?"

Poppy looked at the email that had come in just before she received the clip from Marlee.

Dear Ms. St. Martin-Dubois: We are pleased to announce that you are the recipient of this year's award for diversity in programming...

She felt like a fraud.

"We need to fix this," Poppy insisted.

"That's why I'm trying to find more footage—"

"No," Poppy said. "We've done so much wrong."

"Do we have to do a public apology, like Geoff?"

"No, no." Poppy brushed the thought away. "This is about Sarah. We're done telling her story for her. She has a right to take hold of the narrative. We've done enough damage."

Chuck was silent a moment, then finally nodded.

"What do you want me to do?"

"We run the competition the way it was meant to be. We let her recipes do the talking."

Winnipeg

"How do you pronounce your name again?" Jenna asked.

"SAH-rah," I said. "It's the Hebrew pronunciation."

"I'm so sorry, Sarah," Jenna said, sincerely apologetic. "I've been saying it wrong this whole time. I wish you would have corrected me."

I glanced over at my parents as we watched the recap show. Instead of my usual spot in between them, I sat on the loveseat, hugging my knees to my chest.

"You're right, I should have," I admitted. "It's not your fault. I didn't know what to say."

They switched to my monologue from my interview with Del, the video I asked her to send to Marlee, my only direct connection to the network. They played the words over pictures from my Bat Mitzvah.

"I'm actually half-Ashkenazi Jew and half-Filipino. My mother is Filipino. My father is Eastern European Jewish. I probably should have said something earlier. I don't know, I just, I wasn't sure how to correct it, or even if I should…"

"This is my Baba Esther." On screen I held up a picture album, one of many that were split between my dad and his siblings. I flipped through the pages. "She taught me how to cook. She taught me how to love food."

The camera focused on photos too delicate to remove from the album for scanning. Baba holding me as a baby. Baba holding a brisket. Baba holding my hand as a toddler. Baba sitting at one end of the dining table. I sat to her right as a little girl.

"For my Bat Mitzvah, she gave me her box of recipe cards."

As I continued to talk about Baba, they cut to a rare video of us cooking together, a Passover seder, the most complicated of all traditional Jewish meals. I was twelve. I was shaking a bag with chunks of chicken breast, matzah crumbs, and spices; she kept calling it Kosher for Passover Shake and Bake. I found out later Shake and Bake was a brand of breading. I was making chicken nuggets for my younger cousins.

I looked over at my parents when I started talking about Baba's passing. They both held tissues. My mom leaned on my dad's shoulder.

"...She didn't go right away, but she wasn't here. Not really. A month later, she was gone. At least I got to say goodbye..."

As I watched myself talk about the Shabbat dinners that I missed so dearly, I saw in my peripheral vision my parents glance over at me. I continued to look at the screen. The camera panned over a dinner table with a tablecloth, dishes and glasses; suddenly all the tableware faded away, including the tablecloth, and the table itself was bare. I suppressed a giggle. It wasn't our table. It wasn't our plates and glasses.

I talked about my blog and where the name came from. They showed footage of me looking at the recipes, retyping them into a computer, scanning the cards so I could never lose them.

"...I'm from two different cultures. The blog will be me. Hence, *Fusion on a Plate* was born."

They showed a clip of me holding my mom and dad's hands while we watched Geoff's revolting tantrum. His words were heard in the background, but they didn't replay the footage of him saying them.

"It's embarrassing for me to admit this," I said, my eyes down. The camera held a tight shot of my face. This clip was from a separate interview, a difficult one that required several takes. "But my parents had to point out that Geoff was also referring to me when he talked about skin colour." I raised my eyes to meet the lens. "Truth be told, I didn't think of myself as not White until this show, actually not until that moment.

"Geoff, if you're watching, I'm not mad at you. It was mean and spiteful, but I forgive you. I hope you learned that what you said was wrong. I know I learned something."

The shot switched back to me sitting in the loveseat I was sitting in now.

"Fusion cooking is supposed to be the integration of two dishes, but that's not what I am. I'm lopsided. I'm Jewish, like really Jewish, but I've ignored my Filipino side. There's so much I don't know, so much I want to learn."

I had asked Del to ask Marlee for the footage from my first interview with her. A little note appeared at the bottom of the screen to indicate the source of the clip. The audio was less polished than other interviews.

"I didn't grow up eating a lot of Filipino food," I said. "My mom doesn't cook. My dad is a good cook. We also eat out a lot. Well, a lot of takeout and delivery."

"Do you eat at any of your relatives' houses?" Marlee asked, her face unseen. "Extended family? Lolo? Lola? Debuts? First birthdays?"

"I have cousins, but they live in Penticton, BC. My grandmother lives in BC, helping my uncle and auntie raise my cousins. We've visited my family in Penticton a few times, but I wouldn't say we're close."

"Filipino friends? Family friends?"

"No, I go to private school with a Hebrew immersion program. I was the only Filipino kid in my grade, maybe in the whole school. I hear about Filipinos having this big extended family consisting of actual family members and friends of the parents and grandparents, but that's kind of a stereotype. My parents don't have any Filipino friends. If my grandmother did, I never met any of them."

I took a breath as they went to the next section. Instead of the original footage, I had re-recorded the next part. I'd grown since then and now had something different to say. I was back on the loveseat.

"I cook because I want to share my food, share a part of me, but there was a lot I didn't know. I had to learn that part, learn about Filipino culture and Filipino food. I learned that my upbringing is the complete opposite of the stereotype. That's not a bad thing, but I don't feel like I'm a Filipino at all, and I don't think it's supposed to be this way."

The scene changed to one of me putting together the longanisa ouvo wontons.

"I didn't just learn more about my Filipino culture and Filipino food, I learned things I didn't know about myself, things that were kept from me. And somehow, it leads to food."

The scene suddenly cut to an argument with me and my mother.

"Ever since I started learning how to make Filipino food, you've been avoiding eating what I cook." I yelled at my mother. "Why? Why do you hate my cooking all of a sudden? Why do you hate Filipino food?"

"Sar, I don't hate Filipino food. And I certainly don't hate your cooking."

"But you hate being Filipino."

My mother sat up straight on the couch, watching our argument aired publicly.

"I'm going to kill Del." I heard her say under her breath.

"I don't hate being Filipino," my mother's voice said on the screen. "How can you even think that?"

The shot changed to me back in the loveseat, my confessional.

"I don't know anything about being Filipino. I feel... robbed. When I became a contestant on *Cyber Chef,* I was encouraged to explore my culture, but I didn't even know where to start. My aunt, a professional chef, she taught me how to cook Filipino food. When I learned about the food, I learned about my family. She taught me my lola's recipes, my mother's mom. I never knew my grandmother had recipes. I didn't know I had another grandmother I could learn from."

They cut to video of my bat mitzvah, my grandmother sitting at a table with my uncle and aunt, staring off to the side. The camera pans out, and she's looking at me.

"But I barely know her. And I want to know her. I want to learn from her before it's too late. Maybe we could cook for each other. Maybe we can learn from each other."

I was back to sitting on the loveseat.

"*Cyber Chef* forced me to cook out of my comfort zone. It's made me look at my culture in a whole new light. I think it brought my mother out of her comfort zone."

The shot changed to the clip of my mother trying my Matzah Ball Sopas. A satisfied smile crept across her face.

"It's delicious, Sar," my mom's wistful voice said, barely above a whisper. "My mother used to make a soup that tasted like this. It takes me back to childhood, before things… got hard."

The shot changed to me in my living room.

"The show has actually brought me and my mom closer together. It made me more sure of who I am. I am Filipino and Jewish. I am the integration of two cultures in one. I think I can now truly say, I am fusion."

I turned to look at my mother.

She stood up and left the room.

Chapter Twenty

My baba made braised brisket for Every. Single. Holiday.
Seriously. Brisket for Passover. Brisket for Rosh Hashana.
Brisket for Chanukah. Apparently my lola was the same way
with Caldereta, a salty, savoury beef stew. Caldereta for
Easter. Caldereta for Christmas. Caldereta for birthdays.
I wanted to celebrate each of my grandmother's favourite
braised beef on one platter.

Brisket Caldereta

1 tbsp kosher salt

1 tsp freshly ground black pepper

2–3 lbs brisket, trim some of the fat

1 tbsp vegetable oil

1 medium onion, sliced thin

3 cloves of garlic, minced

1–2 Thai chilli peppers, seeded and minced (optional)

½ cup chicken stock

1 cup tomato sauce

1 tbsp tomato paste

3 bay leaves

2 medium carrots, sliced into thick discs

½ cup canned sliced green or black olives, drained

1 red pepper, julienned

Pre-heat oven to 325°F.

Combine salt and pepper in a small bowl.

Pat brisket dry with paper towel. Rub salt and pepper all over brisket.

Place brisket on a wire rack over a cookie sheet. Let dry 10 minutes.

Heat large cast-iron pan or other heat-proof pan on medium-high heat. Add oil.

Brown brisket on both sides, about 5 minutes per side. You may need to reposition the brisket in order for all surfaces to touch the pan.

Remove brisket and place in a glass dish or roasting pan that fits the brisket snugly.

Reduce heat to medium. Add onions to pan, cook until translucent.

Add garlic and chillies. Cook 30 seconds.

Add stock, scraping bottom of pot with a wooden spoon.

Add tomato sauce, tomato paste, and bay leaves. Mix.

Pour tomato sauce mixture over brisket to ensure top is soaked.

Cover brisket with heatproof lid or foil tightly covering dish, and transfer to oven.

Braise for 3 hours, basting brisket with surrounding liquid once an hour.

Remove brisket, place on platter. Cover with foil and rest for 30 minutes.

Transfer to a cutting board and slice across the grain. Meat will still be somewhat tough.

Carefully add brisket slices back to dish, keeping the brisket's rectangular shape.

Add sliced carrots, peppers, and olives on top. Baste with liquid. Cover with lid or foil.

Return to oven and braise another 2 hours, basting every hour.

Take a small piece of brisket and taste for doneness.
If you want a softer texture, baste again and braise for another hour.

If you are happy with the texture, remove from oven and baste one more time. Tent with foil and rest 30 minutes.

Transfer brisket to a platter. Remove bay leaves. Spoon vegetables over brisket.

Serve over rice or boiled potatoes.

Keep a bowl of the remaining basting liquid if anyone wants extra sauce. (And they will!)

Thirty-three years ago
Winnipeg

"Gloria, galing, your children are so talented!"

"Oh, salamat! Thank you so much! I am very proud!"

"Where is Norman?"

"Oh, he is working, but he will come tomorrow."

Thirteen-year-old Grace rubbed at her temples, leaning back in her seat. Her mother and her friends were so loud. They yelled when they were mad; they yelled when they were happy; they yelled all the time. They had no volume setting lower than yelling.

"Gracie," her mother's friend asked, rolling her R's and stretching out the syllables. *Gray-CEEE.* "Why are you not dancing?"

"I wanted to play soccer."

Two years ago, her parents gave all three kids a choice, soccer or Filipino folk dance. Grace had just tried out for the community league and got onto the higher-level team. That was a big deal for an eleven-year-old. Christoffer and Cherish were still on the little kids' teams. They didn't even keep score. Of course, they jumped at the opportunity to do something else.

Grace didn't realize the big 'recital' at the end of the year was an internationally renowned city-wide cultural festival. Her siblings got to perform for a thousand locals and tourists every night for a week on a real stage with lights and a sound system wearing colourful costumes, performing traditional dances, and singing cultural songs.

Cherish and Christoffer talked about how they played games backstage and held mini-parties. The last show was at nine forty-five pm so they got to stay up late, coming home at eleven pm, which was way past her own bedtime, and she was thirteen! They would get a big bag of candy at the end of the week, along with a barbecue in the park at the end of summer.

Grace loved soccer. She'd moved up to right wing this year! But as she sat in a theatre next to her mother, watching her little sister balance a glass with a lit candle on her head, she sulkily slouched down in her seat. As she watched her little brother expertly step through clapping bamboo sticks in precise 3/4 rhythm, she enviously thought to herself, *I didn't get a big bag of candy at the end of the soccer season.*

Seven-year-old Cherish and ten-year-old Christoffer came running out from backstage. They were back in regular clothing, but her sister's short hair was still slicked back with a fake bun at the back of her head, fastened with bobby pins looking like a black bagel. Both of them wore blush and eyeliner.

"Nay!" Cherish screamed, hugging their mom. "Did you see? I was the only one who didn't drop their glass tonight! And Christoffer tripped on the bamboo poles!"

"Shut up, Cher!" Christoffer snapped. "I got up right away so no one could tell I tripped!"

Why was everyone yelling? Grace thought. She grabbed at her mom's wrist to check her watch. Eleven-o-five pm. No wonder she was so tired.

"Can we go now?" Grace asked.

"Yes, of course," Gloria said. "We will all tell Tatay how good your performance was."

Grace was glad to sit in the front seat on the way home. Her brother and sister kept talk talk talking, coming down from the rush of six days of performing. Both of them were excited about the last night of shows. They were both invited to separate sleepover parties. Grace only went to her first sleepover this past spring.

Her mother sat on a cushion in the driver's seat, a tiny Filipino woman who drove too slowly because she could barely see over the steering wheel. Grace hated the stereotype. Her mother was proud of being the only one of her friends who had her driver's license, but she hated driving at night. Unfortunately, sometimes there wasn't much of a choice. Her dad was working the evening shift at the railyards as an electrician all week. Her mom would drop him off at work and he would get a ride coming home at ten.

"Why are all the lights off?" Grace asked. "Tay isn't home yet?"

Her mom parked nose-first in the driveway. She was always weary of pulling into the garage. Her dad would always back the car into the garage in the morning because her mom was also scared of backing up into the street.

"Wait here," her mom said, the streetlights casting shadows over her worried face. All three kids waited on the front steps, agitated and quiet. Their mother unlocked the front door and stepped into the dark house. The hallway light flicked on.

Then came the scream.

"Go to the car and wait there!" Grace yelled at her younger siblings.

She bolted into the house. She could hear her mother continuing to scream.

"Norman! Norman!"

She found her mother only a few steps from the door. She was leaning over her father, who was lying face down near the hall table. As Grace stepped closer, she saw the blood on the floor. She could tell that her father had collapsed, likely hitting his head on the way down.

Her mother was crying, trying to roll over her husband's hulking body, which was too heavy for her petite frame.

"Help me, Grace!" she screamed through panicked tears.

Grace squatted down and helped her mother roll him onto his back. She already knew from his open eyes that he was gone. Her mother kept shaking him. Weeks later one of her aunts explained that her father died of a heart attack brought on from years of high cholesterol. Hitting his head was incidental.

"Norman! Norman!"

Grace walked into the living room and dialled 911.

We should have been home. We should have been home. We should have been home.

Ten years ago
Penticton

"You want to hang out with us, Sarah?" the ten-year-old twins asked their younger cousin.

"Can I, Mommy?" the little girl asked.

The twins silently pleaded with their Auntie Grace with wide brown eyes. No one could resist their anime-like faces. Their auntie looked them over and then nodded. They each grabbed one of Sarah's hands and led their six-year-old cousin into the rec room in the basement.

"What do you want to play?" Sarah asked.

"Dance party!" the twins said in unison.

Mina ran over to the iPod dock that sat next to the stereo

system and hit shuffle. "Like A G6" started to play, and the twins squealed and started jumping around. They quickly fell into a prepared dance routine they had made up themselves. They shimmied their shoulders and popped out their hips in sync, playing it up for their audience of one. Sarah stared at them with wide eyes.

"Dance, Sarah!" Manda shouted over the loud bass.

"I don't know this song."

"You don't need to know the song," she said while performing an intricate movement with her hands and wrists. "Just move with the music."

"I don't know how," she said.

"I'll switch it," Mina said, pressing the skip button.

Suddenly Kesha's "Tik Tok" started to play. The twins danced around Sarah while she stared at them, bewildered. The song eased into Nicki Minaj's "Super Bass." The twins attempted to twerk their ten-year-old bottoms and Sarah looked visibly uncomfortable, impressed at the fast lyrics but mortified at some of the inappropriate language of the songs that played. Mina hit pause.

"Don't you have dancing in Winnipeg?" Manda mused.

"We have dancing," Sarah insisted. "I just don't know the songs."

"What song do you like?"

"I don't know," she shrugged. "Whatever my mom and dad like."

"What do they like?"

"Um, like Carrie Underwood and Something Flats?"

"Isn't that, like, country music?" Mina asked.

"I don't know. I guess."

"Wow, Tatay was right," Manda said. "You are like a White girl."

The girls giggled. Sarah furrowed her brow and pouted. She didn't know what the words meant, but she knew they weren't a compliment.

"How about karaoke?" Mina suggested. "We have a Magic Mic. It has, like, a thousand songs."

"What's that?"

"You don't have one? I thought every Filipino had a Magic Mic."

"I don't know what that is."

"A Magic Mic or Karaoke?"

"Both."

"Told you she was a White girl," Manda said.

Mina led Sarah to the front of the television set. She picked up the remote to turn it on, then picked up a microphone with a digital display and numbered buttons underneath. She grabbed a binder nearby and looked up a song. She entered a code and Beyoncé's "Single Ladies" started playing, the lyrics scrolling across the screen. Mina started to sing. Her voice was loud against the backing track, with the echo turned up high.

"I think I've heard this song," Sarah shouted.

"Everyone knows Beyoncé!" Manda said.

She grabbed the microphone away from her sister and sang and danced at the same time. Mina jumping behind her and waving her hand in the air. Sarah smiled as she watched her cousins sing and dance, passing the microphone between them.

"Do you want to try?" Mina asked Sarah through the microphone, her voice echoing through the surround sound.

"Okay!"

Sarah took the microphone in her hand.

"Hello?" she said quietly. Her voice echoed around her. She laughed.

"What do you want to sing?"

"I don't know." Her voice echoed again. She squealed in delight.

Manda grabbed the microphone and plugged in a code, then handed it back to Sarah. The opening strains of "Achy Breaky Heart" played.

"I know this song!" Sarah said, jumping up and down, her pigtails bouncing.

"Of course you do!" Manda said.

As Sarah started to sing the song, she danced the accompanying line dance that she had done while copying her parents. Mina and Manda danced behind her, familiar with the dance as they had learned it in school and had heard the song at numerous Filipino parties and weddings. Sarah turned and kicked out her feet, shuffling to the right and left. Luckily the microphone was wireless or else she surely would have gotten tangled in the cord. The three girls clapped at the end.

"I have an idea!" Mina said. "What if you sing and we're your back-up dancers?"

"But I don't know what to sing."

"We'll pick our favourite songs and you can sing them. The words are on the screen."

"You can read, right?" Manda asked.

"I'm six!" Sarah said, a little too loudly. "I'm not a baby!"

"Okay, cool."

Mina added the code for "I Kissed a Girl" by Katy Perry. Sarah sang and her cousins danced around her.

"I like that song!" Sarah said gleefully.

"So do we! Do the next one?!"

"Okay!"

Manda plugged in a new song, and Flo Rida's "Low" started to play. Sarah had more trouble singing the lyrics, but Mina and Manda shouted out the words to her. They even taught her to crouch and get closer to the ground during the chorus.

During the second verse, as they were teaching Sarah to shake her hips, Auntie Grace came down the stairs.

"What are you girls doing?!" she shouted angrily.

The three girls froze. Mina quickly grabbed the remote and turned off the TV.

"We were doing karaoke," Manda said, stepping forward.

"Your parents allow you to listen to this… music?" Auntie Grace asked in an accusing tone.

"Um, yeah."

"Sarah, come here."

She gave the microphone to Mina and joined her mother. She took her mother's hand. She looked down.

"Girls, I'm going to talk to your mother." Auntie Grace looked down at Sarah. "Maybe you should play with Christo instead."

"But he's three!"

"He'll be four tomorrow," she said. "Come on, I think you'll have fun."

Sarah looked back longingly at her cousins as her mother pulled her up the stairs. The twins sat down on the couch, sulking for a minute, until Mina got up and pressed play on the iPod. Britney Spears' voice filled the room. They got up and started to jump around and dance. Britney made everything better.

Winnipeg

"Mom?"

I found my mom downstairs in the laundry room, ironing. She hates ironing.

"Is the show over?"

"Yeah, we recorded it if you still want to watch later," I said. "Dad said I should come down and talk to you."

"Okay." My mom put the iron down on the ironing board, the hot plate facing forward. She remained standing. "How are we going to deal with this?"

"Deal with what?"

"The show has manipulated your image enough. Now they're messing with your family. Should we talk to Del? Should we go higher up? Maybe Chuck, the director? Who else is there? Marlee? Poppy?"

"Mom, no," I said, waving her accusations away. "They didn't have anything to do with it. This was my idea. I came up with the narrative."

"WHAT?!"

Her face went as red as the caldereta brisket I had made for dinner. I thought she was going to burst.

"I wanted everyone to know who I was, who I am," I explained. "I wanted to tell my story and not let them tell it for me."

"At my expense."

"It's not a big deal," I said. "You're barely in it."

"The entire country now thinks I hate being Filipino!"

I blinked.

"But isn't it true?"

She stepped back as if I had slapped her in the face. She switched off the iron.

"Mom, why do you hate being Filipino?"

"I don't."

Her voice was shaky. A part of me was afraid of pressing forward. The protective walls that had been built around me my entire life had started to show cracks long ago. What if they fell inwards? What if they buried me? I continued to pull out the bricks.

"It's more than Filipino food, Mom." I took a breath and worked up the courage to keep going. "You never talk about Lola. You don't know any Filipino, but Auntie Cher and Uncle Christoffer can speak it and they understand. You never had Filipino friends. You never dated anyone Filipino. It's like you avoided it as much as you could."

"I told you, I was bullied—"

"I was bullied too, Mom. Everyone gets bullied, for being different, or being too short, or having black hair, or having a dad that doesn't look like you, but I don't hate anybody for it. I moved forward, like you taught me."

She shuffled her feet. I could see the excuses whip through her mind behind her eyes, as if she were dealing out cards. I wanted to pull the entire deck away.

"Please, Mom." I stepped towards her. "Tell me the truth. Why do you hate Lola so much? Why do you hate Filipinos?"

She pressed her lips together. Like a magician, the deck of excuses disappeared.

"I don't hate them. I don't hate my culture." Unshed tears hung at the edge of her eyelids. If she closed her eyes, they would fall. She took my hand. "Come."

She led me to the bookshelf in our rec room that held old family albums, put together during a time when people still printed photographs and held them in bound books that no one ever looked at. She pulled a yellow album off the shelf and sat down on our old couch. She patted the seat next to her, and I sat down. I had flipped through this album before. The pages were sticky with some sort of adhesive. The pictures couldn't be removed. I'd tried.

She opened the album a few pages in. She stopped at a picture of a little girl wearing blotchy blue make-up, a blond wig, and a white beanie.

"When I was six, I wanted to be Smurfette for Halloween." She must have noticed my puzzled expression. "You don't know who that is, but it's from a kid's cartoon. Smurfette was a blue elf-like creature with blond hair."

Auntie Cher was in a stroller, wearing a blanket that looked like a watermelon. Uncle Christoffer had a top hat and a magician's wand.

My mother turned the page, skipping over photos of birthday parties and Christmases. She stopped at another set of Halloween photos.

"When I was eight, I wanted to be Barbie. My mom used the same wig."

She showed me a picture of a slightly taller girl with a pink dress, the blond wig a little worse for wear. Auntie Cher wore her brother's top hat, a white shirt and black pants, holding the wand in a tiny fist. Uncle Christoffer was a ninja.

"When I was eleven, I wanted to be Madonna. She was the most popular singer at the time."

She turned to another picture near the end of the book with an even taller girl wearing a short platinum blond wig, a black dress, plastic beads, and dark red lipstick. I knew who Madonna was, but I didn't think this was what she looked like. Auntie Cher was a ninja. Uncle Christoffer wore a Transformer's mask and an Autobot t-shirt.

"They were all blond," she continued. "It's all I ever saw. It's all I ever wanted. I wanted to be pretty and beautiful like the characters in cartoons, and dolls, and on TV."

"You wanted to be blond?"

"I think I wanted to be White." She closed the album. "Whenever I was bullied or treated differently or was picked last, I blamed it on not being White. Sometimes it was true, sometimes it wasn't.

"When I was seven, there was a boy in my class. He came from the Philippines. He didn't speak much English. His first day of school, the teacher made me sit next to him. She said we should be friends. I was teased mercilessly. The other kids said we should get married."

She closed her eyes. I could almost hear the taunts of children haunting her from the past. She opened her eyes again and looked at me.

"At seven years old, I decided I would never marry a Filipino man."

She stood up and put the album away.

"A couple months later, I was teased about my lunch. It snowballed from there," she continued. "I avoided making Filipino friends. I was sulky and often rude when my parents would bring me to a Filipino party. By the time I was ten, whenever there was an event with their group, they'd leave me at home. Parents did that in the eighties.

"I hated those nights alone. I'd be scared to go to sleep. I'd stay up until my parents would come in carrying Cher, who always fell asleep in the car. They'd place her on top of the sheets in her own twin bed across the room and leave. They wouldn't even check on me.

"Christoffer and Cher had plenty of Filipino friends. Maybe they went to school with nicer kids who didn't make fun of them as much. They took Filipino folk dance classes. I chose soccer. They developed an interest in learning words in Tagalog and Ilocano. I did really well in French. Their friends made me feel different and awkward. I didn't fit in with them.

"And then there's my dad…" My mother hung her head in her hands. She took a deep breath. "My dad… he died while we were watching a Filipino dance show." She wrung her hands. "I never forgave my mom for making me go. She never made me come to anything, but she wanted me to watch that one show. She thought I would learn something."

Tears ran down my mother's face. I scooched closer to her on the couch. I took her hand.

"I never dated a Filipino guy. I wasn't into the same music. I didn't dress right. I went through a grunge phase; I wore baggy plaid shirts and had scraggly, unwashed hair. It was a thing in the nineties. I annoyed my mother to no end.

"When I met your father, he was basically the complete opposite of what my mom would've wanted for me. He wasn't Catholic, he wasn't even Christian. But he was nice, and kind, and good looking. I think my mom liked the idea of having a half White grandchild. Filipinos love 'the look'. I have to admit. A part of me also liked the idea of having a child that was half White. Not for 'the look', but for the idea that a part of me would carry on as something that wasn't the thing that made me so angry.

"When I decided to convert to Judaism, I thought, maybe this will erase the past and I can be Jewish and not... whatever I was before."

She wiped her tears away with the back of her hand. My eyes looked like hers. She closed them, and another row of tears cascaded down her cheeks.

"Everything painful that I remember about childhood seemed to stem from being Filipino." She looked at me. "Sar, I don't hate being Filipino. It hurt being Filipino. And I didn't want to hurt anymore."

Tears were running down my face, reflecting her own. The brisket we ate for dinner sat like a rock in my stomach. My chest felt tight. One question burned inside of me, a question that had been simmering inside of me my entire life. It was finally boiling over.

"Mom, do you wish I was White?"

She widened her eyes and took my face in both of her hands.

"No, Sar! Why would you even think that?"

"It's like..." The thought in my mind was a spark. I needed to fan the flame. "It's like my whole life was mapped to go in only one direction. Every time I tried to stray one way, you nudged me back the other.

"Every time I asked about Lola, you wouldn't really answer. You didn't like it when I played with my cousins. Anytime I had to learn about my culture, you'd make me focus on dad's side of the family.

"I remember one time when we visited Penticton, Lola brought one of her friends to the house. Mina and Manda and Christo took the lady's hand and they lifted her knuckles to their foreheads. When the lady came to me, she gave me her hand, and I started to copy them, but you slapped her hand away and said, 'Jews don't bow to people.'"

"It's from the story of Purim, when Mordechai refused to bow to the King's advisor," my mom started. "Jews only bow to God—"

"I know that now, Mom, but you were rude." I started to wipe the tears with the back of my hand, but my mother reached over to the end table and gave me a tissue. "It was embarrassing, and I was scared, like *I* was the one who did something wrong. You could have explained the story. You could have explained to me what the bowing to the knuckle thing is. I had to Google it years later. It's called mano. It's a form of blessing for elders. Lola was so angry with you, but I thought that she was mad at me."

"Lola would never be mad at you."

"I always thought Lola didn't like me, but then I see a video of Lola looking at me during my bat mitzvah. Dad found the footage on Facebook. It was a random video under my bat mitzvah hashtag."

"Your Lola loves you."

"How do you know? You don't even talk to her."

"Because she asks about you all the time. Your dad talks to her. They email regularly. He thinks I don't know, but he's always leaving his laptop open. Maybe he does it on purpose. She loves you very much."

"Then why won't you let *me* know her?"

My mother took my hands in hers.

"I had a child's anger towards her for so long. I was angry at her for my childhood, for my father, for leaving, even though Cher and I always argue about which one of us drove her away. I blamed her for so much and I dragged that anger down into your relationship with her. I thought I was sparing you from pain, but I never realized how much I was isolating you. I'm so sorry, Sarah."

My mother pulled me into her arms. We both cried. And cried. And cried.

Minutes or maybe hours later, my dad slowly came down the stairs, unsure of what he would find. My mother and I were a snotty mess on the basement floor, laughing and crying with open photo albums all around us. She shared stories of her childhood and I shared stories of mine, many I had never shared before.

"Everything okay?" he asked.

"Yeah," I nodded. "I think so. Dad?"

"Yes, honey?"

"Can I have Lola's email address?"

My dad looked at my mom. She nodded.

"Of course, but on one condition."

"Whatever you want."

"Is it okay if I make a sandwich with the leftover brisket?"

I grinned widely.

"Yeah, I actually have some atchara, um, pickled papaya, that would go great on a sandwich."

"That sounds awesome!"

"I'll have one too," my mom said, surprisingly. "But we're going to clean up first."

My dad headed back upstairs as my mother and I cleaned up the used tissues. We left the albums open on the floor so we could come back to them later.

Chapter Twenty-one

I don't remember much of my zaida (Yiddish for grandfather). He died when I was only four but I have a vague memory of him wearing my baba's apron. My grandfather cooked. My baba taught me his blintz recipe, a type of Jewish crepe stuffed with a creamy filling. My lolo (Filipino for grandfather) died when my mother was a teenager. He didn't cook, but he would mash avocado and condensed milk as a treat for my mother. I wanted to create a fusion plate of both my grandfathers' love.

Avocado & Macapuno Blintzes (stuffed crepes)

Crepes:
4 eggs
1 tbsp sugar
1 cup flour
1 cup milk
¾ cup water, plus extra
1 tsp vanilla
Pinch of salt
Oil for cooking crepes
3 tsp of butter for cooking blintzes

Filling:
¾ cup ricotta
1 ripe avocado (might need two if there isn't a lot of flesh and the pit is too big)
1 tsp lemon juice

¼ cup condensed milk
½ cup of macapuno, (coconut strings in syrup), drained,
    syrup reserved
Pinch of salt

Topping:
A small container of raspberries
Reserved macapuno syrup
¼ cup macapuno
Condensed milk for garnish
Mint leaves for garnish
Freshly ground black pepper

Prepare the ricotta:

The night before, measure out ricotta and place in a
colander over a bowl.

Refrigerate in the colander to allow it to drain overnight.

Prepare the crepes:

Mix all crepe ingredients in a blender or with a mixer
until smooth

Pour into a bowl and refrigerate for thirty minutes to allow
the bubbles to settle.

Prepare the filling:

In a deep bowl, roughly mash the avocado with lemon juice.
Leave it chunky.

Add ricotta, condensed milk, and salt. Mix.

Mix in drained macapuno.

Place bowl in refrigerator for mixture to thicken.

Prepare raspberry topping:

In a small bowl, mix raspberries with macapuno syrup and ¼ cup macapuno. You can smash the berries if you wish but they look better if kept whole. Set aside.

Cook the crepes:

Tear twelve pieces of parchment paper the size of a dinner plate. Put the first piece on a plate.

Heat a 10-inch non-stick pan on medium.

Grease pan with a small amount of oil. Pre-heat for three minutes.

Gently stir the crepe batter before measuring out.

Pour the ¼ cup of batter into the pan. Tilt the pan to spread the batter to cover the bottom. Consider the first crepe as a test. If the batter doesn't spread well, finish cooking the crepe and place aside. (They're a nice snack with jam.) Add a tablespoon of water to the batter and stir gently. Try making another crepe.

Cook crepe until the bottom is lightly golden, the edges are slightly crispy, and the top is sticky but dry.

Do not flip. Slip crepe onto the parchment paper, golden side down. Cover with another piece of parchment paper.

Make more crepes until the batter is finished. Make sure you stir before measuring out the batter of each crepe.

If the batter starts to get too thick, (which can happen as the flour settles to the bottom of the mixture) mix in another tablespoon of water.

The batter should yield about 12 crepes, depending on how many 'test crepes' you had to make.

Assemble the blintzes:

Place a blintz on a plate or cutting board, the golden side facing upwards. The easiest way to do this is to take the parchment paper with the crepe stuck to it and place it light side down. Carefully peel off the parchment from the crepe and the golden side should be facing up.

Add a heaping tablespoon of avocado macapuno filling on the lower third of the crepe.

Fold the bottom edge towards the centre over the filling.

Fold in both sides towards the centre.

Then roll up like a flat burrito, tucking the end underneath. Place on a plate.

Repeat until crepes and filling are used up.

Cook the blintzes:

Heat the non-stick pan on medium.

Add a teaspoon of butter until it froths. Use a spatula to evenly spread butter across pan.

Place four blintzes in the pan, seam-side down, and brown for about ninety seconds.

Flip over carefully. Brown the other side another ninety seconds.

If the filling leaks out of a blintz, remove and wipe the pan immediately with a paper towel.

For each batch of four blintzes, add another teaspoon of butter to the pan.

Plating:

A serving can be two or three blintzes, depending on if you are serving dessert or brunch.

For each blintz, serve seam-side down, topped with the raspberries and macapuno syrup.

Add a sprig of mint for garnish and a drizzle of condensed milk.

Finish with a couple of grinds of black pepper. Yes, seriously. So good.

Winnipeg

"It doesn't taste right."

"Tastes great to me," Del said, finishing her third blintz.

I was working on the fillings. When my baba made blintzes, she used the raspberries she grew in her backyard. I wanted something more, though. The avocado, ricotta, and condensed milk mixture needed texture.

"I have an idea, but it's too late to go to the store."

"I can go pick something up," Del volunteered. "Just tell me what you need."

"I want to add macapuno."

"I have no idea what that is."

"Hold on."

Chair

do u hve macapuno in ur house

yeah u need?

can u bring over asap

pls pls pls

"My aunt is coming over right away."

"You're not supposed to get help, Sar."

"It's not help," I said. "I'm allowed to shop, right? Even if it's not Pangea?"

"Yes, of course, but—"

"And lots of stores have delivery services. This is like getting a delivery from a grocery store. And I never told her what it was for."

Del sighed in defeat.

"Fine. It's a product Pangea sells?"

"Most definitely." I quickly checked the website and breathed a sigh of relief. I showed her my screen. "Yup! It's on sale for another two days."

I tidied the kitchen and saved the macapuno-less blintzes for my mother. This was her favourite dish by far.

I covered the stack of crepes I had already made. In preparation for recipe testing, I had made twenty-four. I was down to eight. I assessed the eggs and ricotta in my refrigerator in case I had to make another dozen. The doorbell rang. I ran to answer it. Auntie Cher stood on the doorstep with a plastic shopping bag full of jars and cans. The cheap plastic strained under the weight.

"I brought macapuno, pandan, ube jam, coconut jam, jackfruit—"

"You read my mind."

She started to hand me the bag, but the bottom ripped out.

"Oh no!"

The cans and jars tumbled out across the entrance of our house. Luckily none of them landed on my toes and none of the glass jars broke. Cans and jars rolled around on the floor, one rolling down our front steps. Del ran over as my aunt and I were picking up the aftermath.

"Everything okay?"

I handed her two cans and bent to pick up another.

"Bag malfunction," I said.

"I think I got all of them," Auntie Cher said, walking into the doorway, holding a jar and three cans awkwardly. She smiled. "Oh, hi."

I looked at the two of them, my tough and scrappy aunt and tall and lithe Del. I took two cans from my aunt.

"Auntie Cher, this is my media manager, Del." I pointed with my head since my arms were full. "Del, this is my Auntie Cher, the head chef and part-owner of Mosaic. You've been there, right? Both of you, help me take these into the kitchen. Oh, wait," I said. "Auntie Cher, you can't go into the kitchen. We're recipe testing. You can't see any of what I'm making, but I can bring you one of the things that didn't work out, as long as you don't ask what's in it. That's okay, right, Del?"

"Yeah, of course."

"How about you wait here in the living room and I'll bring you a blintz, okay?" My eyes opened wide. "I'm sorry, I shouldn't have said what it was."

"I didn't hear a thing, Sar," Del said.

"I didn't hear a thing either," said Auntie Cher.

Without waiting for an answer, I rushed into the kitchen to drop off the cans I was holding and came back to grab more from Del and my aunt.

"If they're like your baba's recipe, they'd be delicious," my aunt said.

"I think you'll really like what I have so far."

I took a quick look at Del, wondering if she would bite.

"Del?"

"Sure, I could have another blintz."

I walked back into the kitchen, more slowly this time.

"Chair?" Del asked, checking the pronunciation.

"It's short for Cherish."

"Cherish and Grace?"

"My brother's name is Christoffer," Auntie Cher explained. "As in 'Christ Offer'. My parents were very religious."

"Del is short for Odellia. It was too fluffy for me."

"Exactly how I feel about Cherish," she said. "Could be worse. My niece's name is Amanda Lynn."

"A mandolin? That's just cruel."

They both laughed. I turned the corner into the kitchen and smiled to myself for a job well done. I put the jars and cans into the pantry, adding to the macapuno jars that were already stacked in the corner. I took my time putting together the blintzes as laughter trickled in from the other room.

Took long enough.

Three days ago...
Or two weeks...
Or a week before that...
Penticton

"It's on!" Mina shouted. "Hurry up!"

"Coming!"

Manda ran into the den, almost tripping on the long pajama pants that she seemed to always be wearing. She was holding a bowl of one of her favourite recipes, her cousin's furikake popcorn. She took her place on the loveseat next to her twin sister.

Their parents came in after her and sat down on the couch. For dinner they had made Sarah's Kimchi Java Fried Rice with Spam & Eggs as well as chicken wings with her Adobo Glaze. They planned on making the White Chocolate Chai Cookies for dessert after the show ended. Their dad passed by the twins and grabbed a handful of popcorn.

"Tay!" Manda stuck out her tongue in annoyance. Their parents took their place on the couch.

Mina looked over at Lola, sitting in the armchair that no one else was allowed to sit in. She always took her seat ten minutes before the show started.

"Welcome to *Cyber Chef: Next Gen*!" the annoying host said.

As she said each contestant's name, Lola beamed with pride.

"That is my granddaughter!"

She said it every single time they watched the show. Mina and Manda both proudly thought to themselves. *And that's my cousin.*

Winnipeg

"You're Jewish?!" Gary said incredulously. "Did you know this, Chuck?"

"Of course. She's a member of the tribe," Chuck said, frustrated with Gary once again. "Focus on Sarah, please."

"But you cook pork so well!"

"We don't keep kosher," I said. "Well, except during the week of Passover."

"You're lucky. You get the best comedians plus bacon," he said, ever the joker. "Mazel tov!"

"Thank you for not saying anything anti-Semitic, Gary," Chuck commented.

"But the night is still young."

"And now you're done." Chuck rolled his eyes. "Robyn, you're up."

"You're finally bringing us your true self, and it shines in your recipes and stories."

"Thank you," I said, grateful for the compliment.

It was a risk to fuse Filipino and Jewish dishes, but nothing represented me more than these foods. I was glad the judges understood what I was going for. They accepted me and my recipes as they are, including the correct pronunciation of my name.

The judges hadn't seen the recap show, so they didn't understand my whole journey. The judges didn't watch each week and were instructed to keep off social media related to the show. Their decisions were based purely on the quality of the recipes. I had to explain the whole Jewish/Filipino thing. I probably wasn't as eloquent as my speech from last week's clip show. Chuck said they would be inserting some snips from the recap episode anyway.

"I only wish we got to know the real you, sooner," Robyn said. "Can you explain how each dish relates to the theme of Culture?"

"I wanted to bring together my two cultures and create something new. I wanted to take traditional Jewish recipes like matzah ball soup, brisket, and blintzes, and create a remix with Filipino dishes like sopas, caldereta, and avocado with macapuno. I also wanted to pay homage to my baba's recipes, and my lola's favourite dishes. These are cultural and traditional, and now are part of me and my culture."

"Well done, Sarah," Chuck said. "Kelly?"

"Sarah," Chef Kwan said, trying my name out. "I think you finally understand true fusion. They're not just two dishes put together. It's an amalgamation, a symbiosis of flavour. The Matzah Ball Sopas felt like a natural fit. The Brisket Caldereta had a perfect traditional texture with a solid punch of flavour. I want to know more about the use of avocado in the blintz. The macapuno is traditional, so why not use ube or pandan?"

"My grandfather would mash together avocado and condensed milk. It's a popular dessert in the Philippines. And I love the black pepper. It's one of my mom's favourite ways to make flavour pop in desserts. I wanted to put a bit of her in my dish as well."

"It's a good combination. Well done."

"Thank you."

"Okay," Chuck said. "I think we have what we need. We'll connect with Kendra now. We'll see you tomorrow on the live show, Sarah."

"See you tomorrow."

I looked up at Del. She gave me a thumbs up.

Toronto

"Congratulations on your retirement, Victor!" Poppy said sincerely. "If we could have held a banquet in your honour, I would have given a toast."

"Thank you," Victor said.

He held up a coffee cup to the camera on his laptop, as if trying to toast to the screen. Poppy nodded and held up her mug of matcha green tea.

"Cheers!" she said to the image.

"Let's not be premature. I still have two weeks to go." He put down his mug. "I haven't congratulated you on the diversity award. Good job as always, Poppy. You've brought our network into the twenty-first century. You've rebuilt our roster of talent and you've created one of our most lucrative shows to date. You deserve to be recognized."

Poppy knew she was expected to say something like *I had a great team* or *we did it together*, but that wasn't her style.

"Thank you for acknowledging my hard work and vision."

"I like you, Poppy." Victor took another sip of coffee. She wondered if there was more than just coffee in the mug. "You have more ambition than most men, sorry, most people I know."

She nodded, accepting the compliment.

"Thank you, Victor."

"I'll get right to it." He put down the mug again. "If you haven't heard already, Roger Eddington will be vacating his position as VP of Programming."

She smiled. She knew Roger would be Victor's pick to replace him. The only reason he could be calling would be to name her as Roger's replacement. She prepared herself to give in to a moment of humbleness.

"I've hand-selected Roger's replacement, one that fulfills the need for representation, yet will also lead us in technology and in diversity." He paused a moment. Something about the wording. She realized she would be disappointed. "I think you know Noella Belanger. You worked with her over a decade ago when you were at Home & Life."

"Yes." Poppy's heart fell to the floor. "I was her assistant over twenty years ago. She's very smart, forward-thinking."

"Both of you have come a long way since then. She has a focus on digital programming. Noella will also be our first Indigenous executive." He looked as proud as a dog who'd performed a new trick. "She'll bring a new perspective to the table, just like you have all these years. You'll work well together."

"Thank you for letting me know." She tried hard not to let the disappointment spill into her voice.

"And that brings me to my replacement. I would like to recommend you to the position."

She felt her mouth open in surprise. She did not expect this. She put herself back together.

"I thought Roger was replacing you."

"Roger? Oh, heck no," he laughed. "He's a dinosaur! You brought the network into the twenty-first century. He'd never keep up. I don't think he even understands how Twitter works. Mind you, I don't understand how it works either. I thought you knew he was retiring. We're going to spend our days playing golf or ice-fishing, depending on the weather."

"I…" She was speechless for the first time. "Thank you, sir!"

"No, Poppy, thank you."

Her mind whirled. She had so many ideas and had already crafted a couple of proposals, ready to present to Roger as she had been expecting to be named VP of Programming. She even had a mind-map prepared, knowing she would have to explain the idea in detail because he wouldn't understand the technology involved. Now she could green-light her own project and assemble her own team. She would want Marlee, and that girl, the smart one, Tanizia. She knew others she wanted to recruit.

"I've already talked to a few people on the board," Victor continued. "I give them your Yes and it'll be announced the day after the *Next Gen* finale. So, what do you say?"

"Yes!"

"Excellent. I'll make the call now. Congratulations again."

When Victor ended the call, Poppy did something she hadn't done since she was a kid: spun around in her chair, squealing in glee.

"Uh, you okay, Mom?" Leng nudged open the door to the office. "I was just going to ask you if we could buy a wood-burning oven. Would the condo board allow us to have one on the balcony?"

Poppy got up and hugged her daughter, catching her by surprise.

"No, they would never let us get a wood-burning oven for the balcony." She pulled back and looked into her daughter's disappointed face. "So let's buy a house."

Winnipeg

"You're coming tonight?"

"You sure it's allowed?" Auntie Cher asked. I could hear noise in the background, likely the staff cleaning up after their popular Sunday Brunch to-go. She covered the mouthpiece of her phone for a moment. The background noise quieted down. I assume she ducked into her office. "What about the whole NDA thing?"

"It's the last episode. I don't even know how it's going to end," I said. "We've filmed all the judging segments. The final decision will be aired live. The network wants my family there and you're family."

"Does that mean Del will be there?" I could hear the coy smile in her voice.

"Yes, she'll be here," I said. "And yes, she asked about you."

"Oh! I—Okay." She let out an uncharacteristic giggle. "That's good, I mean, that's nice."

"Can the restaurant manage without you tonight?"

"I run such a tight ship, it can always get by without me," my aunt proclaimed with pride. "That's the whole reason I wanted my own restaurant with actual employees, so I could leave once in a while."

The doorbell rang. My parents were out buying snacks and dinner for tonight. Del said she didn't want me cooking, and the kitchen had to remain spotless.

"I gotta go. Be here by six!"

I looked out the window and saw it was a delivery van. I grabbed a mask and hurriedly put it on as I opened the door.

"I have a package for Sarah Dayan-Abad?"

"Um, that's me, thanks."

He handed me the package and stared for a moment. He looked down at his tablet to look at the name again. His eyes crinkled happily in the corners as he looked up at me again in recognition; I could tell he was smiling under his mask.

"Hey, good luck tonight!"

"Thank you."

He tipped his baseball cap as a form of acknowledgement and headed back to his truck.

The box was smallish but very heavy, a little bigger than a shoe-box. I took it into the kitchen and cut the tape with one of our cheaper knives. When I opened the top flaps, I found a couple of tins of specialty tea, some spice shakers, and a jar of raw honey. The combination of scents was striking. I found a folded handwritten note on beige cardstock. A quote was written on the outside.

"These are a few of my favourite things."
The Sound of Music

The song instantly ran through my head. I was humming the notes as I opened the card. A smile spread across my face as I read.

No matter what happens tonight, you've already won.
Let's keep in touch. For real.

Your mentor and friend,
Lai

I hugged the card to my chest, then put on the kettle to make one of the specialty teas. Mmm, goji berry.

Winnipeg
"That should do it."

Del had finished putting together the lighting gear that would illuminate Sarah's face. She had already set up the still camera in the other room. Sarah's family would be watching in the den just off the kitchen, so she and Sarah had to find another area to set up for the last portion of the finale's video feed. Grace's office was a good size and had a nice backdrop of a bookshelf stacked half-full of books and a painting off to the side. The painting was a little too big for its placement in the room, but Del realized Grace must have staged the background to look good for work video calls.

More importantly, Del knew she could stand near the door with the handheld camera over her shoulder. If Sarah won the competition that night, Del could get a shot of her standing up from the desk and follow her down the hallway to the den, where she would get a shot of her being hugged by the family. If Sarah lost, at least she could be in a room by herself to grieve for a moment while Del got her parents and informed them of the results before it came through after the six second delay.

Del was glad to hear that Cher was able to come. Sar didn't know it, but tonight would be the third time they saw each other. Del had stopped by the restaurant the other night. It was on the way home and she was hungry. Yes, she had a fridge full of leftover pizza and the fixings for sandwiches, but none of it appealed to her. She hadn't really been into good food until she started working with Sarah, but she wanted to check out the restaurant that night. Luckily Cher was there.

"Del?"

Sarah sat at the desk, wringing her hands. She looked small sitting at the big desk. They had gotten a lower-backed chair from the dining room and tucked the office chair in the corner. Del wanted to avoid the temptation for Sarah to spin while broadcasting live. She would be watching the live feed on the monitor.

"Yes, Sar?"

"Do you think I could actually win?"

"Does it matter?"

"What you think, or if I win?"

"Both."

Sarah tilted her head and did that weird thing with her mouth. Del was glad she was able to break Sarah of the habit while on film, most of the time.

"No, it doesn't matter," she admitted. "But I still want it."

Winnipeg

Lena

wut colour u wearing 2nit

Y

i cant wear the same clr as u

not if im gona b on tv

ul be on tv 4 a sec

seeeeee

i need 2 look gooooooood

im gonna wear a blu vnek n dark jeans

k

ill wear pink and white leggings

u realize j will prob wear a bb jersey

as always

gud

i like being the qt friend

Toronto

"Ready for the live feed in 5, 4, 3, 2, 1. Go."

On Chuck's mark, the video technician switched to the live feed.

"And we're live," he said. He perched on the edge of his seat, ready to make quick switches when required.

Kendra's feed appeared on the left. Sarah's image appeared on the right. Both contestants appeared to be sitting in home offices. Whether it was the host or the judge who was speaking, Chuck was ready to instruct the technician to switch, or even cut off the feed when necessary. He already knew who the winner was and had all his shot calls prepared in advance.

"Host camera," Chuck said. "Go."

Chuck continued to call the shots as Jenna spoke.

"We are now live with our two finalists, Kendra from Montreal and Sarah from Winnipeg. Welcome and congratulations to you both."

"Thanks, Jenna!" Sarah said in a nervous but chipper voice.

"Merci, Jenna," said Kendra, cool as a cucumber.

"We're going to hear from each of our judges who are also broadcasting live from their homes. They are going to give their final impressions of your overall performance this season. We're first going to hear from Judge Robyn Douglas from popular food channel Byn There, Baked That. Robyn?"

"Hello, ladies!" Robyn said, a little too loudly. Chuck instructed the sound technician to make the necessary adjustments. "I'm elated to see you both. I am also in awe of the culinary journey that both of you have taken us on.

"Kendra, thank you so much for sharing your family's dishes. Every single dish has been well-executed and well-written, flavour-forward, and vibrant with heat and spice and variety. I have to admit, I've made your Jerk Chicken Tenders a couple of times since I first learned the recipe. Bravo.

"And thank you, Sarah. You have improved vastly over the course of the season. You've been on-brand by bringing us recipes that fuse traditional Filipino flavours with other classics. And some of your dishes, such as the Longanisa Wontons, blew me away with their technical skill. I can't believe you're only sixteen!

"In the end, for me the choice came down to consistency. Sarah, you've had high highs and low lows. Kendra, you've been the most consistent of all our contestants and your performance has been solid. I vote for Kendra."

"Kendra's family feed," Chuck said. "Go."

The screen suddenly switched to the audio and video of the still camera pointed at Kendra's family sitting on the couch and floor of their living room. There were about seven people in the room, three of them young children. They applauded wildly and cheered.

"Host feed," Chuck ordered. "Go."

"Thank you, Robyn," Jenna said. "Now let's hear from Judge Gary Jonas, Toronto comedian and television writer."

"Thank you, Jenna!" Gary said exuberantly. "Ser-rah, oh, sorry, SAH-rah. Sorry, gotta get used to that. I'm going to keep this short, unlike Robyn. Kidding! Kidding!

"Kendra and Sarah. You are both awesome. I loved these two months of cooking and eating. I learned a lot from both of you, about technique, and flavour. Kendra, I loved your Jamaican patties. Thank you for introducing me to this cuisine. And Sarah, you taught me how to make sushi! I based my decision on what I enjoyed cooking the most and eating the most. I also picked the contestant whose recipes I would cook again and again. My vote is for Sarah."

"Sarah's family and friends feed. Go"

The screen switched to a split screen. One side had the audio and video of Sarah's den with only three adults on a couch clapping and waving their arms. The other side had a Zoom feed with two of Sarah's two best friends. The girl bounced up and down excitedly, screaming with exuberance while the boy nodded his head and gave a thumbs up. Kids always made for a visually fun audience.

"Host feed. Go."

"Thank you, Gary. Lastly, let's hear from Chef Kelly Kwan, owner of La Fleur Rouge in Montreal and star of the Food and Drink Channel show, K-Pot."

"Thank you, Jenna."

Chef Kwan's demeanour brought a sudden serious tone. The audio technician was ready to bring up background music for suspense.

"Congratulations to the both of you for a successful season. You are both talented and will hopefully continue to cook and share your love of food. I have learned from the both of you.

"Kendra, from your Jerk Chicken Fingers to your Confetti Rice, you have been on-point in terms of flavour, authenticity, and allowing Caribbean dishes to become accessible to the masses.

"Sarah, you have made an entire nation take notice of the gastronomic wonder that is Filipino Cuisine. I applaud you for continuing to bring us dish after dish that represented your culture. I also am impressed with your honesty when you revealed you were half-Jewish. You brought your heart and soul in your last three recipes. I could feel your baba's and lola's hands in each dish. Your love for family has shone through. I only wish you gave us this gift earlier in the season."

"Audio. Strings. Fade in. Go."

Dramatic music faded in slowly. Chuck counted three seconds, the amount of time he had asked Chef Kwan to wait to create dramatic effect.

"I vote for Kendra."

A wide smile finally broke through Kendra's calm and collected façade. Sarah smiled and gave a little clap, like a good sport.

"Sarah and Judges. Fade out. Go," Chuck instructed.

The video images of Sarah's face and the judges faded out suddenly.

"Kendra handheld. Go"

The shot switched to the handheld camera, following Kendra's movements as she stood up and passed her media manager, who followed her down a short hallway. The shot panned out as Kendra's family surrounded her in the living room. The children jumped up and down, screaming. One of them held a sign that said *Felicitations Kendra!*

Chuck breathed a sigh of relief.

Chapter Twenty-two

Possibly the most important recipe I have ever learned.

Lola's Rice

Use a rice cooker.

Use the cup that came with the rice cooker and add three cups of white rice to the pot.

Fill the pot halfway with lukewarm water or your hand will get cold.

Mix with one hand to rinse the rice.

Pour out most of the water.

Rinse the rice two more times.

Put your index finger into the middle of the pot, your fingertip should touch the top of the rice.

Add enough water to reach the first line on the inside of your finger.

Place pot in the rice cooker, cover, and turn on.

Winnipeg

"You're a celebrity!"

"I don't know about that," I said to Lena over the video call.

I told her that I had been stopped twice at the mall today by people who recognized me from *Cyber Chef.* I was wondering how people knew who I was until I realized I was wearing my FaD mask. The finale was three weeks ago, but I was getting calls for interviews as the new season of *Cyber Chef* started up again.

"Have you seen your Instagram? You think twenty-four thousand followers doesn't make you a celebrity?"

"It was twenty-five thousand last week."

"So what? You'll probably stay above twenty. People are fickle. I only have seven hundred, so you gotta repost me, okay?"

"You're still coming to the barbecue?"

"Of course! Wait till you see my ride!"

After the call Lena posted a screenshot to her stories of me and her making funny faces. She tagged my name, so I made sure to share the picture, adding an animated GIF of the letters BFF.

In addition to the new followers I had on Instagram, I now had nineteen thousand subscribers to my blog, which was about eighteen thousand more than I had two months ago. I would finally make ad money.

I slipped my phone into the side pocket of my purse and stepped out of my dad's car. I had been sitting in the driver's seat for the past ten minutes to talk to Lena. I didn't want to be rude to my guests who were waiting at a nearby picnic table. I could see the smoke from the concrete barbecue pit near the table.

Luckily some restrictions were lifted to allow outdoor gatherings in public areas as long as we remained masked and kept to groups of five or under. I grabbed the tray of lumpia I had picked up at the Filipino restaurant located inside the mall, with a two-litre jug of Earl Grey milk tea tucked under my arm. The plastic container of sago in arnibal syrup was still in the car, secured in a plastic bag to ensure no leaks. Del rushed up to take the tray from my hands. Auntie Cher waved as she looked up from the grill.

As I arranged the food on the table, the milk tea, the rice, the lumpia, the first batch of barbecue pork skewers, and a platter of liempo, I took a few pictures from above and from the side. As I scrolled back to see how they turned out, I zoomed in on one photo. I caught Del and Auntie Cher in the background, their backs to the camera, looking at the grill, their pinky fingers interlaced. I looked up to see their fingers still intertwined. I held back from squealing in joy.

"Sarah!"

I looked up to see a red car approaching. The windows were rolled down and EDM was turned up loud. Lena was waving her hand out the window at me from the passenger's seat while Jay was at the wheel, nodding his head in time to the music. He slowed down and pulled over.

"Sup," he said nonchalantly as I ran up to the car. He turned down the volume.

"You finally got it!" I said. It was a four-door sedan, not new but in good condition. Perfect for the three of us.

"Last night."

"Does that mean you're done working at the restaurant?"

"Nah," he said. "Need gas and insurance."

"We're going to take one more loop through the park," Lena said. "Get in."

I turned to Del and Auntie Cher. "We'll be back in five!"

They both waved. I'm sure they were fine without me for a few minutes. I jumped into the back seat and slipped on my sunglasses. Jay cranked up the music and we took off for a slow loop around the park. What a beautiful day for a picnic.

Two weeks ago
Toronto

"I wanted to apologize," Poppy said over the phone. Somehow a phone call seemed more intimate than a video chat. She was nervous as she spoke to the girl.

"You don't have to," Sarah insisted.

"We should have been more cognizant of your dual culture," Poppy insisted. "And pushed less."

"Pushed is a strong word. I'd say it was more like... encouragement than pushing."

"I spoke to Chef Kwan," Poppy said. "We talked about the space that BIPOC chefs occupy on our network. She says she felt that she has always been 'encouraged' to cook Korean food. K-Pot is a very popular show, however she pointed out that she's a classically trained chef. La Fleur Rouge is a French restaurant, yet she has never been able to show off her true skills to cook French food on-air. I think we may have done the same thing to you, and to other BIPOC contestants. I acknowledge this mistake and I want to apologize."

Sarah's silence worried Poppy. She pictured the girl thinking, maybe doing that strange thing with her mouth again. After a moment, she finally spoke.

"I'm glad I was given the opportunity to explore Filipino flavours," Sarah said. "I learned more in the past two months about my culture and my family than the rest of life. I do agree with Chef Kwan, though. I am Jewish. I am very, very Jewish. I wish I had felt strong enough to be myself throughout the whole competition. I don't know if that would have changed the outcome, but I would have liked to have been able to really shine. So I do accept your apology for taking some of that strength away."

Poppy felt that pang in her chest. She looked over to her bookshelf where she had placed the oblong glass plaque etched with the words ...*for the promotion of cultural diversity on Canadian television.* She wanted to work towards being deserving of that award.

Reparations.

"Sarah, other than to apologize to you, the reason I'm calling is to let you know that I've recently been promoted to Network President at Food and Drink Channel—"

"Oh, congratulations, Ms. St. Martin-Dubois!"

"Thank you, Sarah. I have ideas of how I want to expand the

network. I specifically want to create a digital platform that will connect selected bloggers and content creators with a focus on diversity. I would like you to be one of our contributors."

"Wow, that sounds great, but I'm still in high school. I'm actually in the middle of exams."

"We're only looking at a bi-weekly or a monthly contribution for now," Poppy explained. "Whatever you can handle. We have former CC contestants on board. Nessa and Lai will be providing weekly content. Cindy graduates in a week and will be a regular contributor. Li and Harriet and Kendra, of course, will provide content when they are able as they are also saddled with school commitments. Chef Kwan and other FaD chefs will also participate. You're graduating next year. Are you considering a career in the food space? Maybe going to culinary school?"

"I love cooking," Sarah admitted. "But I've seen the sacrifices my aunt has made. It's a grueling career to be a chef, I'm actually considering going into marketing, but will probably still be involved with food."

"I have a marketing degree." Poppy smiled. "It's given me some amazing opportunities. If you decide to be part of our digital platform, you'll have access to similar experiences, whether in front of the camera or in the background, influencing from behind the curtain.

"Of course, you will be well-compensated for content and just like *Cyber Chef*, traffic will continue to be driven to your blog page, however FaD will receive a commission for affiliate links." Poppy realized she'd started to sound like the fine print. "It'll be fun, I swear. And you can make whatever you want. No strings, no pushing."

"What about Geoff?" Sarah asked.

Poppy didn't expect the question.

"Don't worry, he's not included."

"Well, maybe you should consider him," Sarah continued cautiously. "People can change. People can grow. You won't know unless you give him the opportunity."

Poppy thought for a moment.

"You are a far bigger person than I am, Sarah."

"I believe in second chances," she said. "And forgiveness."

"I will certainly give it some thought," Poppy promised. "But what about you? Would you like to be a part of the FaD family?"

A beat of silence.

"Yes."

"Excellent!" Poppy said, happy to have her onboard. "I wanted to tell you. My daughter is a subscriber to your blog, even before *Cyber Chef.*"

"Really? Cool!"

"We make your White Chocolate Chai Cookies all the time. In fact, I have one in my hand."

As if to prove a point, Poppy took a bite. She closed her eyes for a second to savour the flavours. It was the perfect fusion of exotic spices and simple sweet.

Winnipeg

"Sar!" my mom called out from her office. "Open the door!"

I got up from the couch in the den. I was so tired. Lena and Jay and I had gone for a drive last night and ended up in a parking lot sipping Slurpees till late. I had to wake up early this morning for the school awards ceremony. I made honour roll but just barely. Surprisingly I received a merit award for class citizenship. I was considered a role model for the class, a good representative of the school and my generation. I never thought of myself in that way before. It was kind of cool.

After lunch, I just wanted to lie down and relax. Yes, I was on my phone, but I was watching Chef Kwan's new video on eggs

Benedict. Technically, it's research for my new job, right? And I needed to do research. I was saving up for a car.

I dragged my feet and opened the front door. A small Filipino woman stood on our doorstep wearing a bright floral mask.

"Lola?"

"Anak!" she said, wrapping her arms around me. I hugged her tightly.

"Why didn't you tell me you were coming when I talked to you yesterday?"

"Surprise!" my mom said from behind me. My dad was parked in front, pulling suitcases out of the trunk. "Welcome to our home, Nanay."

I put my elbow out to help Lola up the step and through the doorway. My mom stepped forward and embraced her tentatively. Baby steps. They both turned to me.

"Lola is going to live with us for a little while," my mom said.

"Really?" I said, my heart swelling with glee.

"Mina and Manda are grown up, and your Auntie Mimi can take care of Christo on her own," said Lola. "You need me now."

"Yes, I do. I do," I said, holding her frail, petite frame once again. Tears of joy filled my eyes. I pulled back and took her hand. "Come, you have to see our kitchen."

"Oh yes, I want to see the famous *Cyber Chef* kitchen!" she said with a wide grin. "I have so much to teach you. Do you have a rice cooker? I want to show you my secret trick for making rice."

I didn't tell her that Auntie Cher already taught me her technique.

In fact, I decided I would forget everything Auntie Cher taught me over the past few months. Caldereta, Halo-halo, Sopas, all of it gone. I wanted to start over from a blank slate and learn directly from my lola, starting with the basics, like white rice.

Acknowledgements

Almost twenty years ago, while conducting research for my play, *Shades of Brown*, I interviewed a group of young women regarding their experiences with identity and cultural belonging. One girl's story stood out. She was Mestiza: half Filipinx and half White. She said she felt like she didn't belong anywhere; she was "too brown to be white and too white to be brown." Her words have stayed with me all these years. Since then, I have wanted to tell a version of her story. Thank you to that Mestiza girl who spoke so frankly two decades ago. I hope you have found a place to belong.

Over the past few years, I've been involved in food media through my Instagram blog @pegonaplate. I mainly focus on local restaurants and products and have only dabbled in recipe creation. I am lucky to have listened to a lot of food podcasts and that I have supportive friends in the food content community. Thank you to Vanessa of @zestandsimmer for all of your insights into the world of food blogging and advice on recipe writing; and thank you to my friends of the Foodie Collective and the Winnipeg Foodie community for your support on this journey. I promise to make these dishes for you soon.

Thank you to Mel and Catharina (and for a short time, Sam) from Yellow Dog. I wrote my first manuscript when I was twelve years old. (I admit now that it was terrible.) After attempting to send it to a few publishing companies, I received two rejection letters that broke my heart but not my spirit. Thank you for your confidence in me and my writing, and for making my childhood dream come true.

After writing plays for over two decades, I now know that writing a novel and writing a play are very different skill sets and I have a new respect for those who have mastered either craft. Thank you to my editor, Genevieve Clovis, for easing this transition. I have grown as a writer in our months together.

Silas, thank you for your patience this year; I couldn't read your bedtime stories every night because 'Mommy is writing'. You have been understanding and kind. I enjoyed having you sit quietly next to me while I typed away. I promise we will read this book together. There are no talking animals but I think you will still enjoy this story.

Jericho, thank you for your ideas and for helping my teenage characters sound more like actual teenagers. Thank you for your honesty and for being my sounding board. I challenged myself to write a book that will enrapture you the way books used to captivate your imagination, before you discovered Netflix and YouTube. Maybe you'll even make a video review, which I know is the highest compliment I could possibly receive.

Josh, thank you for your love, support, patience, and proof-reading. You have always been my biggest cheerleader, my shoulder to cry on, my critical sounding board, and the kite string that allows me to soar without losing myself in the clouds. With three writing projects this year, you have shown to me how much of an amazing partner, husband, and father you are, stepping in to the places where I have had to step away. As I continue on this journey as a playwright and author, I am thankful I have you to support me. Just think, this is only the beginning.